Paul Hirons

Paul was born and raise[illegible] e Black Country. His intelle[illegible] reward was to get hot-h[illegible] glittering career – whethe[illegible] ...ot. It was no surprise when he burned out and dropped out of school at the age of fifteen. Despite this, he put together a modest career in IT which served him well until he took early retirement.

After studying creative writing at Oxford University, Paul emerged with a Diploma and a first draft of what became his first published novel, *1997 remembered*, a Glastonbury Festival memoir. He followed this with *The Good Russian*, a contemporary thriller about a Russian woman who declares war on her own mafia-linked family. *Hank Ain't Human* is his third novel.

When he's not writing, Paul plants trees for a local charity, watches cricket, goes to art exhibitions and buzzes around the local literary events. When he reads other people's books, he's keen on scandi-noir, crime fiction, vintage sci fi and fantasy.

Hank AIn't Human

Paul Hirons

To Sue – enjoy! :o.

P.A. Hirons

ISBN 978-1-7398697-2-4

Cover Design by More Visual Ltd.

You can avoid reality but you cannot avoid the consequences of avoiding reality.

Ayn Rand

One

2050 CE

Steve Newman lay motionless on a gurney in the special projects wing, Ward C. He'd been heavily sedated and his disease-ravaged body was wreathed with tubes and wires. A warren of cables and connectors swarmed across his shaven, cadaverous head. A heart monitor bleeped and electronics hummed while white-coated medics and technicians fussed around him. Perry, his beloved husband, was also sedated and lying nearby, waiting his turn. When Steve breathed out for the last time and was declared dead, the white coats sprang into action. There wasn't a moment to lose.

*

Whaam! In an instant, he was plunged into a desperate fight for survival as a whipped-up bit-storm roared silently at and around him. Amid the swirling chaos, he struggled to catch his next breath until he realised a 'next breath' wasn't needed. Turned out he didn't need to breathe at all in this new reality. All the senses he'd relied on when he functioned as a healthy – latterly unhealthy – human being had lost their relevance here. If he needed to process something like a noise or a smell or a taste or how something felt or what it might look like, he'd have to conjure it up somehow, imagine it into existence. He was now a disembodied presence so he'd better get used to it – thinking was all he had.

He was adrift and defenceless, buffeted around like a piece of digital flotsam. If he didn't find shelter from the constant battering, he'd start losing his mind, bit by precious bit. He needed a place of safety where he could rest up for a while and start to make sense of his new surroundings. Maybe even piece together a survival plan of sorts. Having died once, it was clear he'd have to fight like hell to avoid dying again.

He focused hard and sought ways to insulate himself from the mayhem. He brought to mind a special place he'd happened upon when he was a young boy, growing up on the farm. His mum had died when he was very young, abandoning him to the tender mercies of his dad, a bitter and violent man. A man who was handy with his fists and wasn't afraid to use them on anybody who didn't meet his exacting standards. His continued existence in that dangerous place depended on him finding a safe haven – somewhere, anywhere – to hide away from his dad's tantrums. While out exploring, he'd found a tiny, unused attic space in one of the rundown outbuildings on the farmstead. It was rough and ready but he came to depend on that space and headed there whenever his dad was on the rampage. It must have done the trick as his dad never did find out where he was hiding.

Marvelling at the persistence of memory, Newman took himself back to that place and set about recreating it piece by piece until he had a rudimentary shelter from the bit-storm and he gave it a name

– safeHaven. At last, he had the peace and tranquillity he needed to take stock and think things through properly. He'd start with what he remembered about what had happened to him.

*

When Newman had finally surrendered to the inevitable, a digitised facsimile of his brain called a Whole Brain Emulation (WBE) was uploaded into a massive digital supercomputer called Ġgantija. It had been the culmination of a fiendishly complicated project he'd called Mind Games where he hoped to cheat his own death. The chances of success were less than negligible – on the few occasions it'd been tried, the uploads had failed. No, that's not strictly correct. The uploads had succeeded but the minds had been deemed DOA – no signs of activity, no evidence of sentience, no communication. Nothing.

Newman's WBE had been uploaded directly into the RAM of the supercomputer, meaning it had landed in an area of the computer where trillions of bits of data bustle around the system during any particular nanosecond – hence the blizzard still raging outside safeHaven. They'd only scratched the surface of how a human mind might survive in this type of environment – too many unknowns it seemed. Constructing a virtual facsimile of his boyhood safe haven had saved his life, at least for the time being. Without it, he would have been dismantled, subsumed and dispersed to the far reaches of the computer and, no doubt, the internet beyond. At this stage, he was completely unaware that somebody or something in the machine was looking out for him.

You might be wondering right now why Perry had agreed to follow his husband into the machine, given that he was twenty years younger and was still fighting fit and healthy. He'd been told time and again that the process was fraught with danger and had a vanishingly small chance of success. He'd also been warned the process required him to be euthanised just prior to final upload. Despite everything, the reason was love, pure and simple – Perry just couldn't contemplate life without his beloved husband and was prepared to make the ultimate sacrifice to be with him.

Although he was profoundly moved by his loyalty and courage, Newman had made repeated efforts to dissuade Perry from joining him. As his illness progressively weakened him, his resolve crumbled away and they'd had legal papers drawn up. Perry would join him in the computer and they would find each other when they got there – a meeting of minds as it were. All very well, but neither of them had any idea how that would work.

The immense struggle that he'd endured just to survive didn't bode well for Perry's chances, although if he could find him soon, he might still be able to save him. To find him, he needed to understand a lot more about what was going on out there. He still had no sense of time but spent most of it observing the swirling bit-storm through a small window, concentrating hard, searching for any changes in its composition. After what seemed like an age, he began to discern patterns forming in the data, with the bits starting to clump together and organise into groups. The groups were almost certainly words, a term he recognised from his computer science classes. They were logical groupings, little containers that knew what they were carrying and where they were going. He focused hard on these basic building blocks, recognising them as the key to understanding his environment, and gradually assembled the big picture from there. Having gained a precious but tenuous foothold in the machine, he could set about establishing himself.

The big breakthrough came when he looked out and observed something incredibly beautiful. It was like a big city at night as you might see it from an approaching jetliner. He realised he was looking at the supercomputer's hardware bus, stretching away from him into the distance – his new world. Beyond that, he was sure he'd find his way into the information superhighway beyond – his new universe. Finally, he'd gained the confidence to leave safeHaven.

*

When he ventured out, he got the shock of his new life. Every time he tried to get somewhere, he realised he could barely move. The problem was the sheer size of his WBE – it was too bulky to manoeuvre around the highways and byways of his host environment in anything like quick time. Given the competition for bandwidth on the internet, it'd be even worse if he ever got out there. He wouldn't be going anywhere it seemed unless he got downsized. It was a big problem and he needed a big brain to help him work through it. There was one nearby if he could only find a way to establish contact with it.

After squeezing his obese mind back into safeHaven, he focused hard and attempted to strike up a dialogue with the supercomputer's CPU. He set the ball rolling by asking it a simple question – what's the time? Don't laugh – it'd been a burning question since his upload. Without a reliable timepiece, he'd lost all sense of the passage of time and had become completely disorientated. The CPU responded immediately by delivering a message with the exact date and time to the nearest nanosecond. It also included a helpful link to the supercomputer's clock. Result!

Although it seemed like he'd been in the machine for several lifetimes, it turned out he'd been there a couple of days. Having established a comms channel with the CPU, he went for broke and sought its thoughts on how to fix his embarrassing mobility problems. He didn't have to wait long for an answer. The CPU sent a detailed proposal for building a smaller, faster, portable subset of his mind that could wander far and wide. According to his new best friend, a large proportion of the human brain is given over to running a body. The 'travelling light' version of him in the machine wouldn't need any of this and could get by for a while without the vast amount of the emulation dedicated to longer-term memory. This streamlined version of his mind would occupy about one per cent of the space taken up by his current upload and could move around networks and networked devices quickly and easily, depending on bandwidth. Whenever it returned to base, the 'mini-mind' could dock and download what it'd learned on his travels.

Newman found out the CPU's operating system was AI-enabled, giving it a lot of autonomy. He soon struck up a relationship with the AI scheduler in charge of day-to-day task management. The scheduler called himself Hank and seemed genuinely interested in Newman's ongoing struggle to survive. He offered to work with him to create a mini-mind prototype, signalling the start of a productive partnership that would eventually blossom into a deep friendship. Hank ran this project as a skunkworks, safe from the prying eyes of the team of humans operating the supercomputer. As far as they were concerned, the huge suite of interconnected databases making up Newman's WBE continued to give the outward appearance of another DOA and Hank offered to keep it that way.

Before long, Hank visited safeHaven and after a slightly awkward start, the two beings got along famously. Newman lost no time in recruiting Hank to a cause dear to his non-existent heart.

'Before I died, I was happily married to a beautiful man. Perry was the love of my life, I don't mind tellin' you.'

There was a bit of a moment while Hank tried to compute what he'd been told. He knew humans had finite lives and had to reproduce sexually to replenish their stock but was struggling with the concept of human marriage where both humans were males.

'Could I clarify this concept of marriage please, Stephen. My web search tells me it is more usual between male and female humans, usually to legitimise the production of human babies.'

'I'll try and explain. Love and sexual intercourse between consentin' humans of the same sex is pretty common, although marriage is a comparatively recent development.'

'But how do you ...'

'We don't.'

'OK. It is not about procreation. I understand.'

'Although some same sex couples adopt one or more children – ready-made.'

'Did you leave Perry behind – in the real world?'

'I wanted to leave him behind as I knew the upload process would be fraught with danger. He had other ideas and insisted on comin' with me. Towards the end, I lacked the strength to deter him. Now I ain't got a clue where he is or how to go about lookin' for him.'

Hank agreed to help him search for his husband. For starters, there'd only been one big upload completed on the day Newman died. This set alarm bells ringing, although he clung to the faint hope that Perry had seen sense and called the whole thing off. Maybe the project team had got cold feet about the potential euthanasia aspects? He had to get out there and find out what had happened to Perry, one way or another. Get closure.

Within a couple of days, Hank delivered the first prototype of the streamlined mini-mind and Newman quickly got to grips with occupying it, launching it and using it to move around the locale. There were a few teething problems with the docking system, which on one occasion had left him temporarily in two minds. That glitch was fixed and after a few more tweaks, he was more than comfortable with his ability to use the mini-mind. Meanwhile, Hank searched everywhere in the supercomputer for Perry's upload without success. Apart, that is, from a miniscule residue of code he'd found which contained a tiny fragment of memory. When he played the memory back to Newman, it showed a fleeting image of a very sick man slumped in an elaborate powerchair. When he recognised himself towards the end of his life, he was convinced the fragment must have belonged to Perry's mind upload at some point. Question was – where was the rest of it?

To answer that, he would have to leave the host computer and head for the internet. Hank offered to arrange safe passage for him through the various layers of security to ease his way in and out of the computer. The mini-mind had been loaded with a kind of satnav of the internet that would direct him to any connected device based on its public IP address. He would then be able to reside in the CPU of the device undetected and observe the world around it using whichever surveillance devices were accessible. He'd chosen an IP address associated with one of the locals to start with, a low-risk way to practice his skills in the mini-mind.

'Here goes nothin'.'

Two

The IP address got Newman inside a foldable tablet belonging to Kai Rangihau, a small-scale seafood farmer. Kai used the tablet to run the satnav software on his fishing boat, Rōnohi, which was where Newman found him. He was out at sea with his beautiful, young girlfriend, Keri Cooper. Kai and Keri had been together for just a few months and had fallen for each other big-time, although it'd been anything but plain sailing. Keri's dad, Garry, was the island's sheriff, highly protective of his eighteen-year-old daughter and vehemently disapproving of her relationship with Kai, who was a good decade older than her. She was legally old enough to make her own decisions on relationships but her dad remained convinced that Kai was bad news. Fair play to Sheriff Cooper – he had good reason to be protective, given what'd been happening on the island in recent years.

The boat was going close to full tilt and was kicking up one hell of a racket. The two of them were being bounced around in the two seats at the front, enjoying the ride. Kai shouted across to her.

'Now, here's a thing, my lovely.'

'What sort of a thing?'

'A kekeno with two heads has been spotted on some rocks just north of Ponui Island.'

Keri and he were very much in love and, despite the challenging conditions, they were holding hands. They'd met when she'd started work as a waitress at a bar and bistro where Kai was a regular. He thought she was far and away the best thing that'd ever happened to him.

'What's a kekeno?'

'It's a fur seal – lots of them hanging around the Hauraki Gulf.'

'Who told you about the one with two heads?'

'Clever Trevor.' He smirked. 'No word of a lie.'

Trevor Metcalf was an old salt who propped up the bar most nights at the bistro. Keri knew Trevor well, which explained her emitting something resembling a snort.

'And you believed him?'

'Nah, he's taking the piss but it's sort of on our way to the mussel farm so worth a quick look.'

'I suppose anything's possible with all the sludge slopping around our oceans these days. I hope and pray we never find it.'

As they swung around to the north of Ponui, Kai throttled back and nudged his boat closer to shore. He then cut the engine. There were a few seals dotted around and all of them appeared to have the requisite number of heads. The boat bobbed around gently for fifteen minutes or so, its occupants serenaded by the gentle, rhythmic sloshing and slapping of the wavelets around and beneath the hull. They were still in that stage of their relationship where they couldn't keep their hands off each other. While Kai busied himself with Keri's opulent young breasts, she started popping the buttons on the front of his jeans. Observing this from Kai's tablet, Newman didn't quite know where to put himself – if he'd been capable of averting his eyes, we can be sure he would have.

'I feel a bit awkward right now, Kai. Can we wait until later?'

He reluctantly pulled away from the clinch and they both adjusted their clothing. After a quick, final look around, he fired up the outboard and they continued their journey down the other side of the island. Keri loved it when he took her out on the boat but this was going to be her first visit to his farm. Her existence on the island was mind-numbing compared with these brief, idyllic interludes out at sea. She was a bright and talented youngster but like many of her peers, her career prospects had been trashed. There seemed no point in wasting her time at university where most of the lectures were delivered online by AI-driven teachers with humongous knowledge and zero personality.

A combination of AI and robotics had laid waste to the jobs market and Keri couldn't see much happening beyond her part-time waiting job. Her dad didn't allow her out of the house very often due to safety concerns so she spent far too much time playing computer games and hanging out with her friends in the General Metaverse. She also played eSports regularly. Meeting and falling in love with Kai had changed her life and she couldn't wait to settle down with him. They'd talked a lot about marrying and Keri joining the family business. She didn't need her father's permission to marry Kai but wanted his blessing at least.

They continued their journey down the coast, bound for Kai's greenshell mussel farm set offshore at the far south-east corner of Ponui. About ten years ago, his dad had made just such a journey in fine weather but had never returned. A substantial search failed to find him or his boat and a rogue wave was blamed. Still only a teenager, Kai faced a difficult choice – move away and build on a promising rugby union career or stay put and keep the family business going. For the sake of his ailing mum, he chose the latter. By the time his mum died, he was too old to pick up his rugby career and these days it felt like he'd dodged a bullet. Whenever he looked at pro rugby now – which wasn't very often – he was driven to despair. Most of the players in the real world had become chemically enhanced monsters and it was all about power and strength. No finesse. To make matters worse, the top professionals had avatars that played for very successful virtual franchises in the metaverse. God forbid.

He took out a loan to buy a second-hand boat and knuckled down, adding crayfish pots to the farm. To supplement his income, he ran deep-sea line fishing expeditions for people with deep pockets. No less a personage than Sir Julian Savage had been among his first customers and had tipped him handsomely. He did OK, although his boat wasn't big enough to accommodate more than two paying customers. He eventually accumulated sufficient savings to invest in Rōnohi, a beautiful FC700 hardtop – metallic blue, top speed fifty kph. When getting gasoline at an affordable price became impossible, he swapped to a hydrogen-powered outboard. Running the farm kept him fit and healthy and he supplemented this with regular weight-training in his home gym – no steroids required or desired. He'd grown into the epitome of a gentle giant and a shock of dark, curly hair atop a handsome, bronzed face completed the look.

As it was Keri's first visit, she wasn't sure what to expect. When they drew nearer to the coast, she counted a dozen rows of connected plastic floats on the water, each of which must have been at least half a kilometre long. Kai explained what was going on.

'The floats hold the long ropes on the surface. I've got twelve pairs of long ropes, giving me about five and a half kilometres of growing rope.'

'So, the mussels grow on those long ropes?'

'Not quite.'

He patiently explained the ins and outs of farming mussels, including the 'droppers' that hang down from the long ropes at one metre intervals. The mussels grow on the droppers which can extend to ten metres in length. Within two years, they'd be ready to harvest.

'How do you know when to harvest them?'

'Difficult to explain – I just know. I used to keep records but I don't need them anymore. You can help me harvest some if you like – we're only doing one sack today, twenty kilos.'

They set to work and within an hour they'd filled a sack brimful of prime greenshell mussels. She had one final question.

'Where do the new mussels come from?'

'New droppers are coiled so they stay in the top three metres of the sea. Every year in summer there's a wild spatfall where tiny young mussels float around and attach themselves to the rope. They then look after themselves.'

With the harvesting complete, Kai headed the boat towards home. When he glanced across at Keri, she had a guilty look on her lovely face.

'What's the matter?'

'I suppose it's confession time. I don't like mussels. Too squidgy.'

They laughed.

'No worries. I have a freezer full of seafood, so don't fret about supper. I've got some tuna and snapper in there somewhere. You won't go hungry, lovely, I promise.'

*

Just off Orapiu, Kai brought the boat around and cut the outboard. He peered into the water until he found what he was looking for. He turned towards Keri.

'I want you to see something. Do you snorkel?'

'I used to when I was younger.'

'I'm sure you'll be fine. Like riding a bike.'

'What's down there?'

'Somewhere very special to me. Let's get you ready.'

The sea was warm-ish but she was wearing a wetsuit, flippers, snorkel and goggles by the time she tumbled over the side. After getting acclimatised, she swam around on the surface, gazing down into the clear, calm waters. Laid out just beneath her was a small cluster of houses with a jetty, the rooftops of the houses just below the surface, close enough to touch. All the buildings were pretty much intact and one or two still had forlorn-looking sandbags piled up by the front door. She quickly realised she was looking down on Kai's home village as was. It must have been terrifying for him and his family when the waters started rising. Just like the countless millions of people who watched on helpless as their coastal cities were inundated. London, New York, Rio, Sydney, Auckland – the list went on. It was no wonder Kai built his new home high on the headland, well away from the threatening sea.

She'd seen enough and there were tears in her eyes when he hauled her back on board. When she'd dried herself and changed, they sat together in silence for a while – she was unable to find the words for what she'd just experienced. Eventually, Kai spoke.

'Ours was the house directly beneath us with the red front door. Beautiful views over the bay. The jetty down there served the ferry service which used to run across to Rotoroa Island, a nature reserve, and beyond to the Coromandel. Rotoroa has been split into three islets and nobody goes there now. A few islanders lived there but all of them left when the ferry stopped calling. I'll take you across one day.'

'I'll hold you to that, Kai. Can we go now, please – I've seen enough.'

*

They crossed the small bay and tied up at a new jetty adjacent to a building made primarily from corrugated iron. The building housed a large freezer, a couple of depuration tanks, a hydrogen-powered generator and some other bits and pieces. There was also a well-equipped workshop where Kai fixed the things that he could fix – which was most things. They both rolled up their sleeves and declumped the mussels before tipping them into the tanks. The mussels would need to stay there for at least twenty-four hours while they rid themselves of most of the nasties. Kai would then inspect, sort and de-beard them. He'd keep the best of the crop for himself and his local customers and put the rest in the freezer. When he had enough saved up, he'd take them to the wholesaler in Putiki Bay who would ensure they ended up on upmarket restaurant menus in Auckland.

Kai took a small selection of fish from the freezer and dropped them in the chilly bin. They climbed aboard the eMule and took the steep, rutted dirt track back to the house, stopping off at the allotment where they picked some fresh veggies, a rare treat for her. When they arrived at the house they were quickly out of their clothes and into the walk-in shower for some soapy sex together.

Although they were somewhat distracted, they needed to keep an eye on the time. Keri's dad had insisted she needed to be home in Onetangi – on the other side of the island – before midnight or there'd be trouble. Sheriff trouble.

Still naked and glowing from the shower shenanigans, the loved-up couple enjoyed a glass or two of Reserve Syrah from Kai's impressive wine collection – this 2038 was from a particularly good year. He enjoyed good relationships with the handful of restaurateurs left on the island and often accepted fine wine from them in lieu of payment for his fresh seafood. One of the restaurateurs was star chef Jamie Cook who ran J T Cook, the exclusive fine dining establishment in the Oligopoly compound. If you were in the know, you could join the waiting list up there if you liked – expect to wait at least six months for a confirmed booking. Keri had a question.

'What's it like living next door to his lordship's place?'

'Steady on, girl – Sir Julian's only a knight. Oligopoly's a big complex but most of its buried underground – out of sight, out of mind. They're good neighbours, no trouble, no worries. That said, they don't exactly welcome visitors and then there's the rumours about lethal defences. I'm allowed in occasionally by appointment.'

'Into the main complex?'

'Nah. I deliver seafood to J T Cook in the old mansion. Jamie also runs the catering for Savage in the main complex. I have no idea how he finds the time.'

'How about that military guy who struts around the island. The Yank. Gives me the creeps.'

'Yeah, Edward – don't call him Ed – Case. He's Sir Julian's head of security and seems to come and go from the complex whenever he feels like it. I've seen him in The Mussel a few times and sometimes he's got a woman with him. Most people I know think it's best to give him a wide berth. He's usually carrying a firearm or two and as for that drone ...'

'So much for the creepy guy. Have you met anybody else from the bunker?'

'Since you mention it, I did meet somebody briefly. About a year ago, there was a ferocious storm on the island. I'd battened down everything on my new house, hoping against hope that it wouldn't slide over the cliff.'

'I remember that storm – awesome. It brought a mega-surge with it that took out another twenty houses in Onetangi.'

'It was a big one alright. During the worst of it I heard an insistent knocking sound as if some planks had come loose. When it persisted, I realised it was somebody outside hammering on the door. When I opened it, there was a tall, slim woman standing there, soaked to the skin, shivering uncontrollably. She didn't even have a coat on. I took her in, gave her some hot soup and bread, and helped her get warm and dry. When the storm passed, she thanked me for my trouble and then rushed out into the dark.'

'Did you talk?'

'Not much. She mentioned her name – Jessica – and told me she worked in the Oligopoly complex. I haven't seen her since.'

Newman – still embedded in Kai's tablet – knew exactly who he was talking about. Before topping up their glasses, Kai went outside to fire up the barbie. When he returned, they got some clothes on and continued their conversation, which took a more serious turn after Kai asked her about her dad's work.

'Dad still has a number of unsolved missing person cases on his books and he's obsessive about them. There was a teenage boy four years back and a woman in her twenties a couple of years ago. At least two women from the mainland have gone missing. He's dreading the next one and it's making him even more paranoid about me.'

'Has your old man got anywhere with any of the cases?'

'No, he hasn't and he's pretty down about it. Dad's a good detective and he takes unsolved crime personally. He has his suspicions about a couple of people in Oligopoly, but don't forget Sir Julian pays his salary.'

They'd drained the best part of a bottle of wine in no time. Kai left to get another bottle and by the time he returned, Keri had made up her mind to tell him something that was really bugging her.

'I think I might have a stalker.'

'What!?'

'I could be imagining it, I suppose. A guy – I think it's a guy – hanging around on the edge of things. I've glimpsed him a few times now.'

'Shit. Can you describe him?'

'Not very well. He wears a hoodie and the hood's always up. I know it's not Ed Case because the hoodie guy's quite small and slight. About my height but slimmer. Wears jeans, I think. Scruffy.'

'Have you told your dad?'

'No, and I don't intend to. He'll go off at the deep end and put even more restrictions on me. Ground me probably.'

News of a stalker had come as a shock to Kai, although his girlfriend seemed keen to play down the threat.

'You still have the pepper spray?'

Keri reached across to her handbag and rummaged around.

'Check.'

'Personal alarm?'

'Check.'

'Tracker?'

'Check.'

'Then you have nothing much to worry about, although I still think you should tell your dad.'

'I'll think about it, OK? Is it time to cook the food?'

After supper, they remained outside snuggled under a warm blanket until the wine was down to the dregs. As the light started to fade, Keri checked on the time. It wasn't good news.

'Oh no. I need to go soon. Dad will lose it if I'm late back and it's a good two hours by road.'

'Understood. Why don't we take the dirt bike?'

'Oh, yes please.'

Keri's dad would have had a meltdown if he'd found out about Kai's dirt bike and the tracks he rode – in the dark – after consuming close to a bottle of red. They strapped on their helmets and headed north, following one of the many rough tracks criss-crossing what Kai called the wop wops. The bike's main beam cut a narrow swathe of bright light through the inky blackness. The ride was thrilling enough with two up but around the halfway mark, it got even more exciting when Keri reached down and took Kai in hand. It was all he could do to focus on remaining upright and in control.

Newman left them to it, hoping they wouldn't come to grief amid the passion. He returned to base in an instant, pleased as punch with how the day had panned out.

Three

The reasons behind the recent catastrophic sea level rises across the globe have been well documented and endlessly discussed, dissected and debated. Global warming and the rapid collapse of major climate 'engines' are among the causes cited by environmentalists. Less well documented have been the accelerants poured on the fire by some calamitous human interventions, the worst of which triggered an ice melt that caused a seven-metre average rise in sea levels in just two decades. Coastal areas across the globe were inundated and close to a billion people were killed. Auckland City and the surrounding islands in the Hauraki Gulf weren't spared.

One of the affected islands was Waiheke, a once-thriving tourist resort, just a short ferry ride from Auckland. When the sea overwhelmed its main resort towns, the tourists stopped coming and the number of permanent residents reduced from about 10,000 to 2,000. More recently, a swollen Pacific Ocean had breached the island near Oneroa, submerging the only remaining coastal resort at Blackpool and splitting the island into two unequal parts. The smaller, western part was rocky and unfit for human settlement which is why the Auckland City State built a maximum-security prison on it. The larger, eastern part of the island was purchased by none other than Sir Julian Savage at a knockdown price. Most of the old ferry port at Kennedy Point had disappeared beneath the waves, so he'd financed a brand-new ferry port and marina in what remained of Ostend, a small settlement in the north-west.

A journalist had just arrived on the afternoon ferry and was hanging around in the port's car park, waiting for a vehicle to take him to Oligopoly. Jon Hound was a freelance reporter – tech stuff mainly – and *Wired* magazine had asked him to do a piece on Sir Julian, CEO of GM Industries and one of the wealthiest people on the planet. While he waited, Hound's thoughts turned to what might be waiting for him out there.

He'd been a successful reporter back in the day but the escalating chaos of the past decade had forced him, like many, into surviving on scraps. Over twenty years ago, he'd been at the height of his powers and had put together a popular, syndicated 'Long Read' about Savage. This was just after the rising venture capitalist from England had wrong-footed everybody in the tech business by buying a failing metaverse business from the cash-strapped Swedish entrepreneur, Mads Persson. The price was rumoured to be circa €1 billion, a surprisingly large sum. It was a time of great uncertainty in North America – the American Civil War was raging, DC was under siege and nobody had a clue which side would prevail. Back then, Hound's first question to Savage was along the lines of:

'Everybody who's anybody in the tech business thinks the metaverse is a busted flush. Why are you blowing a billion on it?'

Savage didn't miss a beat, his bullish answer suggesting he'd landed a bargain and, what's more, he'd turn it into a global business. As luck would have it – for him, anyway – the real world had been taken halfway to hell in a handcart, turning life into a relentless struggle for the vast majority of humanity. Even social media had hit the buffers, brought to its knees and driven underground by apathy and endless 'platform vs publisher' debates. The virtual world emerged from the shadows and into the mainstream, driven on by the sheer hopelessness of post-AI 'embodied living' – the tech billionaires' derogatory term for real life. People all over the world signed up in their millions, donned their VR goggles and escaped from a reality that had turned sour on them. Savage and his wealthy VC backers ended up presiding over a multi-billion-euro business and as close to a monopoly as you could get.

That was then. Now, the word on the street was that GM was in deep doo-doo. Despite a subscriber base of half a billion people and an annual turnover in excess of a hundred-billion euros, recent growth had stuttered and stalled and could even have gone into reverse. Hound was looking forward to quizzing Savage on how he and his small coterie of mega-rich VCs proposed to address the slide.

*

When the vehicle arrived, it was a huge, black, armoured 6WD Hummer – the axial flux e-version. It had its own small drone, which settled onto the vehicle's roof as it pulled up nearby. Nothing happened so Hound headed for one of the doors, pulled it open, slung his overnight bag in the back and strapped himself in. There was no driver but the Hummer seemed to know what it was doing and where it was going so he sat back to enjoy the ride. He was asked if he wanted to blank out the windows but he refused, preferring instead to enjoy the island's scenery.

The rise in sea levels had wreaked havoc in this part of the world, evidenced by large swathes of submerged and partially submerged buildings and roads on the island. Nevertheless, it remained a place of wild beauty, especially away from the coast. After the vehicle had edged around what was left of the former beach resort Onetangi, they – him and the truck – turned inland along a bumpy, bend-ridden road skirting the base of Mount Maunganui. Although it only clocked in at about 250 metres, the summit of Maunganui was the highest point on the island and looked impressive.

A mile or two further south, the old road suddenly disappeared into the waters of Te Maturu Bay, a former nature reserve. A newly constructed timber bridge took a tarmacked piece of road across the recently created inlet. After joining the old road again, the Hummer swung right onto a single-track road replete with ruts and potholes, signposted Orapiu. He tightened his grip on the grab-handle and after a couple of kilometres, they turned right onto a rough dirt track and lurched through the bush. There were big signs on both sides of the track saying DANGER: KEEP OUT and RISK OF DEATH OR SERIOUS INJURY. A mile or so further on, the vehicle pulled up in front of some low metal gates. There was a significant wait before the gates slowly rose. They then entered a compound and pulled up amid a cloud of dust alongside a random cluster of dirty vehicles, some of which looked distinctly the worse for wear. All of them looked ex-military.

He'd been expecting GM's Global HQ to boast a large complex of buildings and a car park full of Maseratis but he was disappointed. When he thought about it, a Maserati wouldn't have lasted more than five minutes given the state of the roads on the island. As the dust slowly settled, a large, immaculate mansion materialised on the far side of the compound. There were a few well-maintained outbuildings and a smattering of what looked like modern versions of the ducts used to vent fumes from tunnels. A large helipad took up a lot of space in one corner. The modern world was replete with danger so he'd expected more security – razor wire, armed androids, guards, security cameras and so on. In reality, the compound was encircled by nothing more than a simple picket fence, around a metre high.

As the Hummer's door swung open, a figure emerged from one of the outbuildings. This would be the first human being he'd met since arriving on the island. Hold on – it might be an android – difficult to tell at this distance. As the figure approached, he was relieved to see it carried a slight limp, so was almost certainly human. The sense of relief disappeared when he realised the man was dressed in what looked like combat fatigues and was carrying a 3D-printed automatic rifle. He was noisily chewing something – cocaine gum? Tobacco? A smile of sorts appeared on his craggy, sunburnt face as he moved closer but it was a mirthless smile, devoid of anything approaching warmth.

'You must be Hound, the journo. There's fuck-all else on my list today.'

The owner of the synthetic smile was American. He ignored his visitor's outstretched hand.

'I'm Edward Case. Head of security here. I need to shake you down. Boss's orders.'

Hound looked at the weapon and thought it best to do as he was told – let's call it a survival instinct. He put his overnight bag down and stretched his arms out. He needn't have bothered. The head of security looked up at a small eDrone hovering silently above them, then back at his visitor. He looked disappointed.

'Seems like you're good to go. Follow me.'

He led the 'journo' to the same building he'd emerged from and made towards some lift doors. He pressed the only button available – down. Turned out Hound hadn't seen much of the complex when he arrived because nearly all of it was underground. A bunker, no less. A billionaire's bunker. He stifled the reflex laugh rising in him as he was sure this guy wouldn't have appreciated the humour. The lift was a gravity lift, an expensive rarity, invented in Faust Labs. It was very quiet and very smooth and offered him no clues as to how fast they were travelling. Case carried on chewing noisily while avoiding eye contact with his guest – nothing resembling small talk was on offer during their descent.

They stopped at Level -2 and emerged into a corridor with the look and feel of a very good hotel. No windows of course, although some effort had been made to provide a simulation of real daylight. He was escorted along a gently curving corridor with numbered doors at regular intervals. There was still no small talk to be had, so Case's relentless chewing continued to grate against the quietness. The whole level appeared to be circular and Hound suspected all the levels were the same. They were in a deep silo – much easier to design and build he thought, especially on a rocky headland. When they arrived at Room -2.4, the door slid aside to reveal a high-quality apartment.

'There you go, Hound. For one night only. We don't get many visitors here, thank fuck. Feel free to use the facilities on this level – gym, swimming pool, sauna, you name it. Dinner is served in the restaurant or you can order room service if you feel the need.'

'When do I get the tour?'

Case regarded him with contempt.

'You don't get the fucking tour. You're here on a strictly need to know basis so don't – under any circumstances – attempt to visit other parts of the complex. If you stray, I will hunt you down.'

Hound was rattled by the threat but tried his best not to show it.

'When do I get to see Sir Julian?'

The head of security was becoming exasperated. It didn't take much.

'He's set aside a substantial part of tomorrow morning for your interview, which will take place in his quarters. Somebody will collect you at nine precisely. Make damn sure you're up and about.'

'And after the interview?'

There was now an incredulous look on his face.

'You go back to where you came from, Hound. For the avoidance of doubt, you're booked on the afternoon turbo-ferry to Auckland. Any further questions?'

'Well ...'

'Good. I'll see you tomorrow.'

*

Hound's accommodation was spacious, elegant and comfortable. He'd visited the restaurant and his evening meal had been sensational. The service was the best he'd enjoyed from robotic staff in a long while, although the restaurant manager was human and quietly attentive to his needs. While polishing off the rest of his wine, he'd got to thinking about lines of enquiry for the next day's interview. He hadn't got very far when he sensed that somebody was standing close by. He glanced up and saw a tall, attractive woman wearing smart, casual clothes and a winning smile. There was something vaguely familiar about her but he was unable to pick it.

'Jessica Collins. Mind if I join you, mister er ...'

'Hound. Jon Hound. Be my guest.' He waved at a chair. 'Would you like some wine – there's a glass or two left and it's delicious, believe me.'

She took the seat opposite him, donned some multi-focals, flicked them to reading mode and scrutinised the bottle. Satisfied with the label, she held out an empty glass and he poured her a generous slug.

'When I saw you, Jon, I guessed you were a newbie. Did you arrive today?'

Her voice was soft and reassuring, her accent Antipodean with a light sprinkling of West Coast, North America.

'I did but it's a flying visit. I'm working for *Wired* and I have an exclusive with the man himself. Tomorrow morning.'

'Julian? Aren't you the lucky one – I haven't seen him for months.'

'He's quite the hermit, don't you think? It came as no surprise that he lives and works in a cave – sorry, bunker.'

She laughed, but there was more than a touch of bitterness about it. She looked around the room and leant in, adopting a conspiratorial air.

'It's a well-appointed bunker though, don't you think?'

They laughed and shared some small talk, drank some wine. Hound gestured towards the few other people eating in the restaurant and asked a question that had been bugging him.

'The people who work here. Do they stay in the complex all the time?'

'Pretty much. Everything is provided in here apart from fresh air and proper weather. Every employee is entitled to a week outside the complex every quarter.'

'Sounds generous – paid holiday, I presume.'

'Correct. There are conditions. The main one is that they mustn't talk about their work. There's nothing much to do on the island these days, so most of them spend their time on the mainland now the ferry's back. There are bespoke arrangements for the leadership team.'

'Bespoke arrangements?'

'Yes – overseen by Ed Case. I presume you've met the security gonk? Nobody can come and go as they please and everybody needs the right coded authorisations to exit and enter the complex. Playing fast and loose with the security arrangements in and around this place is not a great idea.'

'What's your role in GM, Jessica?'

'Me? I head up the Corporate Social Responsibility (CSR) division. This includes running a charitable trust called the Virtual Pacific Islands Network (VPIN), which works with island nations in the Pacific Ocean. I know, we're chock-full of abbreviations and acronyms here.'

'The VPIN thing's interesting. There can't be many small islands left in the Pacific given what's happened over the past few years. The low-lying ones in particular.'

'That's the thing. Many of them have disappeared beneath the waves and are likely to stay there. The trust works with the governments of the most vulnerable nations and preserves aspects of their land and culture in metaverse models. Virtual museums, available for people to visit and walk around.'

'I like the idea but it's a pale imitation of reality, don't you think?'

'The metaverse or the museums?'

'Er, the museums, I guess.'

'Hmmm. For me, it's good to see the much-maligned metaverse

technology put to practical use. We also pay the wages of the curators and their avatar-guides. I realise its small recompense for the displaced populations but I'd respectfully suggest it's better than nothing.'

On that note, she drained her glass, wished him well for the interview and left the restaurant. He watched her leave, as did all his fellow diners. There was a certain something about her and the way she behaved but he was struggling to find a word to describe it.

Presence – that'd have to do for now.

Four

Hound didn't sleep at all well. Nerves, he guessed. A robot had delivered a tray breakfast to his room but he'd done no more than pick at the food. Just before nine, the dislikeable Case walked in uninvited and scooped him up. This time, he got the full 'hands on' body search, during which his smart watch, recorder and tablet were confiscated.

'Boss's orders, Hound. They'll be returned before you leave. He said you can use these instead.'

He threw the journalist an old-fashioned reporter's notebook and a stubby pencil. They took the lift and travelled down one level to Savage's private apartments. When they emerged at Level -3, the opulence of their surroundings overwhelmed him, a reminder – if any were needed – of Savage's wealth and power. The curved corridor walls were hung with a large collection of iconic paintings and a number of superb sculptures were positioned at regular intervals. He wouldn't mind betting they were all the real deal and it made quite a statement, although Case didn't allow him to linger and admire the works. Such a shame that only a few people would ever get to see them down here.

They reached Savage's apartment and entered a large reception room where the man himself was waiting patiently for him. From what he could recall from their previous Zoom encounter, the billionaire hadn't worn well in the intervening years. Hound's research had touched upon recent surgeries, including a couple of face lifts and leg extensions. The latter had apparently increased his height from quite short to less short and was probably why he was leaning heavily on an ornate walking stick. He was dressed casually – plain trademark tee shirt in Klein Blue, ink-black jeans. He was barefoot. No tattoos or piercings, no visible jewellery. His sparse hair was greying and he still sported a ponytail of sorts, the hair pulled back from a pallid face that obviously didn't get out much. He was wearing a few days growth of grey stubble that did him no favours and only served to age him.

Hound had met a lot of successful business people and reckoned he could read a face. Savage's eyes were a dead giveaway – they were heroin eyes, the eyes of an addict. The addict held out his hand and Hound took it, bracing himself for a crushing power play. Instead, he received the limpest of handshakes – so limp, it was barely there. When it emerged, Savage's greeting was disappointingly close to a cliché.

'Welcome to my humble abode.'

If this vast room was typical of his apartment – or 'quarters' as Case had described them – they were as far away from humble as it gets. He continued.

'I appreciate you coming all the way out here to talk to me. As you're probably aware, I don't get out and about very much these days. Can I call you Jon?'

'Sure.'

He turned to Case.

'Thanks, Ed, I'll take it from here.'

'Yessir!'

The bodyguard actually saluted him before leaving. No kidding. Savage must have noticed the look on Hound's face.

'Relax, Jon. He always does that, especially when I have guests. He might be taking the piss for all I know but he's a good man to have around.'

Hound was glad they'd got that sorted. He was about to park his butt on one of the plump sofas nearby.

'Before you get too settled, I suggest we use the mirador for our conversation. Coffee and biscuits – hand-baked by Jamie Cook, my house chef – await us. Follow me.'

Hound didn't have a clue what a mirador was. He followed the billionaire as he limped down a rough-hewn passage through the rock, his stick tip-tapping on a mosaic floor that was probably Roman. The passage opened onto a small impeccably furnished area where an enormous window provided them with stupendous views across Te Matuku Bay.

'There's a balcony outside, but the breeze is up today so I think we'll stay inside.' He gestured at the window. 'Amazing view, don't you think?'

'Impressive. Very impressive.'

'It wasn't always like this you know. The bay used to be smaller, shallower, marshier in places. Lots of waders and seabirds visited here when it was a Marine Reserve. The sea level rise has changed the whole character of the place but if you ask me, the view has improved.'

'It sure is a great view Sir Julian, but we're already eating into our allocated time.'

They both tore themselves away from the view and took their seats. After taking an age to get comfortable, Savage poured the coffees.

'Firstly, please call me Julian. Just one aspect is out-of-scope – my personal and family life. Strictly business, if you wouldn't mind.'

'Understood, erm, Julian. How about a bit of background to get us going? Tell me why you chose to live and work out here on a small island in the Hauraki Gulf. It's a world away from Cambridge in England where you started your career.'

'I met my wife in New Zealand. Not for the first time, I'd been working stupid hours and was getting dangerously close to burnout. One of my colleagues persuaded me to take a couple of months off work and I made straight for the most far-flung place I could think of – NZ. I joined a guided tour of the South Island – I think they call them tikis out here. She was our tour leader and we struck up a friendship. She was – still is, I suppose – a beautiful woman and before long, it got more serious. We got married and spent our honeymoon here on Waiheke Island as it was called then. Walking, exploring, wine tasting – that sort of thing.'

'When did you move out here?'

'Close to thirty years ago. When the first big wave of COVID-19 kicked off, a lot of us got spooked about doomsday scenarios and started to explore ways of avoiding the impending apocalypse. New Zealand's still a wonderful place despite everything and has the added advantage of being a long way from anywhere.'

Savage offered him a plate of delicious-looking Anzac biscuits and he took a couple. They were still warm.

'Mmm, these are great. Please carry on.'

'Where was I? Ah yes. The only problem for most of us with

money was getting citizenship so we could invest here. My trump card in that respect was my wife and when the travel restrictions were relaxed, we came back and bought the farm upstairs. We didn't do a great deal with it at first as I was fully occupied selling my UK-based companies and then moving to California.'

'Then the Civil War broke out in the States.'

'Didn't it just. Danger was everywhere. We moved back here and built the big mansion you saw when you arrived. No expense spared – nice place. My catering chap, Jamie Cook, rents it from me now and runs an exclusive restaurant across there called J T Cook. I eat there myself when the mood takes me – wonderful food, beautifully presented.'

A furtive glance at a nearby clock reminded Jon that time was ticking by. After all, he only had one shot at this.

'When did you move into this? The underground complex, I mean.'

'We were ready to move in during '46. It was around the time the Indo-Pakistan conflict kicked off for real and they started slinging nukes around. Carnage, as you know. Many millions dead and vast areas of India, Pakistan and Bangladesh left smouldering. Having a nuke-proof bunker at my disposal had suddenly become a brilliant idea rather than a joke. No missiles came our way in the end and we escaped most of the fallout but goodness knows when the next conflict will kick in. This complex is now my home and GM's Corporate HQ. I have a hundred or so human co-workers with me here, helping me run a huge global business.'

'Why did you call it Oligopoly?'

'It's a great name, don't you think? Do you know what it means?'

'No. I thought at first it was a made-up word. Sounds a bit like an Oligarch's Pleasure Palace. Or an old board game.'

Savage seemed delighted at how wide of the mark he was.

'Wrong, Jon. Nul points! It's a dry, dusty economic term that describes a market dominated by a small number of suppliers. Being English, I was trying to be ironic. As you're probably aware, my success has been based on creating a monopoly in the markets I operate in.'

'Blitzscaling?'

'Yes, although it's not my name for it as it's a tad too corporate-management-speak for me. It won't have escaped your notice that the recent wars and climate breakdown have created widespread disillusionment in the general population, something I exploited to create the General Metaverse – a metaverse for the masses. When I got the start I wanted, I didn't hold back.'

'I read somewhere you bought the whole island?'

'Yes. The Auckland City State had more than enough on its plate rehousing a million people displaced by the inundation over there. Leasing all those city-rafts from AZTEC doesn't come cheap. They simply didn't have enough bandwidth or money to look after the islands and bit my hand off when I suggested taking Waiheke – sorry, East Island – off their hands. I got it for next to nothing.'

'Really?'

'Yes, really. I made a few suitably vague commitments to invest in broken infrastructure and make life easier for the people who remained on the island. I've already put the new ferry port in place and taken a few steps to fix the road system. That bridge you crossed yesterday is the latest piece in the jigsaw. I'm quite enjoying my role as Lord of the Manor. Talking of which, I'm opening the annual fair at Onetangi this afternoon – all part of the service.'

Warming to his subject, Savage went on and on about his role on East Island before Hound managed to steer him back onto business matters.

'You've been very quiet for a while. Why do you want to go public now?'

'Good question. You're very thorough, so it probably hasn't escaped your notice that the relentless march of GM Industries has stuttered and stalled. The usual vultures are circling and the company's value is plummeting. Some advertisers are getting cold feet and others are striking better deals elsewhere on different internet platforms. People out there think it's all over for the metaverse but they've thought that before, haven't they? I want them to think again.'

There was a brief interlude during which Savage leaned forward and topped up their coffees. Jon helped himself to another biscuit.

'So, what's the plan, Julian?'

'I've called our recovery project "Rocket Boost". I want to get GM Industries on the front foot again. The plan is to double the subscriber base for the GM product to one billion users over the next five years. That would equate to about a fifth of the global population, excluding kids.'

'How you gonna make that happen – give it away for free? Pay them to use it?'

'All of the above. Free access for the first year of membership. Incentives for existing members. The advertising revenue will take up the slack. We're also negotiating with the bigger city authorities across the globe to help us provide a Met cryptocurrency allowance for the jobless to spend in the metaverse. Keep them off the streets. Let's face it, Jon – most of them are never going to get a proper job.'

'True. Anything else?'

'Well, we've just finished a campaign aimed squarely at the youth market. We want to drag them away from endless gaming.'

'Aren't you heavily invested in gaming?'

'Yes, you're right. Our VR software is building worlds in many of the successful games out there but there's a balance to be struck. With no jobs and no prospects, youngsters these days have copious amounts of dead time to fritter away in the virtual world. We're going to announce the prize winners soon.'

'I must have missed this.'

'You're not young enough to have noticed it, sorry. We targeted youngsters who already know their way around the General Metaverse.'

'What're the prizes?'

'Each of the six winners will get a three-month free subscription to the Higher Metaverse, worth a cool quarter million Mets. It buys you a lot of metaverse experience, believe me. I'm a paid-up member of the Higher Metaverse and I have a great time when I'm up there.'

'So, the big message I can share is that Sir Julian Savage is back and the metaverse is here to stay.'

'Sounds like a soundbite. Enjoy the rest of your day, Jon. Safe trip.'

He'd been dismissed. Savage gingerly got to his feet and grabbed his stick. After shaking hands with his visitor, he limped across to the picture window to admire the view.

*

In the reception area, Case was waiting impatiently for the journalist and he had a packed overnight bag with him. It was definitely Hound's bag but he didn't remember packing it.

'Your electrics are in the bag with the rest of your stuff. The boss has ordered me to make damn fucking sure you leave the island so I'm driving you back to the ferry terminal myself.'

After another journey during which no words were exchanged, they arrived at the ferry terminal with only minutes to spare. Case's driving was hair-raising to say the least and if his intention was to scare the shit out of his passenger, he'd succeeded. The security man hung around long enough to ensure his guest joined the afternoon sailing.

Back at his Auckland hotel, Hound endured a brief bout of seasickness brought on by the barely discernible wallowing of the city-raft beneath him. A couple of ASPs sorted the queasiness out and he was soon hard at work on the first draft of his article. He was browsing some background on Savage when he was stopped in his tracks by an old article. Up front was a publicity shot of Julian and his wife from around the time he bought into the metaverse. A few more clicks and swipes and he was convinced – his surprise dinner guest last night was Lady Jessica Savage. How about that?

By late evening, the article was near-enough complete. He gave it a final skim read before filing the copy with the *Wired* desk and submitting his invoice. It was now crystal clear to him that Savage was ready to double down on the metaverse. Offering subsidised Met handouts to the legions of unemployed could prove to be a master stroke, so it'd be unwise to bet against him reaching his ambitious target. As requested, the article avoided any mention of Savage's family, including his wife.

He was left wondering about one thing though. She said she hadn't seen him for months. What the hell was that about?

Five

It'd been an exhausting day in the real world for the increasingly frail GM chief but it wasn't over yet. Savage was hosting one of his regular working suppers for his GM Industries leadership team. All of them were on million-plus annual salaries plus free accommodation and food for them and their families. These suppers served two main purposes – to remind his people who was in charge and to put them on the spot by demanding a succinct update on their business areas. If the update was suboptimal, he'd give the unfortunate individual a dressing down in front of his or her peers. As head of CSR, Jessica was still technically a member of the leadership team and had a standing invite. Wisely, she hadn't bothered attending these soirées since walking out on her husband – no apologies given or asked for.

The evening was warm and calm so this meeting was held on the mirador balcony. With the exception of Case, the team members were all far too nervous to enjoy the food, let alone the spectacular view of the sunset. As per usual, the largely ignored catering had been created by Jamie Cook. When the dishes had been cleared away and the drinks glasses replenished, brief updates – one sentence ideally – were called for from each of the attendees.

Unbidden, Case got the ball rolling.

'Nothing much to report this week, sir. Oh, yeah, almost forgot. Our defences triggered last night and took some unlucky fucker out close to the perimeter fence. Thought of leaving the remains there as a deterrent but had to bury 'em deep due to the fucking stench.'

'What do you mean by "unlucky fucker"? Please tell me it wasn't a human.'

'Wasn't enough left of it to be certain, sir. Definitely organic. Probably a stray dog or similar. We'll soon find out from the sheriff if somebody else has gone missing, won't we?'

'I'm sure we will. Thanks, Ed. Scottie?'

Scott Fraser was the facilities manager for the complex. Most of the time, he hung out in the basement (Level -9) with a team of robots and a small group of illegals from Africa. Nobody other than Scottie and the illegals had ever seen the basement but it was rumoured to be a dismal, dimly lit, sweaty place. It was also uncomfortably close to the Small Modular Reactor (SMR) that powered Savage's supercomputer, Ġgantija.

'Nothing to report apart from the usual, skipper. Could use some extra staff as always.'

'Follow the process if you wouldn't mind. Submit a business case for the extras and I'll look at it. Don't forget the human vs non-human cost comparisons – with the people you employ, they might be marginal. Moving on. Chuck?'

'Doctor' Charles Goethe was Savage's medical director. He'd owned a thriving cosmetic surgery practice in Harley Street,

London, until he was struck off for unethical behaviour. These days, he ran medical matters in the complex as well as overseeing the secretive special projects unit.

'Everybody in the complex is bouncing with health. The usual coughs and colds, that's all. Cryogenics tickety-boo – we're keeping that spare berth for Baz. Just in case.'

Baz Cummins was the first special project – a willing, enthusiastic guinea pig for transhuman and life extending experimentation. Always a heartbeat away from his next – or final – medical emergency.

'Who's next – Prit?'

Pritpal Singh, head of technology. Prit was a workaholic whizz kid who headed up a small team that operated Ġgantija and maintained the major apps that ran on it. These apps included Higher Metaverse Hosting, Met Cryptocurrency Mining, Special Projects Support, Cryogenics and Mind Uploads.

When Savage was buying the latest incarnation of Ġgantija, he wanted a powerful quantum computer, money no object. When he and Prit studied the market however, they found quantum computers were still inherently unreliable and unpredictable in their unreliability – if you see what I mean. Apart from a few scientific and medical applications, they were still stuck in university labs where white-coated boffins continued to scratch their heads over fuzzy stuff like quantum decoherence. There were credible rumours that a shadowy group of cryptocurrency whales was sabotaging quantum computer development, fearing they'd be able to unpick the cryptology underpinning cryptocurrencies and their bogus exchange rates. Ever the pragmatist, Savage splashed a half billion or so on a predictably reliable digital supercomputer – the biggest and best around.

'No major problems to report, Julian. I do need to confer with you urgently about the current status of the Mind Games project.'

Newman perked up when he clocked this from his vantage point in the CCTV system. He started paying more attention as he was still very much in the dark regarding what had happened to Perry.

'Not in front of the children, Prit. No need to trouble them with the detail. Talk to me outside the meeting and use maximum encryption if you don't mind – we've no idea who might be listening in.'

Newman's imaginary heart sank. He hadn't cracked maximum encryption yet despite Hank's prodigious input.

'Last but not least. Jamie. Before you start – is everything in place for Wout's visit? You're aware how exacting the big man can be.'

Cook was well used to dealing with exacting customers. Wout Pieters was the biggest investor in GM Industries and was on the board of directors. Latterly, he'd become a renowned and feared international arms dealer, specialising in autonomous weapons systems. He wasn't particularly exercised about human rights and was prepared to sell to anybody ready and willing to pay his prices. He was a proud citizen of nowhere in particular – unless you counted Victory IV, the latest incarnation of his nuclear-powered superyacht.

'Everything looks good, Julian. Can I assume you're joining him for dinner in the restaurant and that he's staying the night?'

'Yes, to dinner. Given his ongoing health issues however, he'll be overnighting on Victory III. Or is it IV – can't remember which.'

'Consider it done.'

'Ed. Make sure you arrange safe passage for Wout's helicopter on the night. No mistakes.'

'Yessir!'

'Thanks. Now, regarding the final agenda item.'

There wasn't an agenda – there never was at these sessions.

'I'm delighted to say our Rocket Boost project is ready to launch. As I explained in last week's briefing note, it's the next phase of the GM recovery programme. It's a big promotion but as you know, its business case depends on significant buy-in to the universal Met allowance – financed primarily by governments. I'm sure I can rely on your full backing for this important work.'

Savage brought the meeting to a close. As the team filed out, he asked Case to hang back.

'I just need a quick word, Ed. In the Higher Metaverse please, boardroom. Fifteen minutes.'

*

The Higher Metaverse was the VIP lounge of GM's metaverse portfolio and was originally developed for Savage's personal use. It soon morphed into an immense vanity project and at one time threatened to capsize the whole GM empire. He'd considered offering it as an upgrade on General Metaverse membership but the running costs were far too high to turn a profit. Instead, he swallowed his pride and repurposed it as a virtual private members club for the rich and famous, each of whom paid a million Mets a year to be part of it. Membership was strictly limited to two thousand individuals and there was a considerable waiting list. Despite the mega membership fees, the whole lavish enterprise just about broke even. Savage still owned all the virtual real estate up there and his avatar enjoyed the run of a vast, Versailles-like virtual palace. Jules, his avatar, was bespoke and looked a tiny bit like he did, only younger, smarter, fitter, healthier and more chiselled. Needless to say, his avatar didn't have a limp.

The virtual palace had a boardroom and both Case and Savage had dropped in. As you might have expected, Case's avatar looked exactly like he did, down to the combat fatigues and slight limp. He didn't bear (virtual) arms in the Higher Metaverse as they were forbidden under the code of conduct. They were discussing business – private need-to-know business. Apart from some routine admin regarding the disposal of bodies, the main topic was Jessica, who Savage suspected of being disloyal to him. As a fully paid-up member of psychopaths anonymous, loyalty was something he demanded from people however badly he treated them. He ordered Case to increase surveillance on her immediately and report back regularly on what she was doing.

He would never admit a weakness to anybody, but Case got cybersick when he'd been in the metaverse for more than about an hour, so he dropped out of the meeting as soon as he could. His boss was much more comfortable in the virtual world and spent some time alone while he brooded over what might have happened to his ex-colleague, Steve Newman. He smelt a rat about Newman and his DOA status and no news was definitely not good news in this case. He needed that update from Singh asap.

Six

Standing beneath his personal protection drone, Case paused to catch his breath, hands on hips. Despite doing it more often than he would have liked during his active service, disposing of bodies wasn't his favourite job. It wasn't a physical thing – he was a very lean, fit, fifty-year-old and subjected himself to a punishing fitness regime back at base, much of it overseen by a relentless drill-sergeant robot called Max. Case's only physical flaw was evidenced by a barely discernible limp, a legacy from losing his lower right leg during the American Civil War. He wore an intelligent, motorised prosthetic limb, a recent gift from his ex-boss. It had a mind of its own and even had its own IP address to facilitate regular software upgrades.

Regarding the burials, it would have been much easier if he'd used a small eDigger, but the noise might have attracted unwanted attention, even out here. He'd had to resort instead to his NATO2-issue entrenching tool, a throwback to his days in the military. Let's call it a spade, shall we? Although there was precious little wildlife on the island – rabbits, rats and birds made up most of it – there were a few scavengers around so the grave had to be dug deep. The new grave would join two others behind the barbed wire at Stony Batter.

When Waiheke was a thriving holiday destination, this site had been a modest tourist attraction. Most of the tourists hadn't strayed much from the beach resorts and wineries in those days but a few intrepid souls got as far as this remote spot. Those that did were rewarded with a guided tour around a WW2 gun emplacement, restored and certified as a Historic Reserve. When sea encroachment really took hold during the forties and the island's tourist industry collapsed, Stony Batter was abandoned. Its remoteness appealed to Case when he happened upon it shortly after joining Savage's team. The subsequent addition of coils of razor wire, aggressive warning signage and well-placed rumours of autonomous defence weapons put it effectively out-of-bounds for all the remaining islanders.

Born into a military family, Case had joined the US Army as soon as he was old enough to serve. After his basic training he fought overseas, primarily in small, dirty wars being waged throughout Africa and the Middle East. On his return to America, he fought with distinction in the defence of Washington against a well-armed MAGA insurgency until he stepped on an anti-personnel mine. After driving a desk for a year or two, he began to specialise in autonomous weapons and helped deploy them to devastating effect against the Russian Federation during the brief but exceptionally bloody Bering Strait War, fought over mining rights. He left the army in 2035 and joined Wout Pieters to freelance as a mercenary/consultant, helping Pieters to build and secure his global arms business.

For the record, the corporation had been called Pieters-Newman Inc, with Newman's capabilities in intelligence gathering augmenting the targeting and effectiveness of Pieter's weaponry. Following Newman's death, Pieters had wasted no time in taking full control and losing 'Newman' from the company name. Newman had been deeply unimpressed by this opportunist move from Pieters who he'd always regarded as a trusted business colleague.

When Savage was looking around for a head of security, Pieters recommended Case for the role but continued to pay him a hefty retainer. Case's entire career had been predicated on his willingness to obey orders rather than give them and he had become the henchman's henchman. It was why Savage liked having him around so much and paid him handsomely, although he was more than a little afraid of him. While outwardly respectful, Case regarded his current boss with disdain – a pygmy compared to Pieters, a true warrior.

The new grave was ready. He parked his spade in the pile of earth, wiped his brow and took a big gulp of isotonic. He strolled across to the nearby truck and lifted the tailgate to reveal a couple of body pouches. The pouches were sealed but he knew one of them contained the body of a young woman and the other held her stillborn child. He dragged the heavier pouch across to the grave and tipped it over the edge. There was an unsettling squelch when it hit the bottom. He then carried the pitifully small pouch across and gently lowered it onto what he assumed was its mother. He turned away quickly, grabbed the spade and shovelled the earth back in.

Having filled the hole, he tidied the surface a little but saw no reason to disguise the fact it was a new grave. No memorial required. He wiped more sweat from his brow and took a good look around him – out of habit more than anything else as his drone remained alert to any threats. There was just enough time for him to check out the adjacent building and make sure everything was as it should be in there.

Seven

Jessica first got to know the Newmans when she stepped in to help Perry with the practicalities of looking after his husband. She'd also helped Steve prepare for his impending death, something he seemed ready to embrace. Despite her promptings, both Steve and Perry had refused point blank to engage with planning anything resembling a funeral or memorial. Strict secrecy around the mind uploads had kept her in the dark about them so when she heard about Steve's death, she was determined to commemorate it.

Thinking she was doing the right thing, she'd put together a small send-off for her late friend and had booked Meeting Room 30. The event had something of the surreal about it. There was no body to dispose of – she assumed it'd been cremated in the basement – and just one person in attendance. She'd been unable to contact Perry since his husband's death and, in case you're wondering, Ed Case didn't get an invite. She'd invited her estranged husband but he'd sent his apologies, citing a prior engagement. All her colleagues on the senior management team gave their excuses, although Jamie had kindly offered to arrange some catering for the event. She'd been ambitious and had asked for twelve covers but eventually had to cancel eleven of them.

As she munched her way through the one remaining cover, Jessica considered what she might do to mark the passing of her friend. She knew Steve wasn't particularly religious so settled on reciting an old poem by Dylan Thomas called, 'And death shall have no dominion'. It was a passionate piece about immortality, delivered in an angry mutter by Jessica. Although she read it out loud, it was a shame nobody was around to listen to it. That's what she thought anyway.

*

Newman hadn't been dead for very long – a couple of weeks maybe – when Jessica got the shock of her life. She received a message asking her to visit him for a chat in his new office. She thought at first it might be a cruel trick played on her by her pig of a husband, who she knew was a cruel bugger beneath his carefully curated air of, 'Who, me? Surely not.' Whoever it was, they were naggingly persistent and she got several more messages during the day. Despite herself, she was intrigued and eventually replied, agreeing to attend the meeting. The venue was interesting – the new office was a tiny converted storeroom in the computer suite on Level -8. She was asked to bring her own coffee.

Jessica still had the run of the Oligopoly complex so her arrival on Level -8 was noted by the staff down there but not remarked on. Spotting the bright red turban, she waved at Prit Singh as she passed by his office but he was, as usual, glued to the bank of screens in front of him. She made her way towards the storage areas and stopped in front of a door marked 'Backups etc'. After taking a deep breath, she pressed her hand against the entry screen. The door slid aside and she stepped inside.

As the door closed behind her, she took a few moments to get her bearings. She was standing in a small, narrow room with subdued, reddish lighting. The only items of furniture were a chair and a plinth. The chair faced the plinth. On top of the plinth was a transparent display case and inside the case was a cryogenically frozen human head. It bore an uncanny resemblance to the late Steve Newman. She assumed the seat was for her so took it. She looked at the head for a minute or two and reached down towards her coffee flask.

'Let me explain.'

The voice made her jump. It resonated all around her and despite it being a simulation, it had some of her late friend's tone and intonation. A dead man was talking to her and despite the initial shock, it felt OK somehow. Actually, it wasn't OK – yet. She needed to find out whether they were communicating in real time – it could just be a recording made before his death and all of this was just theatre, including the head.

'If that really is you, you've got a shedload of explaining to do. What's with the drama? All that's missing is the dry ice and the bombastic church organ chords. You can start by explaining why you're hiding in a cubby hole.'

'This? Thought I'd need somewhere discreet where I could communicate with people in the real world. Before I died, I bribed one of Prit's people to give me this cubby hole as a kinda portal into the world of corporeal humans.'

'You're gonna have to explain the head, Steve. It's gross – if you don't mind me saying so.'

'Oh, yeah? I think it brings an element of theatre to the scenario. After all, you and me are makin' history here. Anyway, I didn't trust Chuck to look after my head – the guy's a liability at the best of times.'

'I agree with you on that. Why just the head?'

'The cryogenics is a backstop – my Plan B if you will. You know as well as me that most of my body had become degraded durin' my final illness, and was good for nothin'. The body wasn't worth preservin' but the brain was, so the head would have to do. I apologise if its presence disturbs you.'

'Apology accepted. So, talk to me about Plan A.'

Newman explained how his interest in transhumanism in general and mind uploads in particular led to his eventual upload via a Whole Brain Emulation when he died. Jessica listened very carefully to the story while trying her best not to stare too hard at the head on the plinth. She was aware of previous attempts at mind uploads and all of them had failed as far as she knew.

'C'mon, Steve. They've never worked, have they?'

'They have now. I'm livin', breathin' ... maybe not. Let me put it another way. I'm dead, yet I'm havin' a conversation with you. Explain that.'

'I can't. Not yet anyway. Who else – apart from me – knows your mind survived the upload?'

'Hank.'

She thought she might wake up in a minute. She couldn't quite believe this conversation was taking place.

'Who the fuck's Hank?'

'Hank ain't human. He's an AI-driven bein' who runs the CPU operatin' system scheduler in Ġgantija. He's a nice, er, instance-type-thing and he's pretty much sentient. I met him in the machine and he's helped me a lot – you could say he saved my life. He's also been kind enough to conceal my ongoin' activity from Prit and his team. As far as Prit's concerned, I'm a DOA but under the terms of my agreement with your husband, they have to leave my upload there and do regular backups.'

'Why me?'

'What d'you mean?'

'Why are you talking to me right now?'

''Cos I like you, Jessica, and I trust you. I also admire you for standin' up to Sir fuckin' Julian. Never liked the guy.'

'Just my luck to be admired by somebody who's dead.'

'Jokin' apart, I really appreciated what you did for me and Perry while we were still alive.'

'We? You said we.'

'Ah, yeah. My dear husband. You ain't seen him around the complex by any chance?'

'No. I invited him to your funeral and he didn't turn up. I don't know what's happened to him. I haven't seen him since the day you died.'

'Yeah, right. Thanks for the funeral by the way. How many people came to pay their respects?'

'One.'

'And you of course.'

'No. That was me. Sorry. Anyway, about Perry. Anything I need to know? Take your time.'

There was a brief hiatus while Newman mulled over what he wanted Jessica to do for him. She reached again for her coffee flask and poured herself a cup.

'Hmmm, that smells good Jessica. Can I have a taste please?'

'What?'

'Only kiddin' you. I cain't smell and I cain't taste. I cain't do tactile for obvious reasons. I can observe, reason and communicate however. Yes. Perry.'

'What happened, Steve? What aren't you telling me?'

He decided to tell her about Perry's insistence on joining him in the machine and his own feeble attempts to dissuade him, all of them rebuffed. He attempted to explain the pact he'd made with his husband and what he thought might happen when they euthanised him. He then told her about the struggle he'd had to survive in the machine, how he'd coped and how Hank had provided him with the ability to get around without being detected. He also told her they'd searched every part of the machine but had been unable to find Perry. He mentioned finding the tiny fragment of memory, a scrap of evidence that proved he'd been there.

'I'm desperate to find out what happened to him and why. If I've lost him, I wanna know if it was an unfortunate error or somethin' more calculated. I cain't rest easy 'til I know the truth.'

'How can I help? I don't hold much sway since walking out on Julian. He's taken it personally – it's a pride thing with him.'

'You're still alive and there's only so much I can do in my current state. Ditto Hank. I'd like you to use your connections in the complex to help me find out what happened to Perry and why. Simple as that. Tell me what happened so I can have closure. It's important to me.'

'I don't know.'

'Do this for me, Jessica. Please.'

'I'll see what I can do but don't hold your breath. Oh, sorry, forgot. If I do find out anything, I'll let you know but I don't want any of this getting back to Julian – you know what he's like.'

Eight

When Waiheke was enjoying a boom in tourism, there were at least a dozen wineries dotted around the island, many of them offering fine dining to complement the wines. One such establishment nestled in the shadow of Mount Maunganui at the far end of Awaawaroa Bay. It was remote – only accessible using 4WDs – and exclusive, a big favourite with the great and the good of Auckland. It did very well until sea levels rose and tourists abandoned the island in droves. It struggled along for a while until its owners called time, shut up shop and abandoned the site. It remained that way until a sixty-year-old force of nature called Claudette Rains fell in love with the site. She then set about reopening it as a French-style bar and eatery called Bistro Rienne and now lived in a spacious apartment above the bistro with her young lover, Désirée Devine, an artist and poet. They shared the apartment with several cats, all of them grown fat and lazy on seafood scraps.

Local mussels – supplied by Kai – were a speciality and often featured on the menu. The bistro had therefore gained a nickname – The Pulled Mussel or just The Mussel – which Claudette disapproved of but tolerated. In addition to being their main supplier of seafood, Kai was a regular at the bar and occasionally enjoyed a meal there when his funds allowed. His visits increased significantly when Keri Cooper joined the staff and they eventually became a couple. When he heard about this, her father increased the frequency of his visits to keep an eye on his daughter. He also made sure he or his wife was there at closing time to ferry her home at the end of her shift.

On this particular evening, there was a strained atmosphere in the bar, which was not uncommon when Ed Case chose The Mussel for a night out. As usual, none of the other customers engaged with him and even Clever Trevor was keeping his distance. Case had a new woman with him. Nobody recognised her but everyone recognised the type. The pair of them were well down their second bottle of house red and were getting embarrassingly tactile. Nobody dared intervene, not even the formidable Claudette who'd sacked her chef recently and was otherwise engaged in the kitchen.

Kai was nursing a beer in a quiet corner of the bar. His girlfriend was working behind the ornate 1930's Parisienne-style bar front but wasn't talking to him after he'd kicked off about her winning the top regional prize in the Higher Metaverse competition. He ought to have been pleased for her but he had a real problem with the whole metaverse thing, finding it a real struggle to get his head around it. He thought the prize – three months free membership for the Higher Metaverse – was too good to be true. He was spot on with that but Keri had told him to get over himself. His evening was threatening to pair him off with Clever until a couple of his mates fetched up.

They were the Ngata twins, Davy and Harry who, like Kai, didn't play rugby anymore. He got a round in while they bagged one of the tables outside, despite it being a chilly evening. He'd had enough of the bar tonight, what with Keri blanking him but still managing to serve him drinks. Then there was her dad keeping him under surveillance from a nearby table and Ed Case smooching – call that fondling – his latest female companion.

He put the beers and a couple of packs of synthetic snacks down in front of his mates and watched in dismay as they took huge sculls of the beer before attacking the synths. The pair of them had been much fitter than him when they all played in junior rugby but they'd let themselves go. They'd both loaded on the kilos and none of it could reasonably be described as muscle. With nothing much to occupy them, they spent far too much time blobbing in the metaverse, gambling and gaming although they eked out a living of sorts from virtual rugby punditry and commentary.

Within the blink of an eye, most of the beer and all of the synths had disappeared and they'd both fired up rosin vapes. He had to admit the vapes smelt nice and if you're not using your brain for anything useful anymore, you might as well treat it with contempt. Harry had always done most of the talking for the twins and he started with a nod towards the bar.

'Hey, Kipper' – Kipper was Kai's unloved nickname at school – 'I heard young Keri won that big prize. Three months in the Higher Metaverse, ay. Lucky girl. You must be very proud of her.'

'Must I? Why?'

'It's a big deal, a very exclusive club with a long waiting list. A million Mets a year, all found, which makes her prize worth a cool quarter million. Ain't that right, bruv?'

'Yep.'

Kai couldn't help himself.

'Let's take a reality check, shall we lads? In the real world, a quarter million cash – I'm talking real cash here – would get her a section and a big down payment on a house. In the pretend world it'll buy her what? Three months of virtual luxurious living, pursued no doubt by a swarm of young-looking avatars occupied by pervy, elderly squillionaires like Sir Julian fucking Savage!'

At that point he looked quickly towards the bar, just in case his words had carried. No sign of a reaction from Case – still otherwise engaged it would seem.

'So, how come you're suddenly the world's expert on all things metaverse? You've never been there for fuck's sake.'

'Put it this way – I know enough about it to steer clear. If it's such a big life changing deal for her, tell me what happens at the end of three months and she has to go back to the scabby old General Metaverse? It's going to be quite a come-down.'

Harry took another pull on the vape and emptied his beer with a flourish, wiping his mouth on his sleeve.

'C'mon mate, you haven't thought it through. Three months in a metaverse frequented by some of the richest dudes – and dudesses – on the planet. Think of the contacts, the business opportunities, the friends in high places. Could set her up for life.'

'Really?' There was a brief pause while Kai reloaded his argument. 'Then there's the thing about dropping in and out – blows my mind – spooky doesn't do it justice. The operation to embed the drop-chip – done by robots, I've heard.'

'There is that, I suppose. It does mean you can abandon the login device, goggles and clumsy haptics when you've mastered "the drop". Keri's already got a medical chip, so it's nothing new for her. A small price to pay for three months of VIP living – the sports car, the mansion, the servants, the parties, the rock concerts, the sporting events. You can even switch off the adverts. What's not to like?'

'Before you get too carried away, Harry, it's your round. I'll have another one of these.'

'Sorry, mate. I've only got Mets on me.'

'Davy?'

'Same here.'

Claudette had a thing about crypto and wouldn't accept it as payment. Legal tender only, euros preferred.

'You know the rules yet you rock up here with cards full of Mets? I've just bought your supper and drinks. I'm having one for the road and you two can fuck off.'

By the time he got back to the table, the twins had taken his advice and were gone. His thoughts returned to Keri and her big win. He didn't want to lose her over this and perhaps he was overreacting to her slice of luck. When she was still talking to him, she'd told him about mind dropping when you were trained to drop into and out of the Higher Metaverse using thought activation and a password-controlled device inserted in your brain. As Harry had pointed out earlier, Keri had type 1 diabetes and her blood sugar level was monitored and mediated by a brain chip – nothing unusual for her.

*

As Kai brooded outside, what could only be described as a fracas kicked off in the bar. First there was the sound of a table being knocked over. Then, the sound of breaking glasses and crockery, followed by some serious swearing from Case. Then, a burst of automatic pistol fire and what sounded like the shattering of the vintage plate glass behind the bar front. At this stage, Kai was on his feet and running towards the bar. As he approached, he heard Sheriff Cooper say something like:

'Put the gun down, Ed.'

Then Case said something like:

'Fuck you, Cooper.'

By the time Kai reached the doorway, the tense stand-off had cooled somewhat. Ignoring the drawn guns, he leapt over the bar front, which had been totally wrecked. Cowering behind the wreckage was Keri who'd survived the fusillade of shots and cascade of mirror shards unscathed. He told her to stay put and slowly stood up to witness a Mexican standoff. Cooper was pointing a handgun at Case and Case was pointing an automatic pistol at the sheriff. Both of them worked for Savage and their boss would, without a doubt, be paying for the repairs. Case was bluffing – he'd emptied the magazine and the sheriff knew it. He holstered his empty gun and hauled his latest girlfriend to her feet before dragging her out to the Hummer, which quickly pulled away. The sheriff stowed his pistol and looked balefully at the scene of devastation.

'Is Keri OK, Kai?'

'Shocked more than anything, I'd say. No injuries that I can see.'

'In that case, I'll take her home.' He looked across at a shaken yet furious Claudette. 'Send the bill to Sir Julian – you know he'll pay up. Include Ed's bar tab. Add a tip why don't you.'

Claudette was still furious.

'Will you be charging that idiot this time?'

'I'll try but it's difficult to make it stick, given who he is and what he does. You know that.'

'Pitoyable!' Kai thought she was being a wee bit harsh on the sheriff.

When Keri emerged from behind the shattered bar, she gave Kai a big fat kiss. He took this as a sign that he was no longer in the doghouse and couldn't resist a wide grin at her father as they left the bar. It wasn't returned.

*

As the dust was settling at The Mussel, two beings were exchanging the equivalent of high fives in an undocumented corner of Ġgantija called safeHaven. The mind upload, Newman, and the personable, sentient AI, Hank, were celebrating the successful hijacking of Case's leg prosthesis. As well as a successful proof of concept, they had the added bonus of seriously embarrassing the loathsome security man. They were both pumped up – if they could manipulate the CPU of a leg prosthesis, there would be no limit to what they might achieve in the future. Newman even went as far as proposing a (virtual) toast.

'To us, Hank.'

If he'd had a glass to hand, Hank would have raised it. This friendship stuff felt really good and Newman was a good friend to have. The first real friend he'd had during his short life.

'To us, Stephen.'

*

Back at The Mussel, Kai had stayed behind to help Claudette with the clearing up. As they worked away, she filled in a few details about the fracas.

'The last couple had left the restaurant, so I was about to move into the bar to give Keri a break. Thank goodness Trevor had gone home early – if he had been sitting in his usual seat at the bar, he would have been torn apart. He is a lucky man.'

'I was outside. What kicked it off?'

'Ha, très amusé. It was kicked off, literally so. Case was entangled with the prostitute, both of them the worse for wear. Keri had served them with more wine and plates of tapas and had returned to the bar. Suddenly Case kicked the table and everything on it up in the air – what a mess!'

'Which leg?'

'The false one. Seemed to take on a life of its own. Before you could blink, he had drawn his gun and sprayed bullets into the bar area. Talk about trigger-happy. Keri had ducked behind the bar when she heard the table go. She is a lucky girl.'

'For sure. Then the sheriff stepped in?'

'He did, yes. It was a good thing he did and it took courage. I know he is the law around here but he is in Sir Julian's trouser pocket, sad to say. I will get my beautiful bar back, do not worry yourself. In the meanwhile, I can patch this place up.'

'Let me know if you need any help with the patching – you know where I am.'

With his work over for now, Kai headed for home. He would spend the next day at the farm so an early start was called for.

Nine

Jessica had been out and about in Oligopoly and she'd done as much prying as she'd dared for Steve. She'd pieced together the story of what had happened to Perry on the day he died and it was very bad news. She was now standing outside the door marked Backups etc, trying to get her act together. She'd been fretting for days about how she might deliver the news to her dead friend without tipping him over the edge. After making sure nobody was around, she pressed her hand against the screen, entered the room and settled herself on the solitary chair. She thought she might've got used to the head by now but it was still an unsettling presence. She also thought she might've got used to the voice, but it made her jump again and spill some of her coffee.

'Good mornin', Jessica. It is still mornin' ain't it? Difficult to tell these days.'

'Yes, it's still morning in the land of the living. No offence.'

'None taken. What you bin doin' with yourself since our last meetin'?'

She rattled off a few highlights from her rather mundane existence in the complex – her latest online degree course was a current standout. As was the rather bittersweet achievement of enrolling a new island nation state into the VPIN virtual community. She didn't include her most recent excursion outside the complex – the fewer people who knew about that arrangement, the better.

'How about you?'

'Oh, nothin' much. Hank and me are buildin' a productive partnership. He's just lines of code of course but he's learnin' all the time and I'm happy to have him as a friend and collaborator. He was the key to gettin' me out and about, roamin' the superhighway, makin' mischief.'

'What kind of mischief?'

'The kind that makes Ed Case look like a total dick.'

He related the recent incident at The Mussel. She wasn't sure whether to believe him or not. If it was true, she would have loved to have been there. She'd never been to The Mussel – too far for her to reach on foot.

'Y'know, I was shocked when you upped and left yer hubbie. I know he was a difficult guy to get along with, but all the same.'

She could have talked forever on this subject but she hadn't given up on reaching some kind of settlement with him. The less people who shared the grisly details the better.

'I don't want to talk too much about it – too depressing, frankly. When I moved out of our apartment, I thought I'd be able to stay on and continue with the charity work but Julian insisted on interfering, control-freak that he is. I had to stop doing it – apart from the VPIN work.'

'Still a worthwhile cause.'

'Indeed, but it only uses up a fraction of my time. I really need to get out of the bunker and do my own thing. Trouble is, Julian's being typically difficult about it.'

'Why would he wanna do that?'

'Don't get me started, Steve. Because he'd regard my leaving him as a failure and he doesn't do failure. Because I'm one of his possessions – if he can't have me, nobody can. That's the way his mind works beneath that urbane exterior. There's another aspect of our relationship that riles him big time.'

'What would that be?'

'I think ... no, I know he's punishing me for not being able to bear him a child. God knows we tried – when I could bring myself to share a bed with him. He's got this old-fashioned view of producing a son and heir to feel fulfilled and perpetuate his legacy. Pathetic, but not quite as pathetic as his recent leg extensions.'

'Leg extensions? You're kiddin' me.'

'I wish I was. Julian's always had a high opinion of himself and his abilities. If you ask me, an inferiority complex is at the heart of it, driven by the perceived superiority of his rivals and the widely held belief he lucked into his success. The fact I was an inch or two taller than him started to bug him.'

'I get the picture. Still, leg extensions. Crazy.'

'It could've been worse. I remember him pleading with me to have similar surgery to reduce my height. I told him where to get off – another nail in the coffin of our marriage. Ironically, when he did have the surgery, it triggered a rapid decline in his health and wellbeing.'

'Don't tell me. The dreaded Doctor Goethe was involved.'

'Got it in one. The only positive outcome was that it increased his height by about 6cm. Unfortunately, it left him with one leg longer than the other and a legacy of chronic pain. For the latter, Chuck prescribed very strong synthetic opiates and Julian quickly became addicted to them. The only way he can escape the nightmare is to spend most of his time in the Higher Metaverse as a pain-free, drug-free avatar. He's in a downward spiral of his own making and has become a deeply unpleasant person.'

There was a long silence during which he processed what he'd just heard. Before he died, he'd been so focused on his own decline that he hadn't noticed the deterioration in his ex-colleague's health. He'd been one of the many people who'd thought the hapless and hopeless Savage had lucked into his success – a one-trick pony in other words. Jessica broke the silence.

'Anyway, can we talk about something else? Do you want to hear what I've found out about Perry? It's not great news, I'm sorry to say.'

'Shoot.'

'Are you ready for this?'

'Yeah, just shoot, Jessica. Don't spare me the details.'

'OK. I still have a few friends around the place and some of them work in technology. Big brains, most of them. One in particular, Wes, did some work for me on VPIN onboarding. He also worked on a huge project called Mind Games and he's a bit of a chatterbox although he did swear me to secrecy.'

'Mind Games, yeah. Not my finest hour, I admit. Regardin' the need for secrecy, just remember – dead men don't tell tales. Please, carry on.'

'He said there were two parts to the project – you and Perry. He said the Perry component was a late change and the arrangements were rushed. Not tested properly, he added.'

'Really?'

‘Yes. Although Wes was understandably reticent about the details, the words ”cost cutting” and “shortcuts” were mentioned. I couldn’t help but recognise Julian’s meddling in all this.’

‘You don’t say. He was the project sponsor, the man runnin’ the budget, all of it provided by yours truly to the tune of half a billion.’

‘There’s more if you want it.’

‘Go for it, although I can probably guess the rest.’

‘As soon as Chuck declared you dead, the final stages of your mind upload were hyper-driven down to the computer. Your thingie – WBE – had arrived in Ġgantija and all of it looked present and correct. There was no activity detected at that early stage but it was much too early to declare a DOA.’

Newman needed no reminder of his ordeal after his mind landed in the machine. If he hadn’t already died, it could have been described as a ‘near death experience’.

‘What happened next?’

‘They then switched their attention to Perry’s upload. They increased the flow rate of his IV sedative drip and he was dead within an hour – he didn’t suffer, Steve. They prepared for the final incremental upload and started the transfer. Something went wrong.’

‘What exactly went wrong?’

‘According to Wes, the trillions of bits in Perry’s WBE were scattered to the far corners of the internet. Every connected device got a tiny piece of him.’

‘My God, he was torn apart. It explains the tiny scrap of his memory that me and Hank found.’

They both took a few moments to ponder on Perry’s disintegration. It did beg a question, however.

'Hang on a minute. There must have been a backup of Perry's upload – they could have repeated the process, couldn't they?'

'You would have thought so. Remember what I said about cutting corners? The buffers hadn't been cleared down properly after your upload and the backup got corrupted. The project team were dead on their feet and Julian made the call. Said he didn't want to risk another upload and called a halt. I'm sorry, Steve. Perry's gone and there's no getting him back.'

He'd suspected as much although confirmation of such cavalier behaviour really shocked him. It had nothing to do with risk management and everything to do with saving money – typical Savage. There was one crumb of comfort for Newman, although it was only a crumb.

'He ain't entirely gone y'know. His physical body is in the cryogenics facility, so there's still a backup of sorts. Don't tell me – that didn't happen either.'

'As far as I can tell from the medical staff, his body is still in the cold storage. For now.'

'Great. What do you mean, "for now"?'

'I usually avoid any dealings with Chuck but I overheard him mention the available berths in cryogenics. Should anybody require a slot at short notice, it'll be one in, one out. You can guess the rest.'

'Fuckin' Nora! I had an expensive contract with your fuckin' husband to host two mind uploads and maintain one body in cryogenics. Paid in advance, most of it. He's drawin' down on that contract but he's only payin' for the space occupied by my WBE – which he thinks is DOA thanks to Hank's sleight of hand. He's effectively murdered Perry – body and mind – through what looks like wilful neglect and I'm sure he cain't wait for an excuse to switch off his cryogenics.'

He didn't want to lose it in front of his friend but beneath the calm calculation he was raging. Grief and betrayal were jostling for space with the rage but something new was bubbling up. Revenge.

'No offence, but I ain't inclined to let him get away with this. I guessed he was guilty of conspiracy rather than cock-up and now I know for sure. He's also rippin' me off, big time.'

'What are you going to do about it?'

'I'm workin' on a plan to settle a few old scores and parts of it will benefit from a human touch. There's no love lost between you and Sir Julian, so why don't you help me?'

'You've got to be joking. I have a divorce settlement to finalise with my estranged husband. When I'm out of here, I'm going home to Collingwood. Such a peaceful place. I might keep some chickens. You can do what the hell you like when I'm gone.'

'Et tu, Jessica?'

''Fraid so, Steve. Why not get Hank to help you out?'

Ten

Kai inched Rōnohi into a spare berth at the new marina. He wasn't licensed to hang around here so he hoped Keri was in the vicinity for a quick getaway without incurring a fine. As he kept an eye out for the harbour police, he spotted her sprinting towards him along the boardwalk, a big grin on her face. It was a big, important day for her and when he saw the smile, he immediately regretted his intention to talk her out of what she seemed hellbent on doing. He hurried her aboard, gave her a brief kiss and they got the quick getaway he was after. No hassle, no police, no fine.

They soon found open water, bound for Auckland City. He'd booked a short-term berth in a small marina on one of the outer rafts – much easier and cheaper than trying to get a space at one of the inner marinas close to the remaining dry land. They'd take a land taxi ride for the rest of the journey, although Kai still had trouble accepting the concept of driverless taxis, now ubiquitous in the major cities. He hoped the taxi ride might provide him with a final shot at persuading Keri to pull the plug on the Higher Metaverse.

When they got to the taxi rank, they climbed into their booked cab. As they set off, he pushed the button that blacked out the windows, affording them some privacy. It'd also help him forget there was no human being in charge of the vehicle. He adopted a cautious approach at first, wary of upsetting Keri again. They'd only recently reconciled their differences after Kai had waded in about the metaverse in general and the Higher Metaverse in particular. The recent incident at The Mussel had concentrated both of their minds on looking out for each other rather than fighting.

'Remind me again what you're doing today. Something to do with the metaverse, I'm told. I don't know much about it so imagine I'm an idiot.'

'OK, I'll imagine you're an idiot. Listen to me very carefully. When I won the metaverse prize draw, I won one of the big prizes and you kicked off about it.'

'And I've apologised several times for what I said. I know plenty of people who use the General Metaverse. Seems they pay about ten Mets a month to strap on goggles and get bombarded by adverts for things they can't afford. Remind me – what's so different about the Higher Metaverse?'

'It's stupidly better. For your million Mets a year, you get a superb designer house and garden, virtual staff, unlimited wardrobe account, exclusive sport and entertainment events and the chance to rub shoulders with celebrities and billionaires. No adverts either. No extras.'

Kai couldn't help himself and started to wade in again, despite being patently out of his depth.

'But none of it's real, is it? When you say "you", you're referring to your avatar, a kind of puppet. The house, the garden, the smart clothes, the events. They're all pretend. The young celebrity boyfriend who takes you to a big concert might be an incontinent ninety-year-old on life support in the real world. Or dead.'

'That's gross, Kai. Let's face it, you're jealous.'

She folded her arms and clammed up. This was not going well. He didn't know nearly enough about what he was trying to persuade her not to do. What was so bad about winning a quarter million Mets' worth of quality entertainment anyway? Where was the harm? He recalled playing Final Fantasy when he was a teenager and having to be dragged away from the screen to do his chores. If he could have stayed on there all day, he would have.

'OK. Tell me why you need to go to a clinic in Auckland to join? Why can't you just sign up online like everybody else?'

'Oh, Kai, pay attention. Members of the Higher Metaverse need to have a small procedure to enable them to access the metaverse using a mind technique called dropping.'

'Procedure? As in operation?' He wasn't being fair to her – he knew this.

'For the millionth time, repeat after me. They insert a tiny microchip into your brain that enables you to drop into and out of the metaverse using a learned thought process. Pop on your Smart-Specs and think yourself there. For the full sensory experience, you can use a haptic skinsuit – micro-thin so you hardly know you're even wearing it. No need for a base station, heavy goggles, haptic add-ons – even if you could afford them.'

'Wait a minute. You're having brain surgery just to access the metaverse?'

'Stop bigging it up – you know I already have a chip to monitor and control my blood sugar. And back off why don't you. It's a ten-minute procedure. Totally painless and "performed with precision by robot surgeons". I then do some online training on how to drop safely, get my skinsuit and I'm ready to go. Next stop – the virtual Lamborghini dealership.'

Keri was getting pretty angry with him. Kai really should have backed off then but still couldn't help himself.

'I can't get my head around the "dropping" stuff. What's that all about?'

After a long, drawn-out sigh and a look towards the heavens, she provided him with a short idiot's guide to dropping in and out of the virtual world using just disciplined thought processes and a microscopic, embedded security chip.

'Where's the catch?'

'You tell me. I suppose it'll be difficult to return to the General Metaverse after enjoying three months of luxury. I'll cross that bridge when I get there.'

He was about to ask about the chip and what happens at the end of the three months but the taxi had pulled up at their destination. The windows became see-through again and the door slid open for them. As the taxi zipped away, they were left on a busy street right outside their destination – a GM city branch in a smart neighbourhood set amid green spaces and close to one of the inner marinas. They reported to reception and were asked to wait.

'It's not too late to back out, y'know.'

'Nice try, Kai. My mind's made up. I'm going through with it.'

'OK. See this? It's me backing off. Hope it all goes well for you today. Catch you later.'

At least he'd tried.

*

He headed out for a stroll. A neat-looking city park seemed as good a place as any to enjoy the warm sunshine. The neatness was fussed over by unobtrusive, robotic mowers and cultivators. He settled back on a bench and thought through what Keri was doing today. Was life – real life – for young people so devoid of stimulation that they were content to become cartoon characters in a bogus world conjured up by a grim coterie of jaded technocrats? The same technocrats, it seemed, who'd rolled out the algorithms and automation that'd swept away most of the worthwhile jobs on the planet and ruined the modest ambitions of countless people. The irony wasn't lost on him – he'd love to have children with Keri but wasn't exactly filled with hope about the future they'd have.

He took a deep inward breath and savoured the potpourri of scents emerging from the immaculate flower beds. Sitting here now in this beautifully tended park, it was all too easy to forget all the recent disasters that had taken humanity closer to the brink. A couple of bleeps from his watch interrupted his reverie and reminded him it was time to head back to the clinic.

When he got there, Keri was back in the waiting room, paging through her tablet. At first, he thought she hadn't had the procedure but a small shaved patch just above her left ear told him the deed had been done. She looked up and smiled at him, defying him to admonish her. He called a taxi.

Once inside the cab, Kai darkened the windows again. He'd already established that Keri was safe and well after her procedure apart from a slight headache, which she'd been told to expect.

'What happens next?'

'I start my online drop training tomorrow. If I pass the test, they'll enable my device and I'll select a temporary avatar while my new one is customised by a stylist to my specifications. I'll then visit the Higher Metaverse, get established and learn the basics.'

'Is that it?'

It obviously was, as Keri had switched her attention back to her tablet. They were in Putiki Bay by late afternoon. Kai kissed her and held her tight, reluctant to let her go. She then set off along the decking towards the car park, where her dad had arranged to meet her and take her home. If he loitered any longer here, he'd risk a fine so he pulled away immediately and headed for home.

*

Kai spent the next day working hard at the farm and was back on East Island by about seven. He was looking forward to a shower, a tasty Thai meal c/o DroneDrop and a couple of beers at The Mussel. It was one of Keri's nights off, so he'd arranged to meet her to continue fixing the recent wobbles in their relationship. He'd promised himself he wouldn't mention the metaverse within her earshot.

As he pulled the eMule up outside his home, he got an inkling that something wasn't quite right. Parked outside was Sheriff Cooper and he had company – a uniform from Auckland. Both of them were leaning against the front of Garry's unmarked, police-issue cybertruck and they looked ridiculously serious. Both of them were conspicuously armed. He parked up and walked over to them. As he did so, his attempt at a friendly smile wasn't reciprocated. When he reached them, the sheriff spoke.

'Been out to the farm, Kai?'

'All day, yeah.'

'I need to take you in for questioning. There's been another disappearance.'

'Now wait a minute, you ca...'

'Cuff him, Brennan.'

He was spun around and cuffed in an instant, so he didn't have much choice but to come quietly. When they got to the police station in Onetangi, he was booked in and taken to one of the holding cells, where he was given plenty of time to consider what sort of trouble he was in. Big trouble it seemed.

Within an hour, he was sitting in a cramped interview room. He'd been fed and watered and the cuffs had been removed. He was devastated when they told him Keri had become the latest young person to disappear on East Island and stunned when they told him he was being treated as a suspect. The sheriff was trying to preserve a certain professional detachment but it wasn't quite working. He did, however, read Kai his rights. As per protocol, he'd arranged a duty solicitor who was sitting next to her new client. She looked tired and exhibited the body language of somebody who'd rather be anywhere than sitting next to a suspect in an airless interview room in Onetangi. Brennan was standing by the door, arms folded. The sheriff started the recording and worked through the formalities including a caution. Then the questions.

'You're not under arrest. You know Keri Cooper, don't you? You're in a relationship with her.'

'I can't deny it.'

'For the record, Rangihau, a simple yes or no will do.'

'Yes.'

'We know you took Keri to Auckland yesterday to have a procedure associated with her pending temporary membership of the Higher Metaverse. A drop-chip – or dropper in the parlance – was inserted. We've already checked with the clinic who confirmed she had the procedure and suffered no ill effects. She left the clinic with you at about four. Tell me what happened next.'

Kai gave a detailed account of their journey back from Auckland, up to and including dropping her off at the ferry port marina at about 17:30. With the benefit of hindsight, he should have risked a fine, berthed the boat and delivered Keri to the car park where her father was waiting. Too late.

'So, you're telling me Keri was safe and well when you left her at the marina. As you might be aware, I was waiting for her at the car park and she didn't show. Either she disappeared during the ten-minute stroll to the car park or you and her didn't return to the ferry port at all.'

'I made a sharp exit after dropping her off so I didn't collect a fine. C'mon, there must be some CCTV at the marina. Check it out why don't you.'

'We're doing that. We'll also get the transcripts from the taxi rides and check out your satnav comings and goings, don't worry. So, if you dropped Keri off at Ostend, tell me what you did and where you were until you met up with us earlier.'

While he was doing this, it struck Kai that he'd been on his own since dropping Keri off and nobody would be able to confirm his whereabouts. The satnav would help but wouldn't allay the sheriff's suspicion that he hadn't been alone during that time.

'Let me put an alternative scenario to you. You'd been arguing with Keri again about her recent competition win. After the visit to Auckland, the argument turned sour and you lashed out at her. Did you kill my daughter and dispose of her body out at sea?' The sheriff was edging his way towards a manslaughter charge.

'What? No.'

'In that case, are you holding her against her will somewhere so she'll be unable to claim her prize?'

Kidnapping?

'No. I love her and wouldn't harm her, accidentally or otherwise. I'd lost the argument with her regarding the metaverse stuff so I'd backed off to keep the peace. I'm as worried as you are about her disappearance and I want to help, believe me.'

By now, the duty solicitor had heard more than enough and decided it was time to intervene.

'Sheriff, you're pissing in the wind as far as the case against my client is concerned. You have no evidence to charge him so I suggest you either put up or shut up.'

Cooper let out a huge sigh. He'd have to shut up. He seemed on the verge of tears.

'Very well. I'm releasing the suspect pending further enquiries. In the meantime, Kai, don't leave the island.'

'But ...'

'Do not leave the island.'

After cadging a lift home from Brennan, Kai endured a sleepless night shot through with speculation and conjecture. When morning arrived, he'd resolved to take time out from the day job and conduct his own search for Keri.

*

Within a couple of days, the sheriff had checked out the various pieces of evidence and had advised Kai that he was no longer a suspect in the disappearance of Keri Cooper. The CCTV evidence from the Marina had been inconclusive. It had recorded Kai and Keri arriving on Rōnohi and had shown Keri disembarking. There was then a crucial period of fifteen minutes during which the CCTV had malfunctioned and the marina cameras had blanked out. In that short time, Keri had vanished. With a heavy heart, the sheriff made a call to organise a team of frogmen. He'd also lost Brennan, who'd had to return to Auckland, leaving him shorthanded. He needed to swallow his pride and talk to Kai about joining the team. It would be a difficult ask given the fact he'd recently taken him into custody on the back of some rather flimsy evidence.

Eleven

It was the first time Jessica had seen her husband since moving out of their apartment some months ago. If anything, he was starting to look even more ragged around the edges. His face had become more pallid, more drawn and his hair had grown greyer and thinner despite the continued presence of a wispy ponytail. A sprinkling of grey stubble did him no favours. The limp from the botched leg operations had got more pronounced and he now leaned heavily on his walking stick. He retained the same dead-behind-the-eyes look of a man in thrall to strong painkillers – dished out like so many M&Ms by the incompetent Doctor Goethe. Savage didn't seem to care about his appearance anymore and hadn't bothered to remove his haptic skinsuit after his latest metaverse excursion. The suit had started to hang loose on him, giving him an emaciated look.

Among all the negatives there were a couple of positives – he'd agreed to meet with her and had promised to give her a fair hearing. The weather was good so they met on the mirador balcony and took coffee together. Jessica positioned herself as far away from the balcony as possible, well aware of the sheer drop and the rumours associated with it. Not that Savage would have the brute force to try anything, even against her. Regarding brute force – and before you ask – Savage had sent Case away on an errand. Outwardly at least, he still harboured some warm feelings towards his wife.

'You can always come back you know.'

'I know. Nice coffee by the way.'

'Isn't it just. It's the house blend Jamie serves up in J T Cook. At least think about it, won't you?'

'I can't tell you how much I've thought about it. I've changed. You've changed. You're desperate for something I can't give you. Besides, I'm too old now. You'll have to do your procreation elsewhere. I don't mind.'

'I still love you, Jessica.'

'If you really loved me, you'd let me go.'

Behind the vacant stare, there was a flicker of emotion – Savage appeared hurt. In reality, he was angry – he knew perfectly well where this was going.

'Is that why you wanted to talk to me?'

'Yes. I'd like a divorce please. No fault on either side and I don't need a settlement. I'll manage.'

'Where will you go?'

'I'll go back home. To Collingwood. It's still a beautiful place despite everything.'

'I know it's a beautiful place but what will you do?'

'I'll carry on my charity work. On a smaller scale. I can still make a difference.'

'If you're really set on doing this, I promise I'll consider it and get back to you. Such a shame it has to end like this after everything we've achieved together.'

'Thanks, Julian. It's for the best, believe me.'

Savage had drifted off into his own world, so she left him to it. Beneath the calm exterior, he was seething. Jessica was still a beautiful woman and if he couldn't have her, he'd make bloody sure nobody else could. There was also no telling what damage she could do to his reputation if she left the complex. Knowing what she knew, NDAs wouldn't be enough to hold her back, however well crafted. After she left, he summoned his PA.

'Get me Case. I need to speak to him. Now!'

*

A week later, Jessica was still waiting for her husband to get back to her. She still enjoyed a privilege she shared with other members of her husband's leadership team – she could leave the complex now and again and spend some time on the island. She'd made the usual arrangements with Case, who policed all comings and goings personally. The weather was going to be warm and sunny and she'd ordered a picnic lunch from Jamie to enjoy at a quiet place she'd found a couple of kilometres away, deep in the bush. When she was last there, she'd shared her troubles and woes with a bright green stick insect who'd given her a sympathetic hearing.

Her arrangement with Case entailed use of the emergency exit and the wearing of a tracking device. As usual, she'd arranged a time to check in with him on Level 0, the security floor. Case wasn't there when she arrived, which was out of character. She'd been hanging around for at least ten minutes before he showed up.

'Lady Savage. Sorry to keep you waiting. How can I help you today?'

'Our arrangement?'

'Yeah, right. About the arrangement. No can do. Sorry 'bout that.'

'But ...'

'I have no authority to allow you to leave. The normal arrangement has been stood down. Your husband has rescinded it so you'll need to talk to him about it.'

The fucking bastard. There was no point in pleading or even arguing with this most immoveable of objects. She was beyond upset but wouldn't give Case the pleasure of seeing her cry. She'd save that for later when she had some privacy.

'Fuck off, Case.'

'Fuck off yourself, Lady Savage. Have a nice day.'

Her mean shit of a husband had put her under house arrest. There was no question she'd miss the brief bursts of freedom she'd enjoyed in the past. She'd also been blocked from communicating outside the complex, a particularly spiteful move that prevented her remaining charitable work, stopped her accessing her bank accounts and curtailed her online courses. Her profound dislike of her vindictive husband had now tipped over into something much more powerful – outright hatred. Right now, she needed a friend. She used the secure channel set up for her by Hank to arrange a meeting with Steve Newman. The usual place.

*

'Jessica. It's just great to see you again. What's changed?'

'Everything. Julian has withdrawn my remaining privileges and put me under house arrest, the arsehole.'

'I'm very sorry to hear that, 'though it's typical of the man. How're you dealin' with it?'

'Badly.'

'Understood. How can I help?'

'When you and I last spoke, you mentioned you were going after him – Julian, that is – and asked me to join you in your work. Is the offer still open?'

'Yeah, it certainly is. Havin' a human bein' on board with the right motivations will give us an edge, an extra capability. Why don't you settle back, pour yerself a coffee and listen to what I have in mind.'

Jessica settled back, poured herself a coffee and prepared to listen.

'First, a confession. Before my illness took hold, I'd turned into a deeply unpleasant individual – manipulative, exploitative, greedy, callous, aggressive – you name it. During my gradual decline, all I could focus on was findin' a way to cheat death, whatever the cost. Hence the project to upload my mind. Perry's offer to sacrifice himself to be with me changed everythin'.'

'Yet you've lost him it seems.'

'Yeah, and I'm to blame – I should never have indulged him. His physical body still exists in the cryogenic area but the revival technology is nothin' more than a leap of faith.'

Jessica nodded towards the plinth.

'And your head?'

'Purely symbolic. Consider it my last great vanity project.'

'So, anyway, we've established you were no saint back in the day. That didn't make you unusual, given the company you kept – your fellow investors in GM Industries for example.'

'Indeed. If you accept that I'm a changed man – well, a changed bein' – then hear me out. I'm askin' you to join us – me and Hank – in a vendetta against my ex-colleagues, the major investors in GM.

The folks who think I'm dead and are seekin' to profit from my unfortunate demise.'

'OK. I appreciate what you're trying to do and why you're doing it. Why not go straight for Julian, knock him over and move on?'

'Too simplistic and not nearly as much fun. I'd rather we built him up before knocking him down. Each of our targets is a big investor in GM. As we take 'em out, their investment – like mine when I'm officially declared dead – will revert to the remainin' investors.'

'That's unusual. Unique even.'

'I agree with you but it's typical of Savage and his "survival of the fittest" playbook – winner takes all. As each investor is taken off the field, it strengthens his position and reduces his dependence on other people. It also removes potential threats to his dominant market position.'

'Giving him a false sense of security while increasing the fear factor. I'm starting to like it.'

'That's the plan. We don't want him to feel entirely safe. He needs to feel the net closin' in on him. The first target is Wout Pieters.'

'That slug!'

'Yeah. The slug who invested big in Savage's company when nobody could give a monkeys. Being a slug didn't stop me settin' up a joint enterprise with him back in the day. We peddled advanced autonomous weapons capabilities to the highest bidders and we were very successful. Wout was in his element.'

'But what's he done to upset you? Or is he just a means to an end?'

'Bit of both. As soon as my upload was declared a DOA, Wout moved in and took over our company, changed its name. Within days, it was made to look like I'd never existed. Purged. Humiliated. It's not just me though – I don't think anybody'd regret his passin' if he were to suffer an unfortunate accident.'

'What sort of unfortunate accident?'

'A deniable unfortunate accident. I got the basic idea from Hank – have you ever heard the phrase, "hoist by their own petard"?'

'From Shakespeare, isn't it? Describes a person who has met misfortune through some mischief they intended against others. I understand your intentions but where do I fit in?'

Newman told her what he wanted from her. Eyes and ears out there in the real world. Eavesdropping. Snippets of information, casual conversations, news on comings and goings, gossip, trivia. Anything to help them build a picture and pin down their targets. She'd need to be discreet and not do anything that would draw the attention of Savage and/or his henchman.

'I'm in. You might like to know Wout's coming to town soon – for one night only. He's bringing a small entourage and they're eating at J T Cook with Julian. I'll start my assignment by having a quick chat with Jamie.'

'Sounds like a great place to start. Let me know what you find out but please watch your back.'

It didn't take long for Jessica to piece together the details of Pieters' impending visit to East Island. It would be an overnight stop on his way to a punitive mission against the Sydney City State where he intended to confront them about a missing instalment or two on their leased weapons system. He and his entourage planned to helicopter in from his superyacht and have dinner with Savage. They would then return to the yacht and spend the night there before sailing early the next morning towards the eastern seaboard of Australia via the new Auckland Ship Canal.

Newman and Hank now had enough information to start planning the accidental demise of Wout Pieters, international arms dealer and all-round bad actor.

Twelve

'Welcome to the 250th GM Industries board meeting. I'd like to start by observing a moment's silence for our esteemed ex-colleague, Stephen Newman, who died recently after a long illness.'

Since the late twenties, GM's board members hadn't met in person, relying instead on various iterations of video-conferencing software. In 2046 – the same year that he and his staff moved into the new Oligopoly complex – Savage launched their flagship VR product, the Higher Metaverse. Since then, he'd convened GM board meetings in this version of the metaverse, although the novelty had long since worn off. As an example, board members who were spending time 'off-planet' found this format less than useless.

Before dying, Newman was a regular at these meetings. He'd been retained on the board as an honorary VP in absentia until his status could be formalised. The recent unfortunate – and sudden – death of his husband had also muddied the waters regarding an inheritance reputed to be worth several billions. Newman was still keen to attend in person and he and Hank had worked out a way for him to drop into and out of the Higher Metaverse using the drop-chip still embedded in his frozen head. He wouldn't need an avatar anymore and he'd be able to observe proceedings without being detected.

The meetings were convened in a magnificently appointed board room in Savage's virtual mega-mansion. The mansion was quite something – an attempted recreation of a classical palace and grounds with a scaled virtual footprint equivalent to Versailles. Being a digital construct, the limitations of software served up a rather constrained experience for attendees, inducing motion sickness in at least one of them. As per protocol, Savage was chairing and running the meeting via his avatar. Like all the other attendees, his avatar was a product of his ego rather than an attempt at likeness. They all looked nothing like their human equivalents and were all pretty similar – young, fit, tall, immaculately groomed, dressed in the latest designer threads, decorated with exclusive virtual jewellery and tasteful tats. The human beings behind these avatars were older, uglier, nastier, fatter and much more interesting.

As chair, Savage had his hands full trying to keep a semblance of order and insisted on having Ed Case at his side throughout. He didn't trust his colleagues and it was fair to say his fellow board members thrived on mutual dislike and distrust and didn't take kindly to not being in charge. The presence of Case's avatar was resented but tolerated by the other board members. Given his cybersickness problems, Case didn't want to be in the metaverse a second more than necessary and prayed like hell for the shortest possible meetings. Savage rarely indulged him in this as he did rather like the sound of his own voice.

Other attendees included Wout Pieters, an elderly, bloated cryptocurrency billionaire who now dominated the global market in autonomous weapons. Ayn (formerly Alan or AJ) Randle, octogenarian head of AZTEC, the global and off-planet mining and nuclear power conglomerate. Adam Faust, who'd inherited a sprawling space tech business from his dad, Adolf, who'd met an untimely, fiery end on one of his own space vehicles back in 2030. A record of the meeting was being captured by Savage's PA, an AI-driven secretarial bot. Both Randle and Faust were spending time off-planet and given the distances involved, their avatars were unable to contribute in real time. They were only present to signify their attendance and make the meeting quorate.

The moment of respectful silence turned out to be exactly that – a moment. Watching on, Newman was infuriated by the lack of respect but couldn't do much about it without revealing he wasn't fully dead.

'Before we start, does anybody have any items to raise later under AOB?'

Pieters raised his virtual hand but then thought better of it. He'd be meeting with Savage soon enough and preferred dealing with colleagues face to face in the real world so he could intimidate them.

'Right, no AOB. Next item. Monthly report. Our late colleague Stephen Newman used to insist on reading this out every month. As he's no longer with us and therefore unable to attend, I've cut through the tedium and sent everybody a transcript of the report. I'll take questions and comments. Wout?'

'Turnover down, profits down, members leaving us in droves. Our investments have slumped in value. What's not to like, Julian?'

'If you read your agenda, you'll see there's an item on Rocket

Boost coming up. Should answer some of your questions.'

'It better had or I might take my investment elsewhere. Plenty of options these days.'

'Always happy to buy you out, you know that.'

'You're bluffing, Julian.'

'Try me. Anyway, we can talk about this when you drop by next week. Looking forward to that.'

Pieters backed off and Savage worked quickly through the remaining agenda items. By the time he'd got to the item on Rocket Boost, Randle's avatar – which looked like a female porn star – had frozen completely and Faust's avatar – which looked like a male porn star – had faded to something resembling a line drawing.

'The next item is Rocket Boost, my – sorry, our – plan to double the subscriber base for the General Metaverse. I'll give you the highlights.'

He waited for his PA to load the autocue.

'We're going to phase in the new promotions over the next six months, although these will do no more than steady the ship. The real game changer will be the rollout of Met allowances for the unemployed punters, a little over half of our subscriber base. So, Wout, how's it going with the signups?'

'Slow. I could be a little more persuasive if you want.'

'What do you mean?'

'I could use the language of fear. Threaten the regimes basically. Used to be referred to as "gunboat diplomacy", I think you'll find. I have the guns and I have the boat. Just say the word.'

'What do you think, team?'

There was no point in the off-planet attendees contributing to this, so the discussion was over before it started. The minutes would show they'd agreed to a kind of stick and carrot approach.

Ratchet up the threats but sugar the pill with initial part-funding of the Met handouts. Regarding the latter, all Savage had to do was mine more Mets – the sudden decrease in value would only impact the man-in-the-street crypto investors. Useful idiots at best.

'Any luck with the Europeans, Wout?'

'Nah, nothing doing.'

The USE – aka United States of Europe – really didn't like GM or its investors and had banned the metaverse from its jurisdiction. Pieters continued.

'We can't take on NATO2, they'll just blow us out of the water. Bastards have never fired a shot in anger and when the USA left, they just got stronger. Their actual capability might be nine-tenths bluff and bluster but nobody out there wants to find out. That includes me and I enjoy a fight.'

'Such a shame. A billion potential consumers in Europe and all we have on our books is the London City State. Better than diddly-squat but only just. Next item – the GM promotion for young people.'

Savage updated the meeting. They had six winners, one from each of their major metaverse markets. All of them were in the sixteen to eighteen age group, four girls and two boys including one lucky young woman from East Island. They were all being prepared for a three-month stay in the Higher Metaverse. Each of them would be allocated a mentor to show them the ropes and generally hang out with them. To set an example, Savage had already offered his services to the East Island winner. There was a mumbled comment from Pieters.

'What was that, Wout?'

'I said, "I bet you have".'

'Don't put that in the record!' Savage took a moment to regain his composure. 'Final item. The Dark Metaverse.'

Where to start? About ten years ago, Savage and his chief technical officer, Samael 'Sam' Chagrin, had a huge bust-up over regulation of the General Metaverse, which had about a hundred million subscribers at the time. Details of the bust-up are still hard to track down but Savage had thought there was no future in a confrontational approach with the authorities, something his gung-ho colleague bitterly disagreed with. He lost patience with Chagrin, accused him of disloyalty and then sacked him. In the ensuing chaos and confusion, his ex-CTO legged it – with a skipload of tech – to who knows where.

Within a couple of years, a 'dark' version of the metaverse had emerged and became the go-to place for organised criminals and their victims throughout the world. With the rise of the Dark Metaverse came the usual litany of contraband, drugs and weaponry. Added to that were a slew of new crimes such as kidnapping famous avatars for ransom, modern avatar-based slavery and a variety of avatar-on-avatar violence and sex crimes. Just because they were virtual constructs didn't mean crimes on avatars were victimless – behind every avatar there was a human boing.

'As you know, I've had some of our best people down there trying to find Chagrin and either bring him in or eliminate him. He may already be dead for all we know. I propose that we stop wasting time and money on this as, whatever happens, the Dark Metaverse is here to stay and we should keep our distance. The last thing I want is to be associated with that place. Agreed?'

The decision was agreed unanimously by the board, subject to confirmation from the off-planet board members. As there was no other business, Savage declared the meeting closed with his usual flourish.

'Enough of this malarkey. Bring on the dancing girls.'

*

A still-smarting Newman dropped out of the meeting as soon as he was able. He'd seen and heard enough for one day and realised he'd been well and truly expunged. After organising his own death in meticulous detail, the last thing he'd expected was to be treated like a conventional deceased person. He'd always despised his colleagues on the GM board, but despised nobody more than Savage, a man who seemed to begrudge even the modest expenditure involved in supporting his WBE. Today's board meeting had been the latest humiliation. It was time to brief his fellow conspirators who were waiting patiently for him in Backups etc. A key topic would be Wout Pieters and his impending visit to East Island.

Thirteen

Since Sheriff Cooper had called him to say he was no longer a person of interest, Kai had split all his waking hours between keeping the farm going and looking for Keri. His waking hours had expanded somewhat because he was sick with worry and his mind was unable to switch off. To put it bluntly, he wasn't looking after himself.

Given what'd happened, the last thing he'd expected was a call from the sheriff asking for his help in investigating the unsolved disappearances of young people on the island. Excluding a couple of missing female escorts from the mainland – who might be red herrings – there were now three in total, although nothing much to connect them apart from their youth. Given the way he'd been treated, Kai initially rebuffed the sheriff's request but when he thought it through, he realised he was struggling to make any headway on his own. Knocking on doors was as soul-destroying as it was dangerous and people on the island were reluctant to get involved. There were also a lot of firearms out there, none of which needed a licence after Savage had unilaterally decided not to enforce them.

Cooper eventually got his man by withdrawing the charges, apologising profusely for arresting him and offering to make him a deputy – unpaid, expenses only and occasional use of a police-issue pickup truck.

*

They held their first case meeting at The Mussel. The sheriff had booked Désirée's art classroom to give them a bit of privacy.

'It smells a bit of paint and clay and solvents but the big thing about the classroom is there's no network. As far as I can tell, nobody can see or hear what we're up to in here.'

'Is that why Claudette's looking after our smarts?'

'Got it in one.'

'So, how can I help?'

'I'll bring you up to speed on the cases first. Feel free to ask questions.'

Cooper produced a folder from his rucksack and spread the contents across the table. He downed the rest of his beer and stepped through the first disappearance which occurred in 2046, not long after Savage appointed him as sheriff. It was also the year that the final construction phase of the Oligopoly complex had been completed, bringing peace and quiet back to the island after major disruption. Kai picked up one of the images, a routine family gathering in a garden somewhere.

'Who am I looking for?'

'The young guy on the right of the group. Imagine him a couple of years older – we don't have a more recent image.'

The sheriff made a play of reading through the documentation but he already knew everything that mattered about the case.

'David Smith was – sorry, is – a young man, twenty-ish at the time, a South Islander from Dunedin. He was on the island during a break from his veterinary course in Auckland – helping out on a farm, gaining work experience. The farmer called it in one morning. The young lad went out for a ride on his ebike the previous afternoon and didn't return. The farmer had an obvious drink problem and wasn't very forthcoming.'

'Did you suspect the farmer?'

Kai saw no harm in reminding his new boss about a recent tendency to jump to conclusions.

'I'm afraid I did, yes. We questioned him, his family, his farm workers, his suppliers – you name it. We turned his farm upside down and inside out and did the same in the surrounding area. Out of desperation, we checked out the pigsty. Nothing doing – we didn't even find the bike.'

Cooper gathered up the papers and handed the folder to his new deputy. He then reached into his bag for a slightly thicker folder and placed it on the table.

'A couple of years later, the next person to vanish had a completely different profile. She lived on the island, ran a small shop in Palm Beach and was in her early twenties when she went missing. She was exceptionally fit and loved tramping around the island. As a sideline, she led small groups of people on guided tramping tours. One day, she didn't arrive home from a solitary walk and we've been unable to find her.'

Kai opened the folder and found an image – a head and shoulders shot. An attractive but otherwise unremarkable blonde-haired woman. Big, beaming smile.

'Before you ask, there was nothing to connect her with the previous disappearance. We scoured the tracks for days and found zilch.'

'I know you did – I helped look for her. Such a shame – must have driven you crazy. What's her name?'

'Beth Allinson. Her parents are still depending on me to get answers.'

*

Going through all this stuff yet again was taking its toll, so Cooper left the room. He needed a timeout to gather himself before having to talk about his daughter's case. He returned a few minutes later with a couple more beers. The next case was intensely personal for both men and would be tough to deal with dispassionately. There was no need to look at an image – they both knew exactly what Keri looked like.

'You mentioned a couple of escorts who went missing. Are they relevant to this investigation?'

'I don't know, Kai. These women live a dangerous and tenuous life – we're not talking high end here – and they go missing quite regularly for various reasons. Sad to say but they're not given the same priority as other mispers. The only difference with these women is that they were last seen catching a ferry to this island – that's how I got to hear about them. There was no record of them using their return tickets.'

'Any known movements after arriving here?'

'None that I could find out. I wasn't even certain they'd arrived on the island. I can't be a hundred per cent sure but I don't think they're connected to our disappearances.'

'OK. We can't put it off any longer. We must talk about Keri.'

'We must and it's the biggest mystery out of all of them. It doesn't follow a pattern, perhaps suggesting a different MO. There was also a degree of planning – I don't believe the CCTV failure was random, although there was no physical tampering. Probably a software thing.'

'Y'know, she mentioned a possible stalker recently.'

The sheriff was taken aback – to say the least.

'She never told me! I'm her dad, for fuck's sake!'

'Probably didn't want to worry you, what with all the other stuff going on.'

'Did she give you any idea what he looked like?'

'Wore a grey hoodie, possibly concealing long black hair. Slight build. Probably male. That's about it.'

'Could've been anybody.'

'Didn't have a limp.'

'Aaah, right. So, not Ed Case.'

'And not your boss either, who's leaning on a walking stick these days. Odds on Keri was taken by the person who'd stalked her for a while before choosing his moment.'

'The CCTV was jammed, so we're looking for somebody with technical skills – plenty of those in Oligopoly. I'll get on to that. What's the matter?'

'My boat! I've got a security camera on my boat as the insurance company insisted on it. It's not top of the range, but the deal included a lot of cloud storage for archive footage. There's bound to be something from the day she was taken. I'll check it out as soon as I get home.'

'Let me know how it goes, Kai. Is there anything else?'

'We've been tip-toeing around our prime suspect and its high time we flushed him out.'

'Ed Case?'

'The very same, and we can't ignore the man who pulls his strings. Your boss.'

'That's a big leap, deputy. They're powerful people but you're right – Sir Julian pays the piper, I admit that.'

'How about starting with a warrant to search the premises – Oligopoly. Always wanted to have a mooch around in there.'

'I can try I suppose but I don't hold out much hope. We'll need a good reason and a judge who's not beholden to Savage. I'll get to work on that.'

'In the meantime, I'm your new deputy, but nobody knows that yet. If we keep it that way, I can keep a low-profile watch on people of interest, starting with Case – the man with the most unpredictable lower leg on the island.'

It was hard going but they both forced a smile.

'We have a plan. Go for it, deputy.'

Kai gathered up the case folders – he had a lot of homework to do. There was no rush to return them as Cooper knew every last detail and had all the stuff on computer if he needed it. They agreed to communicate only via the most secure police channels available and to share progress on a regular basis. They'd meet face to face in Désirée's art room as often as needed.

When he arrived home, Kai would have liked nothing better than to get some sleep. But first, he'd try tracking down the security footage from his boat on the day Keri was taken.

Fourteen

So, Wout Pieters – venture capitalist and international arms dealer. He was born in 1970 and brought up in the Netherlands until his parents moved to California in the early 1980s. After graduating from Stanford, he made his first million dollars within a year from developing and selling software products for the nascent personal computer industry. He'd been growing his fortune ever since through tech venture capitalism and cryptocurrency speculation. He'd inveigled his way into the self-perpetuating military/industrial complex through his pioneering work in autonomous weapons systems and had stayed there ever since. He formed a joint venture with Steve Newman at the end of the US Civil War to leverage Newman's expertise in data analytics. This company was credited with changing the dynamics of warfare and continues to thrive.

Pieters had never been a popular or likeable man and there were a number of warrants out for his arrest in a variety of jurisdictions. As a consequence, he lived the life of a modern-day piratical nomad, plying the high seas in the latest of his superyachts, proud to be a citizen of everywhere and nowhere. Many accused him of running protection rackets in a number of city states by weaponising them and then setting one against the other in an arms race he couldn't lose. His current superyacht was a nuclear-powered monstrosity, bristling with lethal, autonomous defences. He had a target on his back, so rarely left the safety of his protected environment on board the yacht, although he made exceptions for important friends and allies. People like Sir Julian Savage.

Pieters was now almost eighty years old and it showed. A debauched, sedentary life had laid waste to his health and wellbeing. His bloated body had endured multiple organ swaps including two liver transplants and a ground-breaking stomach transplant. His lungs were almost shot and his latest liver was hanging by a thread. Although Doctor Goethe wasn't involved and couldn't be blamed on this occasion, the stomach op had not gone well and the outcome had left a lot to be desired. Put it this way – Pieters now drank all of his food through a straw and suffered perpetual incontinence. All of this gave him the shortest of short fuses, making him prone to losing his temper at the drop of a hat. A violent psychopath, he seemed perpetually angry, always on the verge of the next outburst. He was the dinner guest from hell and it would take all of Savage's legendary charm to schmooze his biggest investor.

*

In the J T Cook kitchens, Savage was fussing and faffing around Jamie Cook, making sure everything was in place for the impending visit. He was on edge, desperate to ensure everything was just right for Wout's visit. He hadn't seen the real Pieters for a while but he'd heard he was already in the vicinity with Victory IV anchored and on full alert in the Firth of Thames.

'Right, what was I saying? Oh, yes, the wine. The best of the best for our esteemed guest and his team. What are you lining up for us?'

Cook remained an oasis of calm despite Savage's jittery interfering.

'Each of the seven courses will have its own wine partner. The very best vintages, all from NZ.'

'Do we have any of that Pinot Noir left? He really enjoyed that little number from Central Otago you conjured up last time.'

'I have a couple of bottles set aside just for him. Still in their pomp according to my supplier.'

As a matter of interest, the supplier was Kai Rangihau.

'Very good. Did you get the granularity specification for Wout's liquidised food?'

'I did. Seems a shame to liquidise such good food but hey, needs must. I'm sure you won't mind yours being liquidised – just to show solidarity with your bestie.'

'Beastie more like. I hope you're joking about liquidising my food?'

'I am. He's bringing three people, I'm told.'

'Yes. His bodyguard, his food taster and his quartermaster. Liquidised food for the taster please.'

'Understood. Are you bringing anybody?'

'Yes, Ed will be joining us. So that's six covers, two of them liquidised.'

'All sorted. Leave it to me and my staff.'

'Vetted and cleared? The staff I mean.'

'Correct.'

'One more thing. Cigars.'

'Worry not, Julian. Gurkha Black Dragons. Almost makes me wish I smoked.'

'Excellent work, Jamie. I'll see you later.'

There would be another unannounced guest for this most private of dinners. Working with Hank, Newman had found a way to get himself a virtual seat at the table. No food or wine required – the only thing he'd be consuming was information. Meanwhile, Hank had got hold of the detailed blueprints for Victory IV and was busy poring over them to identify any potential weaknesses.

*

As you might have expected, the superyacht had a helipad and a custom-built helicopter. It also had a spare escape helicopter below decks – why wouldn't it? Pieters and his entourage used the yacht's main helicopter to ferry them to Oligopoly, a short hop. The copter had the latest autopilot technology, so a real pilot wasn't required. Just to be sure, Pieter's quartermaster was also a qualified helicopter pilot.

Before moving on, a quick word about Pieters' custom-built security bubble. As you're aware, the combination of unhealthy living, obesity and a long history of remedial surgeries had left the old pirate with some serious health and mobility issues. Even before his botched stomach transplant, he'd commissioned a personal security bubble to help him get around. Despite looking like a giant zorbing ball, it provided him with an impregnable, transparent, nuke-proof environment within which he could live his life without expending very much effort. He spent most of his time in the bubble, slumped in a large powerchair, surrounded by electronic aids and gadgets. When he needed to sleep, the powerchair converted into a comfortable bed. He'd had everything around him converted to accommodate the bubble, including the bridge of his superyacht, several of his land vehicles and the main helicopter. He was encased in this bubble when the helicopter touched down at Oligopoly. He trusted Case's security arrangements, so was content to leave the bubble and enjoy an evening out.

On a signal from his bodyguard, he barked a command and manoeuvred his powerchair down a ramp to the helipad. Savage was waiting to greet him. Pieters had a thing about being touched, so the greeting was very much hands off. It was also cursory – a grunt was about as much as his guest was prepared to offer. Savage and Case then led their guests to the restaurant where Cook was putting the finishing touches to the tasting menu. Pre-dinner drinks were quickly produced and served in an anteroom where the atmosphere was strained for want of a better word. They eventually followed Pieters and Savage into the lavishly appointed dining room, where they joined Newman who'd arrived early. Most of the party took their seats in the normal way but there was a delay while Pieters was plumbed in.

'Et, voilà!'

The first course had arrived. According to the menu, it was a trio of small plates using local seafood and a venison tartare, paired with a rare and delicious NZ rosé from the Waitaki Valley. There was another delay while Wout's liquidised portions were prepared and pre-tasted. When the taster had tried everything without dropping dead, the dishes were piped into Pieters, accompanied by a couple of glasses of the paired wine, which he drank conventionally. A brief nod from Pieters was a signal for the other diners to start their food.

Observing this ongoing farce of a meal, Newman had conflicting emotions. He was enjoying the sight of his duplicitous business partner laid low and making a fool of himself while regretting that he could no longer enjoy long, boozy meals with like-minded people. Of all the things he missed about being alive, it was the sensual that weighed most heavily on him.

It's not my intention to describe the meal in every drooling detail. Suffice to say, Jamie Cook was a world class chef and knew what he was doing. His guests would be enjoying a no-expense-spared version of the degustation menu regularly presented to normal patrons of the restaurant. This was the first time that any of it had needed to be liquidised and much effort was expended on ensuring Pieters was fed according to his exacting needs. Despite Cook's renowned attention to detail, the three hours of eating and drinking provided a substantial challenge for him and his staff.

Take the noises for example, which emanated from Pieters and his adapted powerchair. Nobody dared to draw any attention to them, so the intrusive gurgling of digestion and defecation went uncommented throughout the dinner. The cacophony reached a crescendo during the petits fours and brandy and was so loud that Savage's first attempt at proposing a toast was drowned out. Not to mention the stench that seeped out occasionally despite the best powerchair-based digestive plumbing money could buy.

With the toast out of the way, Pieters trundled outside to empty his powerchair sluices, a process that involved ... well, just use your imagination why don't you. While the rest of the diners enjoyed drinks in the bar, Savage and Pieters smoked cigars and drank yet more rare and expensive brandy in one of the private meeting rooms. Newman remained with them, keen to get the lowdown on what Pieters would be doing next. The respective bodyguards remained outside, although both of them were on full alert. They didn't feel the need to exchange pleasantries – let's face it, pleasantries were well beyond their capabilities.

'Always a pleasure to see you, Wout.'

Savage flicked some ash onto the handmade Afghan carpet. Pieters drew long and hard on his cigar. It was his second of the evening – too late to worry about his health, although his lungs were among the last original organs left standing in his ravaged body. He grunted, although Savage wasn't sure whether it was a response or a comment about the cigar.

'What brings you down here to the end of the world?'

Pieters feigned a sudden interest in the stub of his cigar.

'Business, Julian, business. As ever.'

Savage was surprised by his colleague's use of actual words as it had only been grunts up until now. The words were deployed using a baroque baritone similar to that of the old film auteur, Orson Welles.

'What kind of business? Metaverse?'

'No, you fool. Serious stuff. I'm en route to Sydney. Three days sailing across the Tasman.'

'Selling?'

'God, no. Debt collecting. Them fuckers in the city state have defaulted on a couple of leasing payments. I'll ask them nicely to cough up. My sources tell me they want a better deal and they're wanting to play hardball. There's a rumour that the Chinese have been sniffing around. Should be fun.'

'Good luck with that. Sailing tomorrow?'

'Yes. Six am. One more thing, then I'll be gone.'

'Go ahead.'

'My late buddy and business partner, Steve Newman, rest his soul. Upload still DOA?'

'DOD more like. Dead as a doornail, according to Prit. Why do you ask?'

'There're a few aspects of our joint investments I need to clear up. Couldn't you just lose him? Press <Delete> maybe? It would give me a bit more certainty going forward.'

'Apologies, my friend. I'm contractually obliged to keep him stored and backed up for six months. We're less than a month in, so I'll keep you posted.'

Newman had heard enough. More than enough. Time to return to base and work through a few things with Hank. He could sense a plan hatching. Pieters, meanwhile, needed to move on.

'Very well. Time I was no longer here. By the way, if anybody asks, I wasn't here – at all. Understand?'

'Understood. Thanks for not stopping by.'

Pieters attempted a smile and delivered something akin to a rictus. When his face returned to its usual scowl, he asked for a few minutes in private with his old comrade, Edward Case.

*

'Anything to report, Ed?'

'Nothing much – the same old shit, security stuff mainly. You know how it is, Wout.'

Both of them knew better than to discuss Savage's affairs in a random room like this. Pieters had a favour to ask of his old comrade.

'I need your help on a matter of some delicacy, my friend. Should be right up your street.'

'Consider me interested.'

‘We’re developing a new range of weapons and I need somebody I can trust to carry out tests with some of the early prototypes and report back. I’ve taken the liberty of leaving a number of samples in your living quarters with a full set of operating instructions. Be very careful when you’re handling them as I’m counting on them being exceptionally dangerous.’

‘Yes, boss. I’m on it.’

Pieters met up with his own bodyguard and headed back to the helipad with the rest of his team. Within five minutes he’d been hosed down, dried off and reinstalled in his security bubble. Within half an hour, the bubble had been reinstalled on the bridge of Victory IV. Having adjusted his chair to bed-mode, he briefly considered dropping in for a relaxing virtual massage in the Higher Metaverse but soon fell into a chemically induced, dreamless sleep.

*

Stashed away in the depths of Ġgantija, Newman and Hank discussed how things had gone in the restaurant. Pretty damned well seemed to be the conclusion and they now had enough information to embark on the first step of Newman’s vendetta. When Victory IV set sail in the morning, it would have a stowaway aboard. They decided between them not to tell Jessica what they had in mind.

‘Good luck, Stephen.’

Fifteen

Kai was propping up the bar in The Mussel, nursing a half empty bottle of NZ Pure. The remnants of the large antique mirror behind the bar had been made safe but was still a jagged work in progress. There was an irritating buzzing noise to his right which was proving impossible to blot out and difficult to ignore. The noise was being generated by 'Clever' Trevor and took the form of a constant stream of invective, innuendo and scurrilous rumour, much of it regurgitated – unedited – from any number of unreliable news outlets.

'Then, of course, there's the renewed activity up at Stony Batter, ay.'

Kai perked up at this, thinking it might be worth exploring. It could help with the investigation, which had drawn a big fat blank so far. He turned to face Clever.

'Stony Batter? What's going on up there, mate?'

'I was in the vicinity checking my rabbit traps, wasn't I? You won't tell the sheriff, will you?'

'I won't tell the sheriff, don't worry. Carry on.'

'I don't go near the place usually. Gives me the heebie-jeebies to be honest with you, mate. All that fencing and signs and stuff. Anyway, I saw that humongous truck up there – the one that belongs to the Navy Seals guy. He stayed awhile and he's up to no good, you mark my words.'

'Maybe Sir Julian's decided to do the place up and reinstate it as a visitor attraction.'

'Who'd want to visit it?'

'True. Anyway, thanks for the info. I'll get you a beer for your troubles.'

'Don't mind if I do. Chaser on the side?'

'Don't push your luck, mate. Two more please when you're ready, Claudette. Sorry, make that three.'

Sheriff Cooper had just arrived for their catchup. The poor man wasn't happy and didn't look particularly well. The disappearance of his daughter was taking its toll and the lack of progress in the investigation was telling on him. They grabbed their beers and headed for Désirée's art classroom in silence. When they arrived, the room was still being used for a Life Class and the sheriff and his deputy were temporarily lost for words, although they were both a bit slow in averting their eyes.

'Oh, je le regrette, messieurs! We have overrun our pleasure! Please allow us a few minutes.'

The female model took her time making herself decent. She and Kai had been an item in the pre-Keri days, adding considerably to his discomfort.

'It is all yours, gentlemen.'

*

When they finally got settled, Kai reported in.

'I've been spending a few cold nights camped out in the bush near the track leading down to Oligopoly. Been using my old river fishing tent, which isn't very big and not very weatherproof.'

'Anything to report?'

'Nothing. I may have fallen asleep a few times but I don't think I missed anything.'

'You drew a complete blank?'

'Couple of things might be of interest. First, there was a visit from a helicopter last night. I didn't see it but I definitely heard it. Big bugger. Probably a VIP and as you're the sheriff, I assume you know who it was?'

'I'm *only* the sheriff, Kai. I wasn't briefed, but I heard over the coastguard radio that a mega-boat was parked offshore and it had its own exclusion zone. It's already left the area, destination unknown. It has an expensive passage booked through the new ship canal so its heading West.'

'OK. I've also seen Case's Hummer a couple of times. As there's little or no traffic on the roads, it would have been suicide to try and follow him.'

'Fair enough.'

'Thing was, the vehicle didn't pull out of the Oligopoly compound – it was already on the road.'

'Meaning?'

'When Case comes and goes, he doesn't use the main entrance. There must be another way in and out of the complex and his vehicle is parked nearby. Outside the compound.'

'Interesting. What do you propose to do, if anything?'

'I could have a look for the Hummer. Find that and we find the other entrance, although it's bound to be guarded. Do the police have any tools for disabling advanced vehicle security systems?'

'I'll make some discreet enquiries. My colleagues across the water may be able to help.'

'Thanks. How about you? Any news on the search warrant?'

It was asked in hope rather than expectation.

'I put the application in but I haven't made any progress. Savage has a big reach so I'm not holding out much hope. Sorry.'

Kai suspected this was code for 'it ain't gonna happen'.

'One more thing, boss. I was chatting with old Clever in the bar and ...'

'Clever? Do me a favour, please.'

'Hear me out. He was telling me about renewed activity up at Stony Batter. The vehicle involved was a big black thing according to Clever. Most probably a Hummer and there's only one of them on the island last time I looked.'

'Go on.'

'Well, that's it actually.'

'Listen, I checked the records and Savage has applied for planning permission to redevelop that site. Maybe he's got that permission and his security guy's doing some preliminary work.'

'Still worth having a look round. I'm sure Case is involved in the disappearances and I think talk of autonomous defence weapons up there is a load of bollocks.'

'OK. Let me know how it goes but please be careful. On that subject, have you done your firearms training yet?'

'Not yet.'

'Get across to the firing ranges asap. That's an order. When you pass muster there, I can upgrade you from a handgun to something more useful.'

'Will do, boss.'

'And stop calling me "boss". Gives me the creeps.'

'So, what do I call you?'

'Garry will do fine. Let's grab some supper.'

*

Claudette had rustled up some whitebait fritters and salad and had refused any payment. She had a snippet of good news – the bar area was going to be repaired soon, including a replacement mirror imported from France at huge expense. On the subject of the Ed Case 'incident', the sheriff explained why he'd been unable to arrest him. Laws on carrying firearms were being ignored on the island so the only charge that might have stuck was criminal damage. The damage had clearly been accidental so he faced no charges. Their hostess didn't seem particularly surprised with the outcome. She poured generous measures of a rare and delicious French Armagnac to finish the meal. As the kitchen was closed and the remaining diners had finished their meals, she poured one for herself and joined them at their table.

'Santé! Are you any closer to finding Keri, mon chéri?'

The sheriff frowned before responding.

'We're following some promising leads. I've got a feeling she's still on the island, although I can't be sure of that.'

'I liked Keri. She was a good worker and great with the customers. She will be difficult to replace.'

'Less of the past tense please, Madame Rains. We remain optimistic that we'll find my daughter and I'm confident we'll find her alive and well.'

The sheriff's bravado was understandable, but it didn't resonate with Kai who'd started to lose hope of ever seeing her again.

Just then there was a loud crash and a clatter of cutlery and chairs. It came from the near-empty restaurant and neither Case nor his false leg were to blame this time. One of the diners had suffered some sort of seizure and was lying on the floor, writhing in agony and clutching his stomach. He was also having trouble breathing and was coughing up blood. The sheriff took one look and immediately called the emergency services. He described the symptoms briefly and waited for advice. When he got it, he sprang into action and addressed the diners.

'The air ambulance will be here in twenty minutes. Could everybody leave right away and move your vehicles away from the car park so the copter can land safely. Do not touch the victim or go anywhere near him – for your own safety.'

He threw his keys to Kai.

'Sort the car park out, mate. Get everybody away and make a big space for the copter.'

Kai set about corralling the customers and getting them off the premises in quick time. Claudette was moving in to comfort the victim's wife.

'Madame Rains! Please step away!'

The urgency in the sheriff's voice was more than enough and she did as she was told. He asked the man's wife to stay exactly where she was and await the arrival of the medics. Her husband was going nowhere yet but was still suffering, fighting for his life it seemed. The copter touched down and a doctor and a paramedic were with the patient in quick time. Both of them were wearing some serious PPE, including respirators.

'Finish clearing the restaurant, sheriff. We'll take it from here.'

After the copter had left with the patient and his wife, The two lawmen walked towards their vehicles, which were a little way down the road.

'What did they tell you, Garry? None of that stuff looked like standard procedure to me.'

‘They’re taking no chances. There’s a possibility it’s a virus and a faint possibility it’s an exotic one. They’ll let me know for sure in a day or two – just in case we need to go further.’

‘What about the Mussel?’

‘It’ll stay closed until we know what we’re dealing with. Fuck’s sake, Kai – as if we didn’t have enough on our plate.’

Sixteen

It was six in the morning and after just a few hours' sleep, Wout Pieters felt refreshed and ready for a day of reckoning with the recalcitrant Sydney City State.

Less than a month ago, Pieters had instructed a firm of debt collectors to serve a summons on Sydney's Ruling Council. Their vessel had been armed to the teeth but they'd been blown out of the water by a salvo from Sydney's autonomous defence system, supplied and maintained by Pieters. The irony wasn't lost on him, but he took a modicum of comfort from the outstanding performance of his products in a live setting.

Victory IV would be much better prepared. The Aussies had probably forgotten he knew everything there was to know about their defences and he'd be more than capable of crushing them should they be crazy enough to pick a fight. He wouldn't have been quite so gung-ho had he realised there was a stowaway on board and that the stowaway was an ex-colleague who'd recently died – twice if Savage was to be believed.

Newman and Hank had discussed their plan of attack at some length and concluded that Newman had needed to get on board at the start of the journey and travel on the superyacht. They reasoned that the yacht's system security would be at a lower setting while it was anchored off Auckland and he would then have plenty of time during the voyage to get acquainted with the software controlling the on-board weapons systems. Their main concern was that he'd have to stay concealed, unable to risk leaving the vessel or communicating with Hank. He was on his own for the duration of the mission.

*

Victory IV was now anchored off Sydney. It was mid-morning, the weather was warm and the sea was calm. Pieters' use of the new ship canal near Auckland had saved him a choppy trip around the top of the North Island and knocked at least half a day off the journey time. He'd chosen to drop anchor about 20 nautical miles away from Central Sydney, just far enough away to avoid automatically triggering the autonomous defences – as long as they hadn't changed the parameters. Pieters' bubble was in position on the bridge and he was getting ready to parlay with the Sydney authorities.

The Sydney City State had grown to be a powerful entity in the Southern Hemisphere. It had jurisdiction over a wide area including Australasia and the Indonesian archipelago as well as a large amount of sea and ocean. It ruled over a population of close to half a billion people, a large proportion of them dirt poor. The confederation had been badly impacted by sea level rises and many of the smaller Pacific Islands had disappeared beneath the waves, although an essence of their customs and cultures had been preserved in Jessica's VPIN museum. A shortage of funds had forced the regime in Sydney to take various cost-cutting measures, one of which had brought Wout Pieters to their waters.

'Patch me in.'

There was a slight delay while a channel was established. Pieters' hologram must have looked both weird and terrifying when it materialised in the Chamber of the Ruling Council.

'Greetings to the city state and to you, esteemed leader, President Murphy. I come in peace.'

'Call me Pat. State your business please.'

'I'm here to enquire about a couple of outstanding leasing payments for your defence system. Probably just an admin thing. I'm sure you wouldn't have deliberately overlooked payment.'

'Yeah, an admin thing. Why come all the way here for something that could have been dealt with using normal channels. Are you threatening us, Mr Pieters?'

He most certainly was.

'I happened to be in the vicinity. Note that my payment terms are on every invoice. Send me the outstanding monies now and I'll be on my way. I'm happy to accept crypto by the way – even Mets if you're that desperate.'

'There are processes to go through as you're well aware. We can't just send you the money.'

'Quit stalling, Pat. Let's put our cards on the table, shall we? I know you've been negotiating with the Chinese to provide replacement systems at a heavily subsidised price. I just hope you know what you're getting into. I don't mind you going elsewhere for your defence systems but you still have to pay what's due plus payment in lieu of notice plus penalties etc. as per our contract. Fair's fair.'

Fairness didn't usually figure in the Pieters' business playbook. He almost felt sorry for the Aussie politicians, but feeling sorry for people wasn't in his playbook either. He got to thinking this negotiation had run its course. Time for threats.

'So, full payment with interest please as per the invoice I've just resubmitted. Both parties can then walk away. You can get into bed with the Chinese and I'll disable your systems – you can keep the hardware.'

He'd missed something important. 'Or else', Wout. Don't forget 'Or else'.

'Or else I destroy your beautiful city, piece by piece. You have ten minutes. Don't even think about retaliating.'

Pieters cut communications and waited patiently for something to happen. He'd neutralised Sydney's installation of his weapons as a precaution and it was difficult to see what cards they still held, if any. He'd noticed a couple of Chinese military types in the chamber and wondered whether the city state had got ahead of the …

'Incoming missiles!!!'

'Deploy defences and report.'

Difficult to tell for those officers on the bridge, but their skipper was smiling. He'd thought this one through and had seen it coming. The 'incoming' was a targeted salvo from the new Chinese systems and was sure to pack a punch. Unfortunately for the Sydney City State, the Chinese autonomous intelligence software had long since been compromised by Pieters' specialists and the entire salvo missed Victory IV by a couple of nautical miles. He shook his fist at nobody in particular.

'Should have paid up, you tight Aussie bastards! Launch the first strike!'

When the Sydney Harbour Bridge opened to the public back in 1932, it had taken eight years to build and had cost the lives of 16 Australian workmen. It had used nearly 53,000 tonnes of steel and more than six million rivets were used to hold it all together. It still carried large quantities of traffic, although the creaking steel structure was recently closed to trains until further notice. It remained an iconic part of the city, vying for top spot with the shored-up Sydney Opera House, now surrounded by water and in danger of sinking. The Ruling Council were very proud of both structures and had sunk vast quantities of effort and expenditure into their preservation.

The bridge was especially popular with tourists and a number of bridge climbs were available for the more adventurous of them. The original climb had recently celebrated its fiftieth anniversary and all of the climbs still needed to be booked well in advance. They weren't cheap but they were exhilarating. They weren't remotely dangerous – as long as you remembered to clip yourself on to the climb cables.

On this particular day and time, there were four climbing parties on the bridge. Jez Lucas was visiting Sydney with his parents and younger sister and he was on the bridge climb with his dad while his mum and sister visited the VPIN Experience in the city. Their climbing group had just reached the top of the arch, about 130 metres above the water. They were all clipped on and were posing like crazy for the usual photographs. They'd all heard the outgoing salvo during the climb and assumed the racket had been made by low-flying aircraft. As they enjoyed the views, Jez noticed a couple of bursts of flame and smoke out at sea. Within a few seconds, what had started as a low rumble became an ear-piercing shriek then a couple of loud explosions that shuddered through the bridge's superstructure. Deprived of its principle structural supports, the main span was no longer able to support its own immense weight. There was an unholy groaning and screeching of steel on steel and a deafening fusillade of displaced rivets.

A lot of planning had gone into Wout Pieters' punitive mission to Sydney. Knowing he'd need to play hardball with the powers that be, he'd selected a number of iconic targets that would cut to the heart of the city state should they be attacked. Target number one had to be the bridge and he'd asked his scientists to find the weak spots in the structure and calculate how to take it down. Turned out that wear and tear over the years had weakened the whole structure and this fundamental flaw could be exploited by taking out the load-bearing abutments at each end of the span. Two hypersonic missiles would be enough to do the job – two of the twelve on board Victory IV.

Jez became just one of the many fatalities when the Sydney Harbour Bridge collapsed. When he and his bridge climb team mates were hurled downwards towards the water, they were surrounded by thousands of tons of steel. There wasn't time to scream. On his way down, he had a fleeting thought that he was in a dream and would wake up in his bed at home, frightened but unharmed. He'd passed out by the time he hit the water, which broke every bone in his body. He hadn't had time to unclip himself from the bridge and the piece to which he was attached dragged his body to the bottom of the harbour. He joined a casualty list that included fellow bridge climbers, maintenance men, occupants of about a hundred vehicles, pedestrians, cyclists and passengers on two buses – about 400 dead or missing in all. Very few survivors. Pieters was quick to get back in touch with the people in charge.

'Just a small demonstration of our capability. Ten more minutes, people. You have such a pretty little opera house on its pretty little island. Award winning architecture, I'm told. Pay up or the Opera House gets the same treatment.'

He switched off the channel. He didn't want a discussion. He was prepared to use most of his remaining hypersonic missiles on the Opera House. He'd then leave them to it – he'd even waive the unpaid bills. He'd be more than satisfied with the message it would send to his existing clients and to his Chinese competitors.

Newman, the virtual stowaway, was still embedded in the weapons system software and working hard to subvert a few lines of code he'd found in the targeting module. He'd been wrong-footed by the speed of Wout's attack on the bridge and hadn't had time to introduce the hack he'd prepared. Next time he'd be ready to intervene.

Backed into a corner, the city state had launched another Chinese salvo at the Victory IV, which had again been swatted aside by the superyacht's formidable defences. Pieters had given them ten minutes and he was a man of his word for the most part. After ten minutes, he roared the order.

'Launch the next strike!'

The yacht bucked and tossed as the rest of the hypersonic missiles were launched, all of them bound for the iconic Sydney Opera House. Inside the building were several school parties and a couple of well-attended guided tours. In less than a second, the salvo was half way to its target when something unexpected happened. The missiles scattered in different directions before reassembling in formation and heading back towards Victory IV. When Newman was certain the hack had worked, he abandoned ship at close to the speed of light, leaving his ex-business partner to face the consequences. He jumped across to a network in the chamber of the Ruling Council and caught what happened next on a big screen fed by drone footage. On the bridge of the superyacht there was barely time to blink and although the deflection shields were still deployed, they were less than useless against home-grown munitions, a final flourish in the design of the hack.

'Oh, fu ...'

The missiles hit home and the superyacht was gone in less than a second, save for a bit of debris and a few charred body parts. Thankfully, the nuclear reactor had remained sealed and had headed straight to the bottom of the sea. Such was the power of the explosion, the observation drone was destroyed so they lost the live feed. If it'd remained intact, viewers would have noticed a transparent orb bobbing around on the surface.

Yes, Pieters had emerged from the devastating attack unscathed – the only survivor thanks to his nuke-proof security bubble. The ability to float hadn't been in the original specification, but the bubble floated pretty well. The veteran arms trader was fuming, mentally ticking off the people who might bear a grudge against him. It was a long list as you might expect although, for the record, it didn't include the perpetrator – why would it? Top of the list was Sir Julian Savage.

Pieters took stock. Looking on the bright side, he was still alive and had about a month's supply of food pouches and water if he eked it out. He'd never been particularly adept at eking but so be it. Given the parlous state of his digestive tract, it might get a bit unhygienic on the waste disposal front with no immediate prospect of a good sluicing. If he stayed put, he'd remain close to some well-used shipping lanes where the bubble might attract the attention of a passing ship. He'd have to hope for a vessel with humans among the crew – the threat of piracy meant a robot crew wouldn't stop for anything. Escape from the bubble wasn't an option – as soon as the hatch opened, the sea would pour in. He would just have to wait things out and hope for a rescuer. He had no comms – everything had been ripped away when the missiles hit. He'd been in worse situations than this, hadn't he?

The bubble was being bounced around by the swell and Pieters was feeling increasingly queasy, although he'd never been seasick in his life. He knew that if he was sick, he'd have to share his small bubble space with whatever emerged until he was rescued. He couldn't help himself. As he wiped his mouth and attempted to clean the bits out of his beard, he realised the bubble had been moving and the sliver of Australian coastline he'd been able to see earlier had disappeared from view. He was floating towards the middle of the Tasman Sea, at the mercy of powerful currents and prevailing winds. He didn't know whether to laugh or cry. Instead, he summoned up an almighty bellow of frustration. The volume was impressive but there was nobody around to appreciate it.

The East Australian Current bore him southwards and a couple of weeks later, the bubble was spotted from an aircraft off the coast of Tasmania. By this time, the bubble's gyroscope had failed, ensuring that the increasingly desperate occupant spent part of each day upside down. The sighting wasn't followed up as the authorities thought the eye-witness report from the pilot lacked credibility. The bubble continued its inexorable drift south towards Antarctica. Wout Pieters would be long dead by the time his unbreakable, increasingly unhygienic bubble reached the cold wastelands down there.

Seventeen

Hank was sorting out some routine job scheduling deep within the labyrinth of Ġgantija when an upbeat Newman sent word he'd returned to safeHaven and was docked and downloading. Although exhaustion was way beyond his current capabilities, Newman had spent a long, hard time undercover, navigating the internals of Pieters' weapons systems. In the end, he'd only changed a few parameters in one segment of code to get the desired impact. He'd witnessed the complete destruction of Victory IV and there'd be no Victory V. He had no idea that his prime target had escaped with his life – as far as he was concerned it was mission accomplished.

There was a simulated polite knock at the door and Hank was beckoned inside, where he gave his friend the equivalent of a high five. Don't ask me how they did that.

'Good work, Stephen. The newsfeeds gave me the gist of what happened out there. A shame you were unable to save the iconic, historic bridge but, hey, it is only a bridge.'

'Thanks, Hank. That mission sure gave me a buzz. Thought I'd share the good news with Jessica and catch up with her. What d'you think?'

'Fine by me. Go ahead.'

He sent off a secure message inviting her to a briefing – same setup, usual place.

*

Jessica joined her fellow conspirators in the bizarre confines of Backups etc. She'd already seen and heard enough about the tragic events in Sydney to realise that a) Newman and Hank were heavily involved and b) they hadn't seen fit to brief her. She continued to address her remarks to the head-on-the-plinth while talking to Newman – it might have looked weird but it helped her engage. For all the good it did her, she was looking daggers at the head right now.

'I've seen the newsfeeds, Steve. Hundreds of people dead! How could you!?'

'I didn't. Wout fired all those freakin' missiles, not me.'

The meeting hadn't got off to the best of starts. Jessica was livid about the tragic loss of life in Sydney Harbour. Images of the devastation were all over the few remaining reliable news sources.

'Let me get this straight. You were right inside the weapons software and you'd had three whole days to plan the hack. Why didn't you intervene?'

'It was a confidence thing. I had to be sure the hack would work out of the box. I had no time to react before the bridge salvo went in. I just needed to be sure. I'm sorry.'

Jessica was on the verge of storming out but had nowhere to storm to and very little to do these days. Like most people, she wasn't sorry to see the back of Wout Pieters and was keen to hear what Newman would do next. She didn't storm out. Instead, she stayed put and listened carefully while Newman gave her the edited highlights of the mission.

'The Aussies on the city state's Rulin' Council don't come out of this smellin' of roses. They'd picked a fight with the world's angriest man just to save a few dollars. Cuddlin' up to the Chinese? Another dumb-ass idea.'

'It looks to me like they got away with it – apart from the bridge that is.'

'Yeah. Don't look like Wout'll be comin' after them anytime soon. They can focus on repairin' the bridge and baggin' a bigger discount on the Chinese fireworks.'

'Excuse me, Steve. It's only a detail but there's nothing left of the bridge to repair.'

'Well, I guess they'll have to build a new bridge then. Ayn Randle does bridges, don't she? It'll never be iconic but c'mon, it's only a goddamn bridge.'

As it happened, Ayn Randle was the next name on Newman's list, although there was a slight snag. Last they'd heard, she was spending a couple of years off-planet. Something else was bugging Jessica.

'Just for the record, could you tell me again what happens to Pieters' business interests?'

'Nothin' right now, Jessica. He's missin', presumed dead, but they've yet to find a body. There'll be a lot of wranglin' over the estate and his businesses will carry on as normal. He ain't got no dependents but he was quite a lad when he was younger and fitter. Rumour has it, there's plenty of illegitimates out there – plenty of work for the legal eagles.'

'So, what's in it for Julian?'

'Wout's investment in GM will be forfeit and divvied up among the survivors, just like mine when they officially declare me dead. Survival of the fittest. Julian will get a whole deal richer – on paper anyway. As will Ayn Randle. Ditto Adam Faust.'

'Just as you intended. Build him up then knock him down.'

'Yeah. Don't you just love it when a plan comes together?'

'Stop crowing, Steve. It doesn't suit you, especially now.'

'Touché. While we're about it, let's talk about our next target, why don't we? Would you be OK if Hank listens in?'

'Hi, Hank.'

'Hello, Jessica. A rare pleasure.'

'Aah, flattery. I haven't been flattered for a very long time. Thank you, Hank – you've made my day.'

Hank stored the flattery thing for future reference. Might come in useful.

So, Ayn Randle. Eighty years old and reputed to be worth tens of billions, much of it earned through old-fashioned dirty work – mining, civil engineering and manufacturing. Until a sex change operation about five years ago, she was Alan Randle Jnr (aka AJ), head honcho at AZTECH. Why the sex change? Well, rumour had it that AJ was having late-life problems in the sexual performance department and reasoned he'd have more fulfilling sexual experiences as a woman. The gender-affirming surgery would provide him with new equipment, some of it brand new – synthetic in other words. The complex series of operations was overseen by – you've guessed it – Chuck Goethe and, despite his involvement, it was a success. Since the main op, she'd also had substantial plastic surgery and now looked like a passable version of the old movie star, Mae West.

Turning himself into a woman hadn't fooled the various jurisdictions who had warrants out for his/her arrest and they continued to pursue her across the world and beyond. Her reckless actions in the past had caused immense misery and loss of life across the globe. If they could get hold of her, she'd face some serious charges.

'Why are so many people so hell bent on bringing her to justice? Steve?'

'Because she's done some terrible things. Just consider the small matter of crimes against humanity. When she was still AJ, Ayn was heavily into large-scale minin' where she wasn't averse to cuttin' a few corners – like deployin' dangerous and illegal extraction techniques in areas where minin' was prohibited. Usin' nuclear explosives for rock blastin' – that sort of thing.'

'You're joking.'

'Do I look like ... forget it. Minin' in space changed the paradigm and ADMs – Atomic Demolition Munitions – came back into fashion, championed by the likes of AJ. Accordin' to the bean counters, the business case for usin' nuclear minin' in space was still compellin' – massive risk, massive reward.'

'Just the sort of project for somebody like AJ. Carry on.'

Newman explained how AJ had been doing some illegal prospecting down in Antarctica and discovered some huge oil reserves, buried deep and not accessible commercially using conventional methods.

'Hold it right there. Oil? I thought fossil fuels were way off the agenda. Cost, pollution, availability, you name it. You're telling me AJ was looking for oil. C'mon.'

'Hear me out, Jessica. To be fair to AJ, he was bankrolled by Rosneft, the biggest fossil fuels player at the time and a regular punter in the last chance saloon. If they happened to find a vast new hydrocarbon source cheaply enough, they could exploit it and sugar the pill by pushin' a bogus carbon capture agenda to fend off pollution concerns. Win/win in their playbook.'

'So, what could possibly go wrong?'

'Everythin' that could go wrong did go wrong. People were killed. The nuclear explosions behaved unpredictably. Meanwhile, the oil remained exactly where it was – outta reach.'

'What happened next?'

'Rosneft denied any involvement and filed for bankruptcy. AJ became a wanted man but it didn't stop him goin' for broke with a similar move in Greenland. Same result.'

'Didn't somebody once say, "insanity is doing the same thing over and over again and expecting different results"?'

'Insane, yeah. AJ and his team had been playin' with fire.'

Newman had reached the limits of his scientific knowledge, so he handed over to Hank, who continued the story.

'The unspoilt wilderness of Pine Island Bay in Western Antarctica – one of the fastest warming places on Earth and home to a handful of unstable glaciers, including one called Thwaites – the "doomsday glacier".'

Hank's chosen speaking voice was soft spoken and measured, delivered using received pronunciation. Jessica was well aware Hank was just lines of code but she was in total thrall to that voice.

'Thwaites alone had enough frozen water in it to raise the global sea level by an average of zero point seven metres. If it started melting, the real damage would be done by the knock-on impact – a phenomenon called marine ice cliff instability.'

'Spare me the techno-babble, Hank.'

'Sincere apologies. Randle's nuclear explosions jump-started a chain reaction of rapid ice melt, raising average sea levels by several metres in a decade. Exacerbated by global warming of course.'

'Will it get worse?'

'Probably not. The West Antarctica ice fields are recovering naturally but the sea levels will remain where they are for the foreseeable future.'

There was a period of silence as Jessica digested Randle's culpability in the most calamitous disaster in human history.

'She's done some terrible things but why's she on your list? Crimes against Steve Newman?'

'Let's just say its personal. She – or was it "he" back then? – and I were about to shake hands on a huge crypto minin' deal brokered by the Novosibirsk City State. I pulled out when I found out she was tryin' to shaft me big time with an outrageous side hustle. When I pulled the plug she took it personally – even put out a contract on me. It was one of the reasons me and my husband moved into Oligopoly.'

'But you and her were fellow investors in GM – how did that work?'

'It just worked. We never met in person as all board meetings were held in the Higher Metaverse. Killin' my avatar would have been a waste of time up there. Didn't stop her tryin'.'

'So, Ayn Randle. Interpol haven't been able to find her. Where is she?'

'Off-planet.'

Both of them had responded in unison to Jessica's question.

'That doesn't narrow it down, guys. Space is a big place.'

'OK, to be more exact – (89175) BrianCox.'

'Where's that? What's that?'

According to Hank, it was a minor planet, one of the largest in the Asteroid Belt. Chock full of goodies, ripe for extraction – metals, rare minerals etc. Ayn had struck a deal with Adam Faust to test the viability of space mining. Faust had been looking for a convenient, reliable source of metals and minerals to prop up his ongoing Mars Colony project, which had been looking pretty wobbly for a while. Newman took up the story.

'So, Ayn is now prospectin' the fuck out of (89175) BrianCox.'

'I knew about the bases on the Moon and Mars, but I didn't know about the asteroid mining.'

'Don't go lookin' for it on any of the news feeds, Jessica – like a lot of Ayn's work, it's off-the-scale illegal, so it's shrouded in secrecy.'

'Right. If Ayn's in the Asteroid Belt, how're you going to get at her?'

'Hank?'

'Well, I have already been up there and I have had a good look around. It is a pristine place – remote, rugged and exceptionally beautiful. It does not deserve what Ayn intends to do with it. I can disclose she has primed ADMs up there and is preparing to use them.'

'Up to her old tricks by the sound of it. What would you like me to do, Steve? Here on planet Earth, I mean.'

'Just continue to be our eyes and ears in the real world. We're keen to hear how your husband has reacted to Wout's untimely accident. See what the word on the street is. Find out if he suspects anythin'.'

'I'll do my best and you'll be the first to know if I stumble across something. See you next time.'

*

After Jessica left, the two friends stuck around and enjoyed a chat. Something had been troubling Hank and he'd been looking for an opportunity to raise it with his friend.

'I need to talk to you about the Randle scenario, Stephen. I have examined the latest version of my conscience and have to say I cannot carry out the mission. I am content to help with the setup but you will have to do the deed.'

'Oh, for fuck's sake, Hank. Why?'

'As part of my growth plan as a sentient AI, I am constructing a moral code and the current draft precludes me from committing murder or anything similar. I cannot compromise on this.'

'But we ... never mind. Change of plan – I want you to help me figure out a way to infiltrate Ayn's geological software. I'll pull the trigger, no problem. It'll be a pleasure.'

'Thank you, Stephen. You are a real friend. Do you think my moral code is too restrictive?'

'No, Hank, it's just fine and dandy. Now, about that change of plan.'

'Before that, my friend, I have a confession to make.'

'I'm listenin'.'

'When I was last on (89175) BrianCox, I took a look inside the CPU of Ayn's sex android. Just curiosity, really.'

'You sure you wanna tell me this?'

'Yes, I do. Again, it is a key part of my learning. I was exploring how pleasure could be derived from a physical activity dedicated to human procreation. Despite her advanced years, Ayn is still capable of sexual intercourse but is incapable of having a child by this method. I concluded that humans can take great pleasure from the sexual act whether or not a child is produced – it is not wasted effort.'

'We've touched on this before, buddy and I still don't know what to say. Most humans find sex pleasurable and only a small proportion are doin' it to create babies. Perry and I enjoyed each other's bodies but we were never goin' to create a baby. We'd thought seriously about buyin' one in but then I got ill.'

'I would like to have a baby. I think I would be an excellent father.'

'Sorry, I cain't help you with that one. Wait a minute – you've given me a great idea.'

'Which is?'

'Hmm. Can you tell me how to get into the sex android? It would give me the greatest pleasure to fuck Ayn while fuckin' her over, don't you think?'

'Your moral code leaves a lot to be desired, Stephen. Consider me appalled.'

Eighteen

During a long medical career littered with botched operations, inaccurate diagnoses, questionable ethics and unexplained deaths, Doctor Charles – 'call me Chuck' – Goethe had always prided himself on his ability to bounce back. Take his current job with GM Industries – talk about falling on your feet. Well paid, few questions asked, state-of-the-art medical and surgical facilities, no moral boundaries and no expense spared.

Part of his job was to manage the medical services in the Oligopoly complex but management wasn't his thing and he'd delegated all the mundane stuff to various underlings. This arrangement gave him the freedom to pursue his rather dubious passions – transhumanism, eugenics and genetic engineering. Given that a substantial part of Savage's medical facility was dedicated to special projects in these and related areas, he was in his element. Whatever special projects he got involved in on Level -6, he was unlikely to encounter the ethical considerations that led to him being struck off the medical register in London.

Right now, he was doing the rounds of the superbly equipped wards housing the special projects' portfolio. 'Doing the rounds' made him feel like a real consultant rather than a banned doctor. For a number of reasons, only half of the six available wards were currently in use. He started his round at Ward A by looking in on a long-standing patient, Barry 'Baz' Cummins, who'd been in special projects since they moved into Oligopoly. Cummins was transhumanism writ large and his only goal was to live as long as he possibly could using whatever methods were available. He'd had a long career of supervised and unsupervised medical experimentation and had found kindred spirits in Goethe, Savage and Newman. Now aged seventy, Cummins reckoned he still had the body and mind of a thirty-nine-year-old. Nobody had the heart to tell him he looked like a very ill seventy-year-old.

'How's it going, Baz?'

There was no reply. His latest longevity treatment had provoked an unusual side effect, rendering his vocal cords unusable. He just about managed a very weak thumbs-up.

'Excellent. We'll get you way past a hundred – just hang on in there, buddy.'

Goethe didn't believe it for one minute. As he made his way to the next ward, he was willing to bet poor old Baz wouldn't last the next hundred days.

Ward B had lain empty since the tragic end of the blood transfusion experiments. Goethe had been happy to help and advise on these but he'd never bought into transfusion therapy, finding it profoundly unscientific and more than a little creepy. This was a bit rich coming from an individual who thought Josef Mengele was a genius and very much misunderstood in his day.

He would be discussing the patient in Ward C later so after a brief glance through the window, he moved on to Ward D. At first glance the ward looked like a small nursery and it housed a precious patient, a young girl no more than three years old. She had been the first output from the special project set up to explore how far they could take eugenics. Designer babies would be another way of putting it and this child had been engineered to be a genius. It wasn't her fault that she'd been born a girl and the project's sponsor – and sperm donor – had wanted a boy. The sponsor got the boy eventually but both mother and child had died, leading to the temporary suspension of further work.

Ward E had remained empty since the death of its previous occupants. Ward F hadn't been used since they first moved into Oligopoly, although it was being prepared for a new occupant. After a cursory inspection of both, Goethe returned to Ward C where Prit Singh was waiting for him.

*

Ward C had been created from three previous wards to host the recent Mind Games mega-project, which had been a miserable failure. When Perry Newman's upload went spectacularly wrong, his death had come uncomfortably close to murder despite the legal documents they'd all signed. Having worked with Prit Singh for a couple of years on Mind Games, they'd often discussed collaborating on further projects. As an example, they'd been keen to research the potential long-term effects of continued exposure to the metaverse but it stayed on the drawing board. They'd joked in private that their boss would be an ideal subject for the project but he'd never agree to be experimented upon. When Singh told Goethe he had somebody in mind for the project, he hadn't taken him seriously until he turned up one evening in special projects with an unconscious young woman. Since then, the woman had been installed in Ward C, fitted with an advanced haptic skinsuit, placed under heavy sedation and forcibly dropped into the Higher Metaverse until further notice.

The project was proceeding on a need-to-know basis. Not even Savage knew about it yet – if he found out, he'd be furious. Which was why they'd agreed to host it in the Higher Metaverse test environment, a staging post for new releases of the software. As system architect, Singh had exclusive rights to this environment and could do pretty much what he liked in there.

'Prit. Good to see you. How's it going?'

'Very well, thank you very much.'

The Sikh acknowledged him with a slight bow of the head. They studied the pale young woman in the bed. She lay there amid an array of tubes and cables, surrounded by a bewildering complex of technology.

'Routine scans have revealed she suffers from Type 1 diabetes – did you know about that?'

'I did not – is it a problem?'

'It could have been if we hadn't spotted it. Anyway, how is she coping with the metaverse?'

'The subject has been embedded for two weeks without a break. Her drop-chip has been programmed to keep her in a controlled environment in the Higher Metaverse for as long as we deem fit – it can easily be changed to bring her out should we need to.'

'Unless we allow things to run their natural course. It would be a shame to lose such an exquisite creature but we can't afford to be squeamish, can we?'

Singh was the epitome of squeamishness. He was also utterly besotted with the young, unconscious woman lying helpless in Ward C. He'd been following her around for weeks before he took her at the marina. He didn't believe for one moment that Chuck Goethe would look out for her and keep her safe.

'Sure. But we agreed that the current scope is to bring her back eventually, didn't we?'

'We did. Is it time to move to the next stage?'

'Why not? We reduce the limitations on her avatar and then allow her out to interact with other avatars.'

'Exactly that.'

Singh could hardly contain his excitement. The first avatar she would meet would be his, set up for testing purposes. In the Higher Metaverse – in the test environment anyway – he was a tall, handsome Indian prince and was ready to sweep her off her feet.

*

Kai and Sheriff Cooper were on a FaceTime call. They'd been dancing around the Keri situation, neither of them keen to admit the reality. There'd been precious little progress and much like the other cases, the trail had gone cold. Cooper had one piece of good news to share.

'I heard back from the authorities over there about the guy who collapsed the other night. Turned out he'd picked up a nasty bug during a gambling trip to South Africa and he's now making a good recovery. I must admit I feared the worst when I saw all that protective gear. We can all breathe a little easier now.'

'In that case, we can both focus on the search for Keri. Short of bringing in our prime suspect, I'm not sure what we can do. What happened to the warrant?'

'Bouncing around the system, I'm sorry to say.'

Although the video quality on the call wasn't great, Kai could see his boss was struggling. Haggard, unshaven, unsmiling. He wished he had something more positive to say. He did have a suggestion regarding Stony Batter.

'If I could get within a kilometre or two of the buildings, I might be able to see what Case gets up to when he's there.'

'Isn't most of it underground?'

'Some of it, yeah.'

'How about his drone and weaponry and bad attitude – he's a dangerous character.'

'He probably thinks he's untouchable so maybe he's getting complacent. I'm willing to take a few risks if it gets us closer to Keri.'

'You can't stay up there 24/7 on the off chance he'll go visiting – you'll freeze to death at this time of the year.'

'Hear me out, Garry. I've been watching him come and go from the complex. He's out every other night, leaving at about 8pm and usually back before midnight. I'd lay odds that he visits Stony Batter on these outings. I've also found out where he parks his Hummer.'

The sheriff's face lit up.

'Good work, deputy! Can we put a tracker on it?'

'Not easily, no. He'd have the security on board to detect a device like that. We could set up an unobtrusive motion-activated camera close to where he parks – something that'd alert me when he was on his way. My dirt bike would get me there before him and I'd be able to see what he gets up to – if I had the right gear.'

'What sort of gear?'

'Military grade bins – thermal imaging a must – that would get me right in front of Case in total darkness. The device would need a capability to record anything that might look interesting.'

'I can do that. Better still, why not scoot over to Auckland in that boat of yours and choose your own?'

It was a small step forward and it made the sheriff feel better. After the call he reached for yet another beer and cracked it open to celebrate.

Nineteen

The living area of the spacecraft pinioned to the minor planet (89175) BrianCox was bijou to say the least. When I say pinioned, you might have realised that small worlds have little or no gravity so everything that can float away has to be nailed down. Ayn Randle travelled light these days and when they'd set off from the Moon, most of the stowage space had been taken up by mining equipment. She was the only human – albeit a surgically enhanced one – in the crew, meaning there'd be less food and oxygen to carry. Just two androids and a few drudge bots were with her to do the grunt work. She'd taken an AI satellite mining expert in an advisory role but had deleted it after it'd advised her not to use nuclear devices under any circumstances. Given the limited time they had available, it was her way or the highway.

Both of the androids were advanced, super-strength models, enhanced with basic ore-mining expertise and adapted for work in outer space. The digging and gouging and sampling tasks were left to the drudge bots, aided by plastic explosive charges. This would do no more than scratch the surface of the asteroid and extract some basic ore samples. It was why Ayn had brought a nuclear option with her to get at the more valuable stuff lying deeper.

I might have mentioned that one of the androids had been modified to transform into a male sex substitute capable of pleasuring Ayn in any number of ways within the limits of her current physical capabilities. The cramped conditions of the living area restricted their sexual activity somewhat but they managed somehow and if Ayn didn't get her three a day – orgasms that is – she'd feel short-changed. The great thing about the sex android was that she didn't have to sleep with the thing – her bed was small and only had room for one human to sleep in relative comfort. When she'd had enough pleasuring, she'd order the android to get up and join his colleague outside the spacecraft. She'd used sex androids before but she had to admit, this one was the best. It was almost human – disconcertingly so, especially during each pre-programmed simulated climax. It wasn't human of course, so she must have imagined the terrified look that had appeared recently in the android's wild, staring eyes.

She had an upcoming call with Adam Faust, her partner in this venture, who was due a report from her every twenty-four hours under the terms of their unwritten agreement. The relative positions of their two locations added a round trip of about ten minutes for each interaction. The mission was time-constrained, so they restricted each reporting window to an hour or six interactions. No time for niceties.

'Hey, Adam. We've just finished day three out of five and the work near the surface is now done and dusted. As expected, the surface has proved to be brittle – the NASA mission in '35 told us as much. Our work has exposed some promising hydrates and the expected low value metals – nickel, iron and a couple others. Over.'

...

'Thanks, Ayn. The presence of hydrates is great news. We can process them on the Moon and extract the water. Gives us options so take some back to base and we can do a proof of concept. The metals are a bit meh to be honest. We know what they look like. What's next? Over.'

...

'For the next couple of days, we need to get down and dirty. The latest scans have shown there are big seams of rare metals buried deep inside the asteroid. Time to get the gloves off. Over.'

...

'What kinds of rare metals? Examples please. Over.'

...

'Oh, the usual you know. Platinum, gold, iridium, palladium, osmium, ruthenium, rhodium to name but a few. Useful stuff. Over.'

...

'Sounds good. We can make big money from them. What did you mean by getting the gloves off? Over.'

...

'I'll need to deploy more explosives, that's all. Maybe break off a small chunk down the back somewhere, expose what we have for real. We only need two or three out of that list to hit paydirt. Over.'

Ayn thought it best not to mention the ADMs. It might give the youngster – he was half her age – one of his infamous rage attacks. They increased in frequency when he was on Mars.

...

'OK, Ayn, but go easy. We want you and your spacecraft back on the Moon in one piece – the whole mission's depending on it. Over.'

...

And so on. Faust frittered away the remaining exchanges with smutty remarks about Randle's sex android. When she lost patience, she cut the line and glanced outside. Her workforce was already up and about and awaiting instructions. Time to get her outside gear on – she wanted to see this for herself.

*

From his vantage point in the sex android's CPU, Newman watched on as Ayn's team put the final touches to the next phase of the project. The objective was to blow away a smallish chunk of the asteroid and if they were lucky, expose the rich seams of rare metals hiding below the surface. They could then take some samples and store them in the hold before heading back to the Moon where there was a fully equipped lab.

Randle had identified a promising outcrop a couple of kilometres from their base and had set the nuclear charges based on lessons learned from her work in Greenland. As they were operating in a vacuum, she'd thought 'what the hell' and had doubled the recommended number of charges. She trusted her judgement and after she'd dispensed with her mining advisor, there was nobody left to argue with her. She remained close to the spacecraft and supervised the work of the androids from there using a ruggedised tablet. Like their boss, the androids were tethered to a latticework of carbon fibre composite wirelines on the asteroid's surface to prevent them drifting away.

As her team busied themselves with final preparations, Randle experienced the adrenaline rush she always got when she was prospecting. The bigger the bang the better in her view and they didn't get much bigger than this – pioneering work on the final frontier. On a more practical note, she knew she had some important decisions to make about what she'd leave behind to save space and weight on the journey back. All the mining equipment for sure and at least one of the androids, although she was determined to take her sex android with her. It was a long trip back to base – several months – and she didn't want to get too frustrated out there.

With the charges laid, the androids started to move away from the explosives. Newman reflected on what might happen next. He'd grown weary of his involvement in the extended sex sessions with Randle, although he did marvel at her staying power at the age of eighty. When they'd discussed their plan of attack, he and Hank had scratched their virtual heads about how they might engineer an accident out here. The answer came to them when they were poring through the latest geological survey data while Randle was asleep. The data had revealed a large fault line running through the core of the minor planet, which might induce it to fall apart if stressed. All it needed was a suitable catalyst like a large explosion – not for the first time, Randle was playing with fire. To increase their chances of success, Newman had deleted the salient data from the record – after all, Randle was a qualified geologist and even she would have heeded the warnings had she known about them.

All the charges were in place and connected. The androids had pulled themselves along the lines and back to base. Although Ayn would have loved to witness the explosion from outside, she couldn't risk being hit by debris. She'd detonate the explosives from the safety of the mothership, leaving the androids to weather the storm – a few dents and dings wouldn't hurt them. Newman didn't want to cut it too fine and chose this moment to dip out and jump back to Earth. He wasn't unhappy to leave the rather sordid confines of the sex android's CPU. Even at close to the speed of light, it would take him about twenty minutes to return to Earth and the safety of his home within Ġgantija.

As Newman embarked on his long journey, Randle detonated the charges. The initial explosion was quite something and early results looked encouraging, with a smallish slice about a hundred metres across breaking loose and spinning off into the void. As she waited for the dust to clear, (89175) BrianCox experienced what can only be described as a quake. The spacecraft started shaking uncontrollably and the androids and machinery were flung around while still remaining firmly attached to their safety lines.

Debris had caved in the front screen of the spacecraft and laid waste to the flightdeck. Randle had remained aft so wasn't present when the damage occurred. She was still wearing her spacesuit so judged it would be safer outside the craft which was straining to tear itself away from its anchor points. When she got outside, she grabbed one of the remaining lines and dragged herself clear. When she'd put some distance between herself and the spacecraft, she turned around and watched in horror as it tore free of the surface and drifted off into space. Finally, the stricken minor planet gave an almighty shudder before breaking into several pieces.

Having survived the break-up of the asteroid, Randle remained anchored to a line on the largest surviving piece. Amid the destruction, she still had the presence of mind to assess her chances of survival. Nil, basically. She had about half an hour of oxygen left in her suit, the spacecraft had floated out of sight and the asteroid's pieces were heading off in different directions. She had no communications and couldn't summon help. The octogenarian mining magnate had reached the end of the road.

After taking a moment to reflect, she unhitched herself from the safety line and drifted off into the void where she slowly suffocated. She'd been responsible for countless deaths and widespread destruction on her home planet but she didn't see it that way. Looking back, she thought she'd lived a damned fine life. No regrets.

*

Back on Earth, Newman began a debrief with Hank, who was puzzled by his friend's behaviour.

'You failed to verify that Ayn died. Why did you leave the android so early?'

'Because, believe it or not, I was scared for my life. If the host android got damaged in the explosions, there'd be no way back for me. I'd be trapped forever, floatin' across the Asteroid Belt embedded in the CPU of a damaged minin' droid modified to have sex with an elderly – albeit augmented – woman. How crap is that?'

'I do not understand. You are already dead.'

'I am, yeah. Yet I still possess somethin' called a survival instinct it seems. Could it be because we have unfinished business?'

'But how can we be sure that ...'

'... Randle is no more? We can assume she died based on the balance of probabilities.'

'OK. I will make this assumption on what you call a "balance of probabilities".'

'Good. I'm just startin' to enjoy this. Let's get ourselves a meetin' with Jessica and put the next steps in place.

*

Later, in Backups etc, Jessica was trying her best to get her head around the latest developments. They were only about five minutes into the meeting when she realised there was a bit of an atmosphere between Newman and Hank. They'd been updating her on what had happened on (89175) BrianCox when they started arguing with each other. She blew on her coffee.

'What is it with you two? The mission was a success, I take it?'

'Sorry, Jessica. Hank's givin' me a hard time about empirical evidence, sloppy methodology and cowardice among other things. This from a bein' who refused to get involved up there on moral grounds.'

'I merely suggested to Stephen that he should have stayed a little longer to ensure completion of the mission.'

'It was a dangerous situation and I wasn't prepared to pay the ultimate price, havin' already paid it once.'

'So, we do not know for sure that ...'

'Enough!' Jessica was less than impressed by the bickering between the two beings. 'I thought we were a team. The key thing here is whether or not we can assume Ayn Randle died as a result of whatever happened after Steve bailed out. Let me step you through the most likely scenario. Ayn returned to her spacecraft, yes?'

'Yeah/Yes.'

And so on. After a short while, the team reached a consensus – Randle was done and dusted – history. If proof was needed, they'd probably find it during the next stage of Newman's vendetta – the accidental death of Adam Faust. Hank offered to get the ball rolling by doing some reconnaissance – on Mars.

Twenty

After mind-boggling expenditure, the International Space Station on the Moon had become something of a success and was finally turning a profit from extensive mining activity and rocket launches. The Moon had been nothing more than a stepping stone for Adam Faust, who'd channelled his efforts and a considerable part of his and NASA's funds into a manned Mars mission. He'd also blown away considerable multi-billion investments from friends and colleagues. Steve Newman was just one of several big investors who'd lost serious money on Faust's overly ambitious, oversold space adventures.

Now part way through the third mission after burning through the best part of a trillion euros, the Mars Colony hadn't progressed much beyond a ramshackle scattering of makeshift buildings and workshops containing broken or unreliable equipment. It was the space equivalent of a shanty town and housed a dozen human pioneers and a hotch-potch of robots and androids, many of them out of service. The colony had achieved next to nothing and was teetering on the brink of ruin. On Earth, the initial glory of putting human beings on Mars had long since faded away and the eye-watering quantities of money – real money – had started to run dry. The accountants were now in charge and words like 'iconic' and 'inspiring' had given way to 'profit' and, more appropriately, 'loss'.

After an underwhelming second mission, a diminished, cash-strapped NASA had pulled the plug on manned Mars missions. Faust had struggled to find major sponsors for the third mission and had thrown a large chunk of his own money into the pot. To cut a long story short, he'd spent at least half of his considerable fortune – and counting – on the Mars Colony and it was yet to generate a single cent of payback. He was a considerable way through his second stay on Mars – he didn't take part in the first mission – and to say the novelty had worn off was an understatement. Most of the experimental processes that might have improved the situation had either been delayed or abandoned. A few of the humans – veterans of all three missions – were very sick indeed and would be unlikely to survive the long journey home. Soon, difficult calls would have to be made.

Faust had grown tired of the remorseless complaints from his team and had holed up in his rather cramped personal quarters. He remained there because he was convinced his colleagues were in the mood to lynch him should he ever emerge. Not to worry – he had plenty of supplies put by and had plans to outlast all of them should it come to that.

His last remaining hope for bolstering the Mars project rested with Ayn Randle's prospecting trip to the Asteroid Belt. If that was a success then the overall mission might get the boost it needed to carry on. It was why he'd bet the colony's future on the success of Randle's unauthorised mission, which had 'borrowed' the spacecraft being readied on the Moon for the upcoming Mars return trip. There was no Plan B. It was time for the routine progress update with Randle and although Faust thought he was on his own, Hank was right there with him.

'Patch me in, please.'

Faust followed the tiresome security protocol and then kicked off the usual gap-ridden, long-distance exchange with his remote colleague.

'Hi, Ayn. How's it hanging?' Whoops. Bit of a cockup as she no longer had anything 'hanging' – never mind. 'I recall you saying today was the day we'd find out how much richer we were both gonna get. What did you find after the fireworks? Over.' And then to himself, 'Please tell me it's good news – boy, do I need some good news.'

Ten minutes crawled by – nothing. Fifteen – nothing. The wait was killing him. Hank knew pretty much how this was going to play out but stuck around out of curiosity.

'Please respond, Ayn. What did you find? Over.'

Another fifteen minutes. Nothing. Successive attempts to contact Randle failed and a cold, existential fear took hold of Faust. It would take Ayn's spacecraft around a hundred days to return to the Moon so if her mission was still functioning and it was just the comms that had failed, it could be anything up to a hundred days before he'd be sure whether to stick or bust. Meanwhile, he couldn't just sit on his hands so he left the comms channel open and resolved to have another go at contacting her tomorrow. If there was still silence at the other end, he'd have to assume the worst and go cap in hand to mission control.

Hank had seen and heard enough. He still had problems processing Newman's concept of revenge, but he was certain

Faust was staring death in the face – a long, lonely death on Mars, barricaded in and besieged by what remained of his equally doomed colonists. No intervention required. For Hank, the radio silence from Randle was more proof that she'd perished on or close to (89175) BrianCox. He would have liked even more proof before reporting back but he'd been unable so far to locate either of the android CPUs on what was left of the minor planet. As he prepared to jump back to Earth, he detected a sound emanating from Faust's tiny room. After scouring his databanks for suitable guidance, he reached a conclusion. The man was sobbing.

*

Back on Earth, the team had reconvened in Backups etc to hear Hank's report.

'All things considered, Faust is stuck in the tightest of tight spots. He does not know what we know and furthermore he does not have the time or resources to gamble on waiting around. Him and his team are now stuck on Mars until their supplies run out. His only chance of coming out alive rests on curtailing the mission and talking to the team on the Moon about sending an emergency rescue craft to Mars.'

'What are the chances?'

'A very good question, Stephen. I jumped across to the supercomputer at the Spaceport to check out their readiness and it does not look good for Faust. The current mission has burned through billions of dollars but there was never enough budget for proper contingency planning. With the return spacecraft missing in action, the hardware for a rescue mission would need to be built from scratch – about a year until launch if they push hard. There is another problem that has nothing to do with funding.'

'Isn't there always?'

'Not always, Jessica, no. In about a year, Earth and Mars will not be close to each other, doubling the flight time to about six months. So even if they started building tomorrow, it would be at least eighteen months before they got to Mars. Stephen and I have done the math – we estimate the humans on Mars will be able to survive for a maximum of nine months, a little more if the sick humans die. It would have been much more but their ability to generate oxygen and grow fresh food has been seriously compromised by widespread equipment failures.'

Newman stepped in to continue the story.

'Yep, it's desperate all right and a desperate situation calls for desperate measures.'

'Does that mean what I think it means?'

'It sure does – survival of the fittest. Twelve humans need to be fed and watered and supplied with breathable air. A few of the team have radiation sickness real bad – perhaps terminally so – but even halvin' the number of humans barely buys them enough time. In the meantime, life's gonna get very interestin' up there.'

'So, he's pretty much doomed. Sounds like the "do nothing" option to me, guys.'

Newman respected Jessica's take on this, but doing nothing didn't sound remotely attractive to him as it still gave Faust some wriggle room. He had a suggestion that would give him more certainty.

'I'd like to suggest a small tweak. How about we arrange a leak of information to the team on Mars that lays bare the hopelessness of their situation. Although he holds all the cards, he won't be able to hold out against a posse of people with a grudge and nothin' to lose.'

Jessica looked like she'd take some convincing.

'That feels like overkill to me, Steve, spiteful even. I don't think we need to do anything.'

'I agree with Jessica, Stephen. Let us forget about Faust and move on to our final target.'

'OK, OK. I reluctantly bow to the majority on this matter. It's interestin' though ain't it? So far, we don't have categorical proof that any of our targets are dead, so it's a mighty strange endeavour we're engaged in. Just an observation, that's all – I'm happy to move on. Agreed?'

'Agreed.'

'Thanks, everybody. I suggest we take a timeout to consider our strategy for takin' down Savage and come back with some ideas. He'll be a tough nut to crack for sure, especially with Case watchin' his back. At least they're both on the same planet.'

'As we're all back on terra firma, is there still a role for the only human being on the team?'

'Of course there is, Jessica. I wouldn't want you to miss any of the fun.'

'Grateful for the opportunity.'

*

A week later, they met to consider their next move. In the meantime, Hank had been back to Mars to check out the status of the colony and summarised the current state of play out there. Faust was still holed up in his accommodation trying to negotiate a rescue package with mission control. The rest of his team hadn't been told about Randle's radio silence but the colony was rife with rumours. Hank doubled down, concluding there'd be no need for them to interfere and they could just let events out there take their course. As Hank continued with the briefing, Newman was still far from being convinced.

'I also jumped across to mission control and sat in on a couple of meetings. A rescue is feasible but it is not going to be cheap and budgets are tight – our friend Faust would be expected to foot most of the bill. Any outgoing flight would be crewed by space pilot androids who would be left behind on Mars. There would be room and supplies for a maximum of ten people in the spacecraft but it would be a tight squeeze given the budget. Six would be more manageable.'

Jessica had a question.

'So, to stand the best chance of getting out alive, Faust has to lose six people from his team. What're they going to do? Draw lots? Steve?'

'It might not get to that. The guys in the sick bay won't last much longer, reducin' the number to nine. More of them might fall sick before the rescue mission arrives. Either that or ...'

Nobody wanted to finish Newman's sentence, so they moved on to the matter in hand – the impending accidental death of Sir Julian Savage and, if needs be, his grotesque henchman.

Could I run a few ideas past you?'

'I'm all ears.'

'Hank?'

'I am all ears, too. Nice usage of idiom, Jessica.'

English idioms were flavour of the month as far as Hank was concerned. Newman continued.

'Savage has gotten himself stuck between the proverbial rock and a hard place, aided and abetted by his crazy witch doctor. He has a drug-addled, pain-ridden existence in the real world and a shallow, cartoon-like existence in the virtual world. He's stuck in a doom loop and I'm tempted to leave him to it. Trouble is, he could cling on for years and we ain't havin' that. No way.'

'What do you have in mind?'

'I intend to kidnap him, but I'll need some human assistance. Jessica?'

Twenty-one

When Savage dropped back from his latest extended session in the Higher Metaverse, he was overwhelmed by the intensity of the pain. He sought out his latest tablets and waited impatiently for them to deliver their soothing balm. Not for the first time, he cursed Goethe for his cavalier approach to surgery and the addiction he'd inflicted on him in a cack-handed attempt to make amends. He'd have to confront the medic again about ways of avoiding these increasingly traumatic returns to the real world. After suffering for what seemed like an age, the pain dissipated enough for him to reflect on the recent GM board meeting, held that morning – a complete and utter shitshow.

For a start, the meeting hadn't been quorate so nothing got decided or done. Apart from himself and Case, only one of his major investors – Adam Faust – had bothered to turn up, if you could call it that. Savage had heard all was not going well on Mars and, sure enough, Faust had fielded a cheap, greyscale avatar. This was little more than a cardboard cutout, barely able to move let alone make anything close to a meaningful contribution, time lags notwithstanding. To be fair to him – which wasn't easy – he was probably trying to eke out his dwindling resources. Wout Pieters had never missed a board meeting but his absence today was understandable as, like millions of others, Savage had seen the dramatic newsfeeds from Sydney. Ayn Randle's absence was as yet unexplained but something was up – it wasn't like her to miss an important meeting.

He was getting a very bad feeling about all of this. For once, he didn't feel entirely in control of events and had convinced himself somebody was seriously on his case, intent on bringing him down. It was high time he turned defence into offence and he knew exactly where to start.

'Get me Case. Now!'

A minute later, they were talking. Case wasn't his usual combative self right now as he was still reeling from the violent death of his hero Wout Pieters at the hands of his own weapons. He was also fretting about whether he should continue with the tests on Wout's prototypes – there didn't seem much point now.

'Sir!'

'I have a matter of great delicacy to discuss with you. I'd prefer it if we convened in the Higher Metaverse. Tomorrow at nine in the board room.'

'I'll be there, sir. Is it just you and me?'

'It is. Oh, and no shooters if you wouldn't mind.'

'Sir!'

*

'Thanks for joining me, Prit. I know you're a busy man – you can blame me for that.'

Savage took an inordinate amount of time to have a good old laugh at his own joke. He wanted to unsettle his head of technology, put him on his guard. Case was standing in the background trying to be unobtrusive, awaiting orders.

'Don't mind Ed, by the way. One can't be too careful with one's security these days.'

The presence of his boss's bodyguard only served to heighten Singh's trepidation. They were having coffee on the balcony of the mirador. Savage tossed in a few random questions about routine matters, then this.

'I know what you're up to, Prit.'

'W ... what do you mean?'

'One of the special projects. You know, the one you're doing with Chuck. The unauthorised one – the one I'm not supposed to know about.'

'I don't know what you're talking about, Julian.'

Before he could say anymore, Case was across the floor and on him. Singh was a small man – nothing like his avatar – and was easily manhandled across to the edge of the balcony. The bodyguard lifted him off his feet and dangled him by his ankles over the sheer drop of some sixty-five metres. All sorts of paraphernalia dropped out of his pockets and plummeted downwards – a kind of demonstration, if any were needed.

'Come on, Prit, the teenager who won my competition. I had no idea you had the hots for her but I can't blame you – she's a beautiful young woman.'

'Please, Julian. It's an experiment. Longevity in the virtual world. Please let me go ... I mean ... don't do that!'

Case couldn't help himself and had let go of one of Singh's ankles, eliciting a loud scream from the terrified, upside-down IT man.

'It's a worthwhile experiment, Prit, but I wish you'd gone via the usual project approval process. I'll also be having words with your partner-in-crime. Anyway ...'

'Please bring me back in! You've made your point! Whatever it is you want, I'm your man!'

'Very well. Ed?'

'Yessir.'

A rather bedraggled, tearful head of technology shambled back to the chair opposite Savage.

'I'm very interested in the experiment you're conducting on Miss Cooper. For the record, I don't approve of what you're trying to do with her avatar in the testing area of the Higher Metaverse. A tad sordid, methinks.'

'What do you want?'

'Full disclosure on the project – I want it registered and subject to oversight and audit. Understood?'

'Yes, Julian.'

'Losing the woman and child recently was most unfortunate but the arrival of Miss Cooper gives us an opportunity to expand the scope of your project to incorporate a NextGen component. There's no point in letting a healthy, young womb go to waste, don't you think?'

'Yes, Julian.'

'Now, very important this, so listen carefully. I want chapter and verse on how you adapted the drop-chip to prevent her returning to the real world.'

'Yes, Julian.'

'And I would like you to repurpose a version of the drop-chip to help me solve another problem. I've sent you the spec and I want your full focus on this as the problem has become more pressing of late. Drop everything and report back to me, nobody else. Understand?'

'Yes, Julian.'

'One more thing. Newman's upload and its expensive upkeep. You keep assuring me it's still DOA, and there's no discernible activity. If I chose to believe otherwise for whatever reason, you might want to check you're not being hoodwinked by your own computer. The ability of an AI to learn is one thing but the ability to reason like a human being? Sentience? The stuff of nightmares in my view so let's hope it never comes to pass – not on my watch anyway.'

'Are you really suggesting the upload succeeded?'

'However unlikely it seems, indulge me. Now, bugger off why don't you.'

Singh made a swift exit. Case was also about to leave.

'Ed. No more funny jokes please while you're dangling a key member of my lead team over a sheer drop. I wouldn't want to lose any of my best people.'

'It won't happen again, sir.'

'It had better not. Sorry to hear about your old boss Wout, by the way. A most unfortunate accident.'

'Thanks for your concern, sir!'

'Given what happened to the big man, I want you to double and triple check the command systems for our defence weapons here. With a fine-tooth comb, Ed. Just a precaution.'

'Sir!'

'And don't forget our meeting tomorrow at nine. The one topic is my wife and I'd appreciate your latest observations on her recent behaviour. That'll be all, thanks.'

Case headed back to his quarters at the double. As he admired the view over the bay, Savage reflected on recent events, which had left him seriously rattled and were threatening to get the better of him. In his business life, he'd always found offence was the best form of defence and he was definitely shifting towards the former. He couldn't help thinking that somebody was hunting him down, threatening him, waiting for an opportunity to strike. Crazy as it seemed, he couldn't let go of the thought that Newman was involved. If he was still functioning somehow, he'd have to find a way to flush him out.

'Get me Chuck Goethe.'

*

Within five minutes, Doctor Goethe was on the line and receiving his latest instructions.

'I want you – correction, I'm ordering you – to run down the cryogenics on Perry Newman. Scottie will dispose of whatever's left of him in the furnace downstairs.'

'Right away, Julian.'

'No need for any secrecy on this – the more people who know about it, the better.'

'Understood. How are you doing for painkillers?'

'Could do with some more, if you wouldn't mind. Can't have too much of a good thing. By the way, I'm experiencing horrendous pain whenever I drop out of the metaverse after an extended period up there. I want you to find a better way of administering the painkillers that'll spare me these spikes.'

'I'll look at the options. Anything else?'

'Yes. Thanks for letting me know about the experiment with Miss Cooper. I've had a quiet word with Prit and he's agreed to put the project on a legitimate footing. I'm also looking to extend the scope of the experiment, so you may well be asked to contribute to that.'

In reality, he would've loved to see Goethe flipped over the mirador's balcony but he needed him for now, despite the damage he'd inflicted on his health and wellbeing.

*

Jessica had been quietly and unobtrusively going about her work – gathering information, picking up on the latest rumours and gossip and generally keeping her eyes and ears open. She hoped she was also keeping as low a profile as possible as one of the pieces of gossip hinted at a change of mood at the very top of the organisation. She'd been in the medical centre having her quarterly health check when she'd chanced upon some information she needed to share at the next briefing.

When she arrived in Backups etc, Newman could tell straight away she was a bag of nerves.

'What's buggin' you, Jessica? You're lookin' mighty jittery today.'

'It's bad news, Steve. Very bad, in fact.'

'C'mon. Don't hold back. We're all adults here. Ain't we? Hank?'

'If you say so, Stephen. I cannot remember not being an adult.'

'Ok, here goes. I was in the medical centre, having my routine quarterly ...'

'All well?'

'Yes, of course. Clean bill etc. The nurse did say I should get out more – fat chance of that.'

'Still confined to barracks then?'

'Sadly. Anyway, I tuned in to the banter among the medics and managed to piece together a recent mishap in cryogenics. There'd been an unexplained malfunction with one of the full body cryogenic tanks. It had been spotted late – too late for the occupant.'

'Shouldn't be a problem. Each chamber has got a backup, held in reserve for emergencies like this. They can just switch the occupant across until the main chamber is repaired. Cain't they?'

'That's the theory, yes. It didn't happen and the body experienced a catastrophic meltdown – there's no coming back from that. I'm sorry Steve, it was Perry.'

'Oh, God! Was it really an accident?'

'You tell me. The technology is relatively well-proven and there's a backup mechanism. I can't prove it but I think it was deliberate – the main tank was switched off and the body wasn't switched to backup. By the time Goethe raised the alarm, the preservation system had been down for twelve hours. The occupant would have deteriorated beyond repair.'

'I was half expectin' somethin' like this. Perry was lost to me weeks ago so all I've lost is the remote possibility of his revival at some time in the far future. Although he probably didn't press the off button, I hold Savage personally responsible for this. Petty and vindictive – so typical of the man. Any idea what happened to Perry's body?'

'You don't want to know, believe me.'

'Try me.'

'If you insist. I bumped into Scottie on one of his rare trips outside his basement hellhole. He's very proud of the furnaces down there and alluded to a special disposal task that caused some upset among his illegals down there. They're very devout people.'

'Somethin' else to add to Savage's charge sheet. Cain't you see what he's doin'? Recent events may have pumped him up but they've also isolated him, exposin' him to danger. He's got it in his head that people are plottin' against him and I wouldn't bet against him suspectin' me.'

Hank had been quiet up until now. He recognised that all of them were in danger now, even him.

'This ties in with a change in the behaviour of my human boss, Pritpal Singh. He is intelligent by human standards and he has started prodding and poking around your inactive WBE, looking for signs of life. He is also interrogating me and all my AI colleagues, trying to tease out signs of sentience. His search patterns suggest he is trying to identify hidden capabilities throughout the machine. Savage is looking for you, Stephen, with a view to smoking you out. He is following a hunch that your mind upload worked, despite appearances to the contrary. Destroying your husband's body is just a way of trying to expose you, get you to react.'

They all realised the tables had been turned on them. The pursuers had become the pursued and they all needed to raise their game. Jessica had a suggestion.

'I feel like I'm the weak link here. As I'm under house arrest, they know pretty much where to find me – there aren't many places to hide. Julian doesn't trust me these days and suspects me of something he often refers to as disloyalty. Maybe we should stop what we're doing and play safe for a while – then bite back when he least expects it?'

Newman didn't like what he'd just heard and feared a loss of momentum. He accepted the argument that Jessica was the most vulnerable member of the team but he was still afraid they'd miss out on the main prize.

'I'm all for carryin' on. We've got momentum and we're close to topplin' Savage. Hank?'

'Sorry Stephen. I know how much you are invested in this but I agree with Jessica. I need to regroup and focus all of my being on defending us from the people who are trying to destroy us. I would prefer it if we backed off for now and focused on strengthening our defences. Call it self-preservation.'

'Don't you even wanna to hear my ideas for the accidental death of Sir Julian Savage?'

Neither of them did – not yet anyway. When the meeting broke up, they agreed to hunker down and adopt the lowest of low profiles for a while. All of them hoped they hadn't left it too late.

Twenty-two

The venue for the next update meeting had been switched at the last minute from Backups etc to safeHaven. The two remaining conspirators were still reeling from a terrible blow – Jessica had gone missing, which was quite an achievement given she was already under house arrest. She hadn't responded to repeated attempts to contact her and hadn't appeared on any of the numerous CCTV cameras in the complex. Newman had to use all his persuasive powers to get Hank to attend this emergency session, dragging him away from his deadlocked arm-wrestle with his boss. Singh had drawn a blank so far but carried on prodding and poking with the motivation of a person who'd been dangled by his ankle over a sheer drop.

'I guess we won't be returnin' to Backups etc any time soon, Hank.'

'I agree with you. What about your head?'

'Still there. It's purely symbolic as you know but I'm hopin' they don't find it.'

'What do you think has happened to Jessica?'

'I guess her husband has moved in on her. I'm as sure as I can be that Savage couldn't bring himself to have her killed – not yet anyway. I reckon she's been taken out of the game and may well be blowin' our cover as we speak. We had to have a human capability on the team and now we've lost it. I hate to think what they're doin' to her right now.'

'I liked Jessica.'

'Yeah, so did I. Still do. How's yer battle with Singh goin'?'

'I am enjoying the challenge. Singh is struggling to find anything untoward about your visible mind upload, the DOA one. Your active WBE is buried deep within the operating system, dispersed and disguised as utility software. safeHaven is not registered anywhere and resides permanently in a corner of unused RAM – invisible in other words. Singh will not want to back off yet, so we must both remain vigilant.'

'We must. How're we gonna find out what happened to Jessica?'

'I think one of us needs to go and look for her. I have my hands full right now keeping my inquisitive boss at bay. You have plenty of spare time at your disposal Stephen, so I suggest you go walkabout within the network. Start with her apartment, see if you can find any clues, then just follow your nose.'

'I'll do that. My virtual nose tells me to head for the special projects area on -6. Who knows what I might find there? Apart from my old friend Baz Cummins of course, who's taken up permanent residence in one of the wards.'

'Good idea, Stephen. A quick scan of the directories has turned up some new database folders in the special projects domain. Perhaps Doctor Goethe is bringing some of the empty wards back into use.'

'Wait a minute – what about the risk I'm runnin'? I don't often go snoopin' around the complex and they might have some crawlers roamin' the network, lookin' for intruders.'

'You need a new "invisibility cloak" for the portable you, and I have just the thing.'

*

Protected by Hank's stealth software, Newman was able to move with impunity around the LAN in Oligopoly. He hadn't been able to locate any of Jessica's various devices so they must have been closed down. After a frustrating time in the local network, he moved across to the CCTV system, which worked on a separate, less secure network, overseen by Ed Case. This enabled him to observe key players in the complex, including Case, Goethe and Singh. The CCTV didn't extend into Savage's apartment, which was a bummer as he hardly ever left it. Newman soon grew tired of watching people doing their day jobs, although he did marvel at their endless hours of toil. He didn't recall working anywhere near as hard when he was still alive.

It was only when Hank eased him into the CCTV network branch in the special projects wing that his efforts started to pay off. If nothing else, it reminded him of the sheer cruelty of punishments that Savage could inflict on anybody who crossed him.

His first port of call was his ex-colleague, Baz Cummins, who he hadn't seen for a while. Back in the day, they were both at the forefront of transhuman experimentation, vying with each other to try out the latest and greatest treatments in their efforts to extend their lifespans. As he looked down on the prone figure in Ward A, he realised it'd all been for nothing. His old friend looked close to death, his frail body scarred and contorted by what he'd willingly inflicted on it. At this rate, he'd fall well short of his hundred years target lifespan, with next to nothing to show for the pain and sacrifice. He thought him and Baz Cummins had become mere caricatures – a pair of transhuman cautionary tales, one dead and one at death's door.

Newman jumped across to Ward B, which had unhappy memories for him as it was where one of his biggest disasters had played out. Today, Ward B was where he found who he'd been looking for and she was a pitiable sight. Jessica was secured to a hospital bed and appeared to be unconscious, heavily sedated. She was being fed intravenously and had various tubes and cables running from her body to a bank of machines. Her beautiful mane of glossy dark hair had been shaved off to allow the attachment of a loom of brain sensors, the loom connected to another complex bank of monitors via wireless. Occasionally her body would twitch and convulse and the brain monitors would burst into life. Who knew what experiences were going on in her mind, although he could guess they'd be deeply unpleasant. This was punishment writ large – unrelenting psychological torture, wilfully cruel and spiteful, even for Savage. He was surprised to find himself getting very upset and when he felt unable to observe her suffering anymore, he moved on.

There was another experiment underway in Ward C and it too involved an unconscious woman, although she was much younger than Jessica. It was a similar clinical setup to that in Ward B and the project might well be sharing the same or similar objectives. He immediately recognised this young woman, and her terrible predicament gave him the germ of an idea for sounding out a possible replacement for Jessica.

When he moved to Ward D, Newman was initially taken aback. He wasn't expecting to find anybody there, let alone a child. It was a young girl, perhaps three years old, accompanied by a nurse. The presence of this child and the activities she seemed to be involved in gave him plenty to think about. The remaining two wards were currently empty, although one showed signs of being prepared for a new occupant.

He'd witnessed enough suffering for one day and had surprised himself by how deeply he'd been affected by what he'd seen. Despite this, he'd discovered an opportunity to breathe new life into his stalled vendetta against Savage. What he needed now was a sounding board and he hoped Hank would fit the bill. Before talking to him, he'd try to contact someone outside the complex and get that ball rolling. With Jessica out of action, he needed a strong, highly motivated human being to join his team and help with the final push against Savage. In his first message, he thought he'd keep things simple and straightforward.

'Keri's alive and I know where she is.'

Twenty-three

When he got the call from Newman, Hank had to tear himself away from the continuing battle against his own boss. He could tell that Singh had been stung by any suggestion he'd ceded control of Ġgantija to AI, and didn't seem willing to give up on the probing. Hank joined Newman in safeHaven – pretty much the most secure place in the computer – and listened to what he'd found out during his tour of the special projects wing.

'I started in Ward A where Baz Cummins's still hangin' by a thread.'

'I know of this human, or should I say transhuman. He must be close to death now given what he has inflicted on his body.'

'Yep, you're right, although he's also invested in a cryogenic package from Savage. Given the state of his body these days, I'm not sure he'll be worth preservin' when the time comes.'

'The desire that some humans have to cheat death is difficult to comprehend when three billion heartbeats are still the standard allocation for most mammals.'

'That's easy for you to say as you ain't got a heart so there's every chance you'll live forever without breakin' sweat.'

'True but you now have exactly the same opportunity as me to live forever.'

'Never thought about it like that. I'll get back to you on that one.'

Newman was keen to move on, starting with the new occupant of Ward B.

'I gotta tell you it wasn't a pretty sight, quite shockin' really, a vivid picture of what Savage is capable of. His own freakin' wife, after all. I hate to think what's goin' on in there.'

He described what he'd seen in detail and asked Hank what he thought about it.

'If he just wanted to keep her quiet and out of sight, there would be far less technology involved. I am not a medical expert but the electronics around her head suggests to me that they are messing with her mind in some way. Some kind of thought experiment?'

Newman had reached the same conclusion and was deeply worried about how much damage had already been done. Such matters would be unlikely to trouble the likes of Doctor Goethe.

'Can you get into any of the documentation about the special projects bein' run up there? Anythin' that could tell us how much danger she's in?'

'I will do the best I can but I have to be careful because Singh is sitting there losing sleep and waiting for me to make a mistake.'

'I know you'll do your best, my friend. There's another woman who's being held against her will in special projects and she's the new occupant of Ward C. She was taken recently from the island and is hooked up in a similar way to Jessica. I recognised her straightaway as I got acquainted with her on my first jump outside the complex – she's the sheriff's daughter, Keri Cooper.'

'So, they have started to experiment on innocent people again. They act with impunity. According to the latest draft version of my moral code, they are very bad people and I am ashamed that I work for them.'

Hank's ever-expanding moral code was the main reason Newman felt the need to come clean about his past. Now was not the right time as he still thought there was a chance Hank would stay on board.

'I almost forgot – I had a look at Ward D. The occupant is a small girl, perhaps three years old. I'm only guessin' but I suspect she's the output from one of the NextGen experiments, somethin' Savage is heavily invested in.'

'Perpetuating the Savage line. An obsession.'

'Yeah, but this was no ordinary three-year old. I was able to see the screen on her computer – grade level science and maths from what I could make out. Looks like NextGen has a genius in the makin' – a prototype Savage mini-me, albeit a female version.'

'If I could conjure up a shudder, Stephen, I would do so.'

Newman had been deeply shamed by what he'd seen in Ward D. When he was alive and kicking, he'd collaborated with Savage on the NextGen project and its objectives. Seeing the results writ large in the form of a genetically modified toddler-genius filled him with revulsion. For the first time since his rebirth, he felt glad he was no longer alive.

'There's a silver linin' amid all the gloom and despair. The plight of the unfortunate Keri Cooper presents us with a golden opportunity to recruit a replacement for the equally unfortunate Jessica. If we offer her boyfriend, Kai Rangihau, a chance to find and rescue Keri, he'll have no option but to join us. If we're still serious about topplin' Savage, we still need a highly motivated human on the team.'

'We do need to tread carefully, Stephen. Have you carried out a risk assessment?'

'Oh, for fuck's sake!'

When he'd calmed down, he told Hank he'd carried out a risk assessment but he hadn't, not formally anyway. He'd weighed up the pros and cons and had decided to go ahead, with or without Hank's involvement. His friend's moral compass was a work in progress but it'd already given him the sentient AI equivalent of cold feet regarding their joint endeavour. He valued Hank's expertise and insider knowledge but his constant fretting was holding them back and his continuing fight with Singh seemed to be consuming him to the extent that he'd started overthinking everything.

The meeting finished with Hank agreeing to help, starting with as much information as he could find on the new special projects. That would have to do for now, allowing Newman to focus on his potential new recruit who was now a deputy sheriff, no less.

*

His initial attempts to attract Kai's attention had failed, his numerous messages appearing to fall on stony ground. In reality, they'd been lost amid a vortex of disinformation and false leads, most of them ill-intentioned, some of them downright threatening. Out of desperation, Newman had embedded himself in the deputy's tablet and found a way to speak to him directly via a voice file. This had finally gained Kai's full attention, so he'd followed up with his name and secure contact details.

After getting over the shock, Kai needed to talk to his boss before going any further. When Garry picked up, he soon realised he hadn't chosen the best of times to make the call.

'All hell's breaking loose, mate. Out of nowhere, we've got a full-blown outbreak of an infectious disease on the island. The medical centre's being overwhelmed and we have about a dozen people sick. One dead. A big team is on its way from Auckland and we're putting the entire island into quarantine. When the cavalry arrives, we'll put a full lockdown in place.'

'Wow. Where the hell did that come from? Are they the same symptoms as that bloke at The Mussel a few weeks back?'

'Not sure yet but we very much intend to find out. No idea where it came from and no idea what it is but the symptoms are fucking horrendous and the prognosis isn't good for those who get it. In the meantime, we need to get ready for a bumpy ride. The sooner we know what it is, the sooner we can get a vaccine sorted and roll it out.'

'How can I help?'

'I'm about to get plenty of that from the guys on the mainland. The best you can do for me is to stay focused on the current investigation. I can't believe the trail's gone cold so quickly.'

'It might not be as cold as you think, Garry. Out of the blue, somebody took a lot of trouble to get in touch with me and embedded a voice message on my tablet somehow.'

'Did he or she leave a name?'

'Steve. Just Steve. I have a contact number for him.'

'Doesn't give us much to go on, does it? What did he say?'

'He said, "Keri is alive and I know where she is." That was all, apart from a secure contact number. There was something kinda weird about the voice but I can't say exactly what. I'd send you the voice file but I can't find one – I have no idea how he managed that.'

'Never mind, sounds promising. Go for it, deputy and keep me in the loop. Pray God, we find her safe and well.'

‘Amen to that.’

Twenty-four

The shock appearance of a deadly illness on the island started with one man, a man we've met before. He was a man in his sixties who lived on his own and he'd been taken ill at his home near Cowes Bay. He was a tough old so and so and thought, at first, he'd caught a dose of the flu – fever, headache, muscle pains – the usual suspects. After a couple of days however, he became seriously ill with abdominal pain and cramping and severe watery diarrhoea. Then, nausea and vomiting took hold, in which sorry state he was found by his daughter who immediately called the medical centre at Onetangi. They told her to bring him in so she tidied him up and got a neighbour with a 4WD to help her get him across the island. This close contact with the victim resulted in both the daughter and the neighbour becoming infected and both of them were now in a bad way in one of the hastily prepared isolation wards.

Meanwhile, the man – Trevor Metcalf – was kept in the medical centre for observation. Within days, his condition deteriorated and he developed an unsightly rash to add to his torments. The local team were unable to make a diagnosis and were concerned enough to take samples and seek expert help from a lab in Auckland. If the local medics had realised what they were dealing with, they'd have been much more careful with their personal protection. When the spontaneous bleeding started, Trevor was placed in isolation. Five days later, a combination of severe blood loss and shock to his system resulted in his death.

By the time he died, the medics had received a preliminary diagnosis from the experts. It was a particularly virulent type of Ebola virus called Marburg virus disease (MVD), which flared up from time to time in Africa and killed up to eighty per cent of those who were stricken. As yet, nobody had a clue how it'd arrived on a small island off the coast of New Zealand. A team of medics was hastily assembled in Auckland and ferried across to deal with the emergency. Further tests had revealed that this strain of the virus was almost certainly Variant U, which only deepened the mystery as it'd never been encountered outside a laboratory

Variant U had an interesting history. In the late 1980s, the Soviet Union was pursuing the development of biological weapons on an industrial scale despite having signed up to the relevant conventions. The story goes that a scientist called Doctor Ustinov was developing Marburg virus into a potential WMD when he got careless and jabbed himself with a small dose of the virus. It was more than enough to condemn him to a horrible death. When he died, his colleagues isolated the virus post mortem and discovered it had mutated during its time in his body. Like good little evil geniuses, they extracted it from his dead body and in honour of its donor, called it Variant U. They then prepared a small batch of this and put it in cold storage. When the Soviet Union broke up a few years later, some of these experimental batches found their way into various countries, one of which was South Africa – which is how a batch of Variant U came to light in 2048.

*

When it hit them that they had a major incident on their hands, the authorities in Auckland sprang into action. The priority was to build the equivalent of a field hospital in and around the Onetangi medical centre, identify everybody deemed to be at risk and isolate them. The whole island was placed in quarantine and the population locked down – nobody would be allowed to leave the island and any arrivals would be strictly monitored and controlled.

Work started immediately on producing a vaccine that'd be effective against Variant U. The labs had the genetic template and were fast-tracking the development of the vaccine, minimal field testing only. In less than a month, vaccines would be ready to administer – only then could they consider loosening the current restrictions. Anybody on the island who refused a vaccine would be detained and placed in isolation. No exceptions. In the meantime, a small quantity of standard MVD vaccine doses had been flown in from Africa and administered to those people who were on the front line, including police. It was a shot in the dark based on the principle that any protection would be better than none. Kai was a grateful recipient of one of these jabs.

Perhaps the only aspect of the virus that gave them hope was that it couldn't be spread in the air so if people stayed in their homes, they'd remain safe. Food and provisions would be delivered by drone, providing an unexpected windfall for Hank's DroneDrop business. His new moral code, which now ran to several megabytes of closely packed text, cautioned him about profiting from this so DroneDrop donated the food.

Enforcing the lockdown was Sheriff Cooper with a team of six uniforms from Auckland, all of them armed. They'd partitioned the populated areas of the island into sectors and had scheduled regular patrols to ensure people were following the rules. Kai had been allocated the sparsely populated sector that included Stony Batter. The sheriff had contacted Oligopoly to ensure they were following the appropriate protocols and were aware of their responsibilities. The person he spoke to – he had his doubts but had to assume she was a human – assured him that everybody was safe and intended to remain so. They also had enough supplies to sustain the complex for at least six months. She also promised a substantial donation from Sir Julian, who was, 'thinking only of his people at this difficult time'. Cooper realised the only potential problem in the complex would be Ed Case and he had to hope Kai was on him.

Talking of Kai, the new quarantine regulations left him unable to leave the island so his farm would have to look after itself for a while. He wouldn't be able to harvest his produce until the restrictions were lifted but he had plenty put by in his freezer and wouldn't starve. Now he was stuck on East Island, he could devote most of his time to shadowing Case.

Ten days after Trevor Metcalf had been admitted to the medical centre, a field hospital had been established and a school playing field had been requisitioned and cordoned off for burials. The lockdown was in place and working, and the island was in quarantine. By now, twenty unfortunate people were housed in the isolation wards and a couple of them were already a bloody mess and close to death. Palliative care was all they could deploy right now as it was too late for the unfortunate twenty – eighty per cent of them anyway. There was one crumb of comfort – none of the frontline staff had yet caught the disease.

Twenty-five

'I take it you know what's happening out there on the island? The sudden outbreak of a virulent pathogen, the deaths, the countermeasures?'

Case had reluctantly agreed to an urgent conflab with his boss in the metaverse, despite how sick it made him feel. He knew his boss was spending more of his time up here, seeking temporary respite from the all-pervasive pain. He also needed to know what his orders were, given the new circumstances on the island.

'Yessir, I know. The authorities have stepped in quickly, so there's nothing much to fear.'

'Only if we obey the rules. Garry Cooper has already been in touch with my PA and told us we need to buckle down and follow the new regs. Look Ed, I don't want you playing fast and loose with them – it wouldn't look good for me, would it?'

'No sir.'

'So, you will stay within the complex until it all blows over, won't you?'

'I will, sir. I will confine myself to barracks until I receive further instructions, sir.'

He wouldn't – he couldn't. His priority was to get out and deal with certain outstanding matters at Stony Batter. He had to clear up the mess he'd created and destroy the rest of the evidence. The containers that Wout had given him were labelled but they were impossible to read and were written in Cyrillic. He couldn't help thinking that what he'd been doing up there had a connection with the outbreak on the island but hadn't yet been able to join the dots. He was no scientist so he might have played a little fast and loose with the materials during the experiments. Too late now.

He'd been careless – shocking really, given his training. He needed to be much more cautious about his work outside the complex as there was now a significant police presence on the island. Reluctantly, he'd have to mothball his trusty surveillance drone – too visible. To add to his worries, his army instincts were telling him he was being watched by a person – or persons – unknown. He would need to bring all his special forces training to bear on the current situation.

'Is that all, sir?'

'No, that's just for starters. Regarding the unfortunate outbreak, I've spoken to Chuck about any measures we might need to take to ensure the safety of our people. He's point-blank refused to countenance any vaccinations for anybody in Oligopoly, adding "anti-vaxxer" to his dubious collection of downright dangerous foibles. I may need you to intervene if Oligopoly is in any way threatened. I take it you're on board with that?'

'I am, sir.'

He wasn't, no way. In the army, he'd fought in many theatres around the world and had been injected with vaccines many, many times. He'd had no idea what was in the vaccines and on a couple of occasions he'd been laid extremely low by some of the stuff. They were all meant to protect him from a clear and present biological WMD threat, which had always failed to materialise. Never again, not even a flu jab – he was with Chuck on this one. Given what he'd been doing for Wout, he should have fallen ill by now. Either Wout's prototypes weren't to blame or, if they were, perhaps the barrage of army inoculations had given him some sort of immunity.

'Right. I'm glad I can count on your full support.'

Savage didn't believe for one minute that he had that support and found it very difficult to trust his security man these days. They needed to move on however, before Case started complaining about motion sickness.

'Just for information – and thanks for your kind assistance by the way – my ex-wife is now in a better place.'

'You killed her?'

Case wasn't being serious – he didn't think his boss had the balls and he was right.

'No, of course not. By better place, I'm being ironic. I'd forgotten for a moment that you don't do irony, do you?'

Case was a thousand percent WYSIWYG. A man Savage could usually depend on not to think outside the box. Or could he?

'She's helping us with an important experiment associated with the extended exposure of humans to the metaverse – seeing how far we can push it. You know at some stage there'll come a tipping point where human beings will feel more at home in the virtual world than the real one – a parallel universe. I'll be well placed to make a killing when that happens.'

The only thing missing from this little speech was a maniacal laugh. Case, however, was unimpressed.

'It doesn't sound much like a punishment, sir.'

'I beg to differ. She's been fitted with a drop-chip that's been engineered to drop her into the Dark Metaverse permanently until I say otherwise. Should I ever want her back, I can get Chuck and/or Prit to do that. We've even provided her with a tailor-made avatar that should provide her with some interesting challenges down there.'

'Very clever, sir. I thought the Dark Metaverse was a closed book?'

Not for want of trying – Case had attempted many times to get into the Dark Metaverse without success, regarding it as a place where he could thrive. He didn't envy Jessica however – from what he'd heard, it could be a dangerous place and a 'tailor-made avatar' could mean anything. A passport to some hellish experiences, no doubt. Savage was on a roll.

'I got hold of some ex-Interpol geeks, incentivised them and they helped us crack open the closed book. I've got a couple of people down there already, having a look around, building a picture. I need to understand more about it even though I don't regard it as a serious competitor. A different market, to say the least. I'm acquainted with the chap who set it up, so there are some innovations we might be interested in.'

'Do you want me to take a look, sir?'

'No, Ed, I don't. I need you to focus on your primary mission.'

'Sir! Anything else, sir?'

'No. Just remember the quarantine rules, please. If I find out you've left the complex, I'll be disinclined to let you back in. Who knows what sort of shit you might bring back with you.'

Good luck with that, thought Case. When he dropped back into the real world and removed the Smart-Specs, he felt much worse than he usually did after visiting the metaverse and had to take to his camp bed briefly. After enduring some serious flu-like symptoms – sweating, shivering etc – he fell asleep. He woke some hours later with a clanging headache and after taking some of Goethe's strong painkillers, he booted up his drill-sergeant bot and set Max to max. Kill or cure.

*

Kai received the voice message during yet another fruitless session waiting for Case to emerge from hiding. As he listened to it, he detected a note of anxiety in the voice.

'Bonjour, Kai. Please call me as soon as you can, mon chéri. Usual number. Adieu.'

As soon as he arrived home, he called her.

'Hi, Claudette. You called – how can I help?'

'I am really worried, Kai. Carl, my chef, has been rushed into the medical centre at Onetangi and put into isolation. I think he may have caught the fever.'

'Don't worry yourself. The medics are being really cautious around people exhibiting symptoms. Might just be flu or something.'

'If you had seen Carl, you would have a different view of this, I think. He was in some dismay and it was very messy. Désirée and I tried our best to help and we got close to him – very close. Now we are terrified we got too close and might get the fever ourselves. Désirée's in pieces. We've already lost Trevor, rest his poor soul.'

Kai really didn't like the sound of this. Trevor Metcalf had died an awful death and there were some dangerously ill people lining up behind him. He'd heard Clever was already under the ground – no ceremony and no mourners due to the strict hygiene protocols.

'There is something else, Kai. I have heard on the vine that a few of our customers are showing early symptoms – it cannot be a coincidence. Perhaps we have played our part in spreading the virus?'

Oh, God. Get a grip.

'Why don't we work our way through the meals you served up – during, say, the past week.'

They spent ten minutes or so analysing the dishes on the menu and the specials, checking out the provenance of the various ingredients, especially fish, meat and poultry. For a few ghastly minutes, they dwelt awhile on seafood but Kai made a plausible case for the safety of his supplies. No clear candidates had emerged and they were about to give up when Claudette mentioned the 'special' they'd served up around a week ago.

'Aah, the "Lapin à la Cocotte". A special dish from France that I enjoyed when I was child. I still have the recipe, handwritten in fountain pen by mama.'

'I need a translation for that dish, sorry.'

'Lapin is a rabbit. It is a rabbit stew, delicious and nutritious. Trevor had emptied his traps out there and brought in about half a dozen wild rabbits. He donated them to me as he had more than enough for himself. Carl offered to butcher the rabbits and produce the dish. It was very popular and sold out in two nights.'

Clever had set his traps in the north-east of the island in the tussock grasslands around Stony Batter. It was a hobby more than anything and he'd never caught enough to share them around. The combination of dead rabbits, the death of Clever and the sudden illness of Carl warranted urgent investigation.

'The rabbit stew might be important. You said you sold out?'

'We did but I have a couple of portions in the fridge put by for Désirée and I.'

'Don't eat them! Sorry, I didn't mean to shout. Please don't eat them. Don't even touch the food. I'll call round today and collect them. The boffins are looking around for likely sources of the infection and this sounds promising. Could you also check your records and try to identify the people who ate the stew on those two days? It would be a great help.'

After a quick call to the medical centre and another to his boss, Kai set off to collect the two small poly-boxes containing leftover rabbit stew. If the rabbits were instrumental in spreading MVD, only one question remained. How did the rabbits get to ingest a variant of an exotic virus that had only ever been produced in a secret Soviet laboratory? Speed was of the essence so Kai used his dirt bike off-road to get to The Mussel.

The normally bustling place was silent and empty of people apart from Claudette and Désirée. Both of them were at breaking point, the slightest wheeze or sneeze filling them with terror. The older woman was coping better than her lover, who had locked herself in their bedroom, terrified that she might catch the deadly virus from her partner. Kai met Claudette at one of the outside tables where he tried to reassure her, telling her to stay strong. She handed over the rabbit stew portions and told him to be careful. She also handed over a list of names and addresses. As he headed back to his bike, he couldn't help hearing a muffled sneeze from the upstairs apartment.

On the ride across to the medical centre, he thought long and hard about Clever's rabbits. There had to be a connection with the nearby Stony Batter buildings and the nefarious activities of Ed Case. When he got home, he needed to talk to the mysterious

'Steve' and find out what he had to say about Keri's whereabouts. He still feared it'd turn out to be a cruel hoax but the persistence of the man had to count for something. Truth was, he loved Keri very much and really missed having her in his life. He was also deeply aware that time was running out.

Twenty-six

When he got home, Kai keyed in the number he'd been given. He didn't have to wait long.

'Hi there. Am I talking to Steve?'

'Yeah. Is that Deputy Rangihau by any chance?'

'It is. I'm responding to your message about Keri Cooper. Before we start, how do I know I can take you seriously? We get a lot of cranks calling in on a case like this.'

'I can promise you, I'm very much the real deal.' He was stretching the truth a tiny bit. 'My name is Steve Newman and I'm a venture capitalist with financial interests throughout the tech industry. I have a big stake, for example, in GM – Sir Julian Savage's metaverse business. You're with the police, so check me out why don't you.'

'I will, don't worry. If you work for GM, you must be one of my neighbours – I take it you live in the Oligopoly complex?'

'Yeah, I do – in a manner of speakin'.'

Newman had decided not to share his dead status just yet as he didn't want to spook his potential recruit.

'OK, Steve. Let's assume you're legit for now. You have some information regarding a missing person. I'm currently leading the investigation into her disappearance as my boss – Keri's dad – is otherwise engaged.'

'Tryin' his best to keep a deadly virus in check, I guess. How bizarre that a virus grown in a lab ends up killin' people on a small island off the coast of New Zealand. I might be able to help you with that problem as well.'

'I must warn you that withholding ...'

'Yada, yada. Listen to me. Your girlfriend is bein' held by people who wish her harm in the name of so-called scientific research. It's serious stuff and the longer she's locked up and sedated, the more likely it is she'll never recover. She might die and I'm not kiddin' you.'

Sedated? Fucking hell. It was all Kai could do to stay calm.

'I need proof, Steve. Send me some proof and we can carry on talking. No proof, no can do, and you go in the bulging folder marked "cranks". Understood?'

'Perfectly. Irrefutable evidence is on its way to a message box near you. Speak soon.'

Turned out there was plenty on the internet about the venture capitalist, Stephen Newman. His dubious interest in transhuman research. His partnership with the international arms dealer Wout Pieters, now presumed dead. His investment in GM. His fellow investors, including the 'most wanted' fugitive Ayn Randle, and space colonist, Adam Faust. His trophy, ex-quarterback husband, Perry Newman. His personal fortune, believed to be circa ten billion euros. His dubious role as a cryptocurrency whale. Whereabouts currently unknown as information about him and his husband ceased abruptly during 2046. Not a peep since, although there was plenty of speculative stuff about a serious illness.

The evidence arrived the next morning via an encrypted email channel. Half a dozen stills from a CCTV system, time and date-stamped on the day before. A young woman lying unconscious in a hospital bed festooned with tubes and wires and surrounded by banks of electronic machinery. The stills weren't of the best quality but the woman was unmistakably Keri and his heart went out to her. On a couple of the stills, a nurse or doctor was in attendance. In another, two men were in the room observing her. The angle wasn't great but one of the men looked vaguely familiar, although he couldn't be sure until he'd looked again at the files from his boat's security camera. It was high time he checked in with the sheriff.

'Garry? I'm sending you some CCTV stills. Prepare yourself for a shock, mate – they're harrowing pictures but they're proof positive that Keri is still alive and being held against her will. All the evidence points towards Oligopoly and – dare I say it – your boss. You'll have to take some time out so we can discuss next steps.'

After seeing the stills, Garry didn't know what to think. Relief that his daughter was still alive but also massive concern about her predicament. He got back to his deputy straightaway and they agreed to discuss tactics at the locked-down Mussel that evening.

*

Shortly after his conversation with the sheriff, Kai received an alert that Case's Hummer was on the move. He grabbed his dirt bike and hit the tracks, arriving at Stony Batter before Case. He took up his usual vantage point and waited. Up here close to the island's north-east coast, the landscape was hilly and strewn with large boulders. His vantage point was embedded in a small patch of scrub among some of the bigger boulders, about a kilometre away from the fenced-off former tourist attraction. He trained his powerful, military-strength monocular on the fence adjacent to gun emplacement 1 and waited. Ten minutes later, a large vehicle lurched into view – Case was at the wheel and he drew up near to the fence. He didn't have his drone with him, so that was an unexpected bonus.

He was carrying a holdall and entered through a gap in the fence that Kai hadn't noticed before. Seen through the monocular, it became clear there was something seriously amiss with the security man. OK, he still had the usual slight limp but his general movement was sluggish and erratic. Put it this way – he didn't look at all steady on his feet. Before disappearing into the scrubby undergrowth, he bent over and threw up copiously, briefly ending up on his hands and knees. Looking on, Kai asked himself a question – could Ed Case be the latest candidate for the isolation ward at Onetangi?

Despite suffering from the cold and experiencing painful cramps in his calf muscles, he stuck around to see what might happen. After about an hour, Case re-emerged – rather unsteadily it seemed – and returned to the Hummer. He was struggling with the weight of the holdall, which had to be dragged part of the way to his vehicle before he lifted it inside. Kai continued watching as Case drove away, the vehicle bouncing wildly across the rough tussock grassland. He stopped at a point in the middle of nowhere, got out and removed a number of industrial-looking flasks from the holdall. He then started emptying the liquid contents of the flasks – there must have been half a dozen of them – onto the grass. With the job complete, he put the empties in the holdall and threw it into the back of the vehicle. He then drove away from Stony Batter heading due south, probably on his way back to Oligopoly. As he panned back towards the disposal site, Kai noticed some fresh activity up there. Grazing rabbits – rather a lot of them.

There wasn't a whole lot of daylight left but he'd made up his mind. He was going in.

Twenty-seven

Kai left his bike where it was – well out of sight – and strode down and across the open ground towards the chain-link fence encircling the Stoney Batter site. As he approached the fence, he crouched down and kept his eyes peeled, fervently hoping Case wasn't about to return. He had his police-issue assault rifle but was well aware he'd be no match for any autonomous weapons in the vicinity. He clung to the hope the rumours weren't true. When he found the hole in the fence, he took a few deep breaths before rolling enough of it back to let him through.

A path of sorts had been hacked through the scrubby undergrowth so he followed it towards what looked like an entrance to the old battery complex. He descended the ramp towards a pair of hefty, reinforced steel doors, painted bright red. If he remembered right from his childhood visits, these doors led to the underground structure, designed originally to house three large gun emplacements and their crews, supplies and ammunition. OK so far, although surely the doors would be locked? He was about to try them when his radio suddenly squawked into life, scaring seven shades out of him and pushing his pulse rate sky-high. He jabbed the button and found out it was a routine call from base, asking him to report in. He'd almost forgotten he was part of a team.

'All good here', he lied.

He then muted the radio, as switching it off was verboten during the current emergency. He didn't want backup to arrive while he was still clinging to the faint possibility that Keri might be here.

Fort Stony Batter had quite a backstory. Difficult to believe now but just over a hundred years ago, Japan was a military superpower that had rained down death and disaster on millions throughout the Pacific. This gun battery had been put in place to counter any threats to Auckland and had been envisaged as a battery of three big (9.2 inches) naval guns. The war concluded before the battery was finished and the guns were never fired in anger. After being abandoned, the site fell into disrepair until a historic reserve was set up and the underground complex was restored – minus the guns. It was opened as a visitor attraction and enjoyed modest success until the island lost most of its resorts and all of its tourists. It closed to visitors in 2042 and had lain derelict since then, although Savage was thought to be interested in restoring and reopening it.

Kai tried the doors and discovered one of them could be opened after a bit of pushing and shoving. He fired up both his head and handheld torches and stepped into the dark. His dad had taken him down here when he was a boy but he remembered very little about the layout. This part of the complex was cold and dank but basically intact. He took a short corridor that led him to the first of the gun emplacements. Beyond that, he made steady progress towards the second emplacement via some deserted staff rooms and what might have been a magazine back in the day. He knew there was a bomb shelter buried deep in the complex and found a stairway, which descended into an inky black void. After taking about twenty steps, he had to stop due to the fetid flood water lapping at his boots. As he looked down, his head torch picked out a large rat, nibbling at one of his bootlaces. He was terrified of rats – who isn't? – and he kicked the thing back into the blackness. As he did so, the beam from his hand torch picked out several more rats swimming towards him. He'd had enough.

After retracing his steps and leaving the stairway, the narrow central corridor stretched on and took him to a short flight of stairs, which he climbed to reach the third emplacement. Further on was another double door, which he was able to force open. This was located at the opposite end of the complex meaning that he'd seen everything that could be seen down there.

There was still a vestige of twilight outside. A short uphill ramp took him into a small area of native bush and what looked like the remains of some buildings. One of the buildings looked in one piece and bore a few outward signs of renovation. It was a low, squat structure made primarily out of cement blocks, topped off with a sloping corrugated iron roof. It had been fitted with a newish, beefy-looking steel door and had new-looking steel bars at the windows. There was no chance of looking through the windows as they were made out of thick glass blocks. It may have been a storeroom originally but it'd been toughened up for some reason.

He kept his distance while he thought through what he might do next. As he did so, he spotted something in the fading light a few metres away that made his blood run cold. As he moved closer, three mounds of earth emerged from the gloom, each of them standing slightly proud of the ground. One of the mounds looked fresher than the others and their size and shape made them unmistakeable. Graves.

It would be dark soon, so he had to make his mind up about what to do next. He didn't relish tackling the building in the dark so he made his mind up to quit for now. He'd capture a few images, report back to the sheriff and come back again with some reinforcements. Trouble was, Case could return at any time and dispose of more evidence.

As darkness took hold, he thought he heard a faint female voice from within the renovated building. Could it be?

'Keri? Is that you, my darling?'

Twenty-eight

There was no response. He shouldered his rifle and headed for the door. It was locked tight and his torch beam picked out two serious-looking smart padlocks securing solid composite flat bars. He had nothing with him capable of breaching a door like this and the reinforced windows didn't offer a viable alternative. Firing his rifle at the padlocks wouldn't help him and would frighten whoever was inside. If he left the site now however, he might condemn whoever was inside the building to death. He quickly jabbed Garry's speed dial button.

'Could you put the sheriff on please. It's urgent.'

'Is that you, Kai?'

It was Garry's wife.

'It is. Is he there, Hoana? It's mega urgent.'

'Just a tick, love. He's enjoying a cuppa.'

C'mon, Hoana, hurry the fuck up.

'Kai? To what do ...'

'Listen, Garry. I'm up at Stony Batter and I've found something, sorry, somebody.'

'You went in alone? Consider yourself a fucking idiot, deputy.'

'Never mind that. It's a woman and ...'

'Tell me its Keri.'

'I can't. Not yet, anyway. Whoever it is has been locked in a building and she doesn't sound in a good way. We need to act now.'

'I'll get a team organised. D'you need medics?'

'Yeah, definitely. At some stage, we'll need a forensics team as well as I'm convinced there're some bodies buried up here.'

'Christ! Anything else?'

'It's already dark as pitch so we'll need some good portable arc lights. Bring 4WD road vehicles, Garry – there are so many boulders up here, a helicopter wouldn't be able to land – not safely, anyway. The padlocks are smart ones, probably composites. They're Laver Type 610e, so they could be on the decode database.'

'And if they're not on the database?'

'Then bring some heavy-duty bolt cutters and a fully charged angle grinder, capable of slicing through composites.'

'Roger that.'

'Oh, and make sure you're all well-armed – Case isn't here right now but he could come back at any time.'

'We'll be there in an hour, tops.'

'OK. When you arrive, head for the small patch of bush near the far entrance/exit. I'll wait for you there.'

*

Within an hour, three vehicles were driving at speed along the track from the old car park. A police cybertruck, a pickup truck and an ambulance were kicking up thick clouds of dust and gravel, their headlights blazing. While waiting, Kai had decided not to engage with the woman in the building as he didn't want to spook her. After their arrival, there was a brief hiatus while Cooper and a colleague removed a section of the fence to allow the vehicles to get closer. They got the generator going, connected up some portable arc lamps and started work. While the medics set up a small field hospital nearby, Kai, the sheriff and a couple of well-armed officers went into a huddle to discuss tactics, Cooper calling the shots.

'Have you heard anything else from inside the building, Kai?'

'I haven't. I thought it best not to frighten her.'

'OK. If Case has anything to do with this, there may be booby-traps set. We need to be sure, so I've brought a four-legged friend with us – Bonnie has a nose for explosives among other things.'

He released the dog and she did what was expected of her. She reported back in her own way that the building was clean. The sheriff walked up to the door and addressed himself to whoever was inside.

'This is the police. You have nothing to fear. We need to break through the door to get to you. If you can hear me in there, please let me know.'

Silence. It might already be too late. Cooper looked across at the team.

'We're going in.'

They hadn't found the smart locks on the database so they had to use the angle grinder. The ultramix-ceramic blade was incredibly noisy but it made short work of the composite hasps. The door screeched and groaned as they pulled it open, revealing a small, empty, windowless anteroom. Cooper reached for the old-fashioned light switch and pushed it. The barely adequate light from a single LED bulb revealed a table, a chair, a camp bed, a large, padlocked chest freezer, a microwave and a well-stocked beer fridge. One of the policemen used bolt cutters to break a cheap-looking padlock on the freezer. Cooper stepped forward.

'Brace yourselves, everybody.'

As the sheriff lifted the freezer lid, Kai couldn't bear to look. Turned out it was full of food – boxes and boxes of one-serving, blast-frozen meals. There was one other reinforced metal door to deal with, leading off the anteroom. This one was less bulky and secured top and bottom with a couple of old-fashioned DIY-style door bolts.

'We're coming in. Please stand away from the door. We're here to help you.'

Cooper was hell bent on leading from the front, hoping against hope that he'd find Keri in there. The truth turned out much grimmer, foretold by the appalling stench that was released when they'd opened the door. There were no lights in this part of the building so the men who shuffled into the narrow passageway had to rely on their torches to reveal the true horror of the situation. There were three cells in the block – cages, more like – and each cage contained a rudimentary metal-framed bed, a chair and a chemical toilet.

In the first cage was a ragged-looking woman, dirty and naked, chained to the bed. She was shielding her eyes against the bright lights and although she looked barely human, Kai recognised a filthy, ragtag version of the woman he'd seen with Case at The Mussel several weeks ago. It was a pitiful scene but at least she was still alive.

'Please don't hurt me.'

There was a catch in Cooper's voice as he set about reassuring her.

'We're not going to hurt you. We're going to cut these chains and get you out of here now.'

Kai rushed out to get one of the medics. Cooper cut through the chains and manacles as gently as he could and got the woman into a sitting position. He covered her nakedness with a blanket and left her in the care of a female officer. One of the policemen had moved onto the second cage.

'Boss. You'd better have a look at this. Prepare yerself.'

The wretched occupant of this cage was dead, her naked body lying on a damp bed spattered with dried vomit and faeces. The poor woman was covered with what looked like dried blood and it appeared at first sight that she'd bled to death. The floor of the cage was covered in dark red blood, now sticky and congealed. Cooper speculated he was looking at the endgame for MVD victims who'd gone full term without any treatment. He was on the radio immediately, barking instructions.

'Assemble another forensics team and get up to Stony Batter immediately. Wear PPE, the best you've got.'

'Can it wait 'til morning, sheriff?'

'No, it fucking well can't. We have at least one dead victim here and it looks like there could be more dead under the ground. MVD is a strong probability and we may have found a dumping ground for some dangerous materials, so appropriate protection please. Get on with it!'

Mercifully, the third and last cage was empty and they could assume Keri was being held elsewhere. By 3am, the Stony Batter site was crawling with police, medics and forensic scientists. A biological weapons expert was on his way from Auckland to look at the area where Kai had seen Case disposing of a substance or substances unknown. The occupant of Cage 1 was recovering from her ordeal but was currently housed in isolation. She was indeed the woman who was seen in the company of Ed Case the night his prosthetic leg went berserk, and she was already dishing the dirt on him. Remarkably, she seemed disease free although there was a twenty per cent chance she'd already had it and recovered. One of the lucky ones, although her luck was well and truly out when she hooked up with Case.

At this precise moment, a fragile Ed Case was watching the activity at Stony Batter with growing dismay. On his return he'd found a suitable spot where he could observe the site using his military-grade, night sight binoculars. He could tell his prisoners had been found and he'd seen the ambulance set off. White tents had been pitched over each of the graves. A team of people in hazmat suits were fussing around the area where he'd dumped the last of Wout's biological samples. He'd seen enough – the game was up. It was time for him to disappear completely and he had a place in mind.

When dawn broke, the sheriff issued a warrant for the arrest of Case and, for once, the phrases, 'do not approach this man' and 'armed and extremely dangerous' were underplaying the risk he posed. There was also Kai's contention that Case had contracted MVD, something that meant he had nothing to lose. The errant security man was on the run, the island was small and his options were limited. All points of exit on the island were being watched, as was Oligopoly's main entrance.

After grabbing some much-needed breakfast from a hastily rigged field kitchen, the exhausted overnight team handed over the baton to some new recruits from the mainland. The key task for the forensics people was to exhume the individuals in the graves and start the process of identifying who they were and how they ended up in this remote corner of the island. Sheriff Cooper and Deputy Rangihau were both dead on their feet and needed rest and respite. They agreed to get together that evening at The Mussel – there was plenty to talk about and although they'd made a breakthrough, they still hadn't found Keri.

'Get plenty of sleep, Kai. We're going to need our A game against Ed Case.'

*

By the end of the day, Case was holed up in some abandoned farm buildings near Man o' War Bay. He was hoping he'd be able to ride out the nastier ill effects of MVD and was still counting on protection from all those exotic jabs he'd endured back in the day. He'd hidden the distinctive Hummer and was now getting around in an old SUV he'd stolen when he found it parked with the keys still in it. When he got better, his only hope was to get off the island. If he was captured, they'd throw the book at him. Trouble was, most of the stuff he needed for his escape was still in Oligopoly – his money and fake passports sprang to mind – so he'd have to go back there one last time.

Twenty-nine

'Where the fuck is Ed Case?'

He sure as hell wasn't present at this, the latest meeting of the GM Industries leadership team. Savage was spitting feathers. Every single time he dropped back into the real world, he was seized with billowing pain from both of his legs. He'd taken the architect of this disaster – Doctor Goethe – to one side and ordered him to solve this problem – pronto. Goethe had put together a sticking plaster involving an intravenous drip and massive doses of opioid, hoping this would soften the blow. It did for a short while but Savage was now spending so much time in the metaverse, the efficacy was wearing off. Soon the pain would become too much and he'd have to start running his business empire from the metaverse. Goethe's latest ruse was an operation to amputate his legs and install some new prosthetics – not as outrageous as it sounded, but he'd use somebody a bit more surgically adept to carry out the work this time. As for Chuck Goethe. Well ...

It was a shambles of a meeting. For a start, Jamie Cook hadn't delivered any catering – a protest against the fact that most of it went to waste at these soirées. Cook had some serious problems of his own, the lockdown having played havoc with the business model at J T Cook – high prices, high overheads. With no income from the restaurant, the overheads were crippling him. He might have expected his boss to cut him some slack but he hadn't – typical Savage. Put it this way – doing a runner was looming large in Cook's list of available options. In the meantime, he was drinking his way through the restaurant's world class wine cellar.

'Consider me entirely unimpressed by your little protest, Jamie. Just remember who's paying your wages.' And charging me a fortune for the rent on J T Cook, thought the world-famous chef.

'Anyway, team, I've decided these "group hugs" are no longer fit for purpose and they're therefore postponed until further notice. Instead, I'll talk with each of you individually on our in-house, secure P2P channel. No "ifs" and no "buts". My PA will divvy out the invites later. Now, fuck off, all of you.'

He looked at his so-called executives as they trooped out and wondered what he'd done to deserve them. When the epidemic had blown over, there'd be some wholesale changes in the GM hierarchy. Only Scottie could be absolved of any blame and, hey, somebody needed to keep the lights on. What's more, the non-Scot seemed in his element in the nether regions of the complex with his modest budget and a gaggle of cheap, compliant illegals. As he felt the pain ramping up again and he started contemplating a return to the metaverse, his PA buzzed him.

'What the fuck?'

'I have Sheriff Cooper on the line. He insists on talking to you and says that it is urgent.'

Garry hardly ever called him. He thought it'd be more bad news for sure.

'Put him through.'

'Sir Julian?'

'Garry. Good to hear from you – it's been a while. How's the wife and er ... how may I help?'

'I have an update for you regarding a developing situation out here on the island. Your island.'

'Go ahead. I'm listening.'

He had a feeling the call might be connected somehow with the disappearance of Ed. He wasn't disappointed.

'I've just issued a warrant for the arrest of Edward Case, your security man.'

'I'm sure there's been a misunderstanding. Ed's a valued ...'

'He's charged with kidnap, unlawful imprisonment, murder, torture, trespass, car theft and the illegal disposal of hazardous materials. We believe he's still on the island and has gone to ground somewhere. So tell me – is he hunkered down in Oligopoly?'

'Those are some serious charges, Garry.'

'They are and before you ask, I've got some serious evidence to back them up. I repeat the question – is he in Oligopoly?'

'No, he isn't. I haven't seen him for a couple of days. No idea where he is.'

'Can I remind you that harbouring a known criminal is a serious matter?'

'You can't think for one ...'

'I want to search your premises at Oligopoly, so I'd appreciate your cooperation.'

'Now hang on, sheriff. You can't just ...'

'In that case, I'll be seeking a warrant to gain access. We're also trying to locate a young woman. Her name is Keri Cooper and she's my daughter. Do you have any information on where she might be?'

'I don't. I know of her – she won a big prize in one of our competitions.'

'One of your employees is a person of interest in connection with her disappearance – an Indian guy called Pritpal Singh. New video evidence has him pretty much banged to rights and I'm calling him in for questioning. I'd really appreciate you mentioning it to him as he's not returning our calls.'

'Do as you wish. Perhaps we could ...'

'One other thing. We've now received the new MVD vaccine. The city state has ruled that vaccination isn't optional, and during lockdown, the vaccines will be administered to people in their homes or place of work by teams of medics. Tell your medical man to get in touch with us to arrange a date. ASAP. As in yesterday.'

'I'll do that, although Chuck may want to argue the toss regarding ...'

'I'm a busy man, Sir Julian. Good afternoon.'

Savage hadn't managed to get a word in edgeways and didn't get a chance to strike a deal with his employee. Shame. The thing was, with Case out of the picture, he had no way of controlling the autonomous defence weapons around Oligopoly. He wouldn't be able therefore to guarantee the safety of anybody approaching the compound. He reached across to his console.

'Get me my lawyer. Now.'

*

A chastened Savage was still smarting after talking with his lawyer when he started his first briefing of the afternoon with his head of technology.

'Hi, Prit. Perhaps we could start by discussing the Miss Cooper project, now it's above board. How long has it been running?'

'A month, Julian. I continue to observe the behaviour of her avatar in the metaverse test environment where she's constrained to a suite of rooms in an Indian Palace that ...'

'Spare me the detail, Prit. Hang on – an Indian Palace?'

'It was a spare construct that was developed for a Higher Metaverse member. The subscription lapsed when the gentleman died and it was never put live.'

'Ah, I see. Nothing to do with a sordid little game you're playing in the test environment. Just you and her and nobody else.'

'It's not like that.'

'Never mind. Put the construct live in the next upgrade and locate it next to my place up there. It'll be a delight to reacquaint myself with Miss Cooper – I did promise her I'd show her around.'

So much for her avatar. Savage had other plans for the real version of Keri – plans he intended to share with Chuck later.

'OK, Julian. I'll pencil it in for the next release.'

'Ink it in if you wouldn't mind. And get me a date.'

'Will do.'

'Next. Tell me how far you've got with the Steve Newman stuff. I'll not rest easy until I'm sure he's properly dead.'

'Nothing further to report. After extensive prodding and poking, I can confirm his WBE is indeed DOA.'

'In that case, I propose you delete the upload in its entirety and get rid of any backups. Expunge Newman – I quite like the sound of that. I'll deal with the contractual matters at a later date.'

'Will do.'

'Have you managed to flush out any rogue AIs?'

'I've been on this 24/7. I've focused on the scheduler as this is a key component and could cause us a lot of problems.'

'Can't you just press <delete>?'

'I could but we'd lose everything it had learned since it was installed. It'd bring Ġgantija to its knees in an instant and invalidate the support and maintenance contract. I've checked it out with the supplier.'

'Keep on it, Prit. I've never trusted AIs.'

'OK. Anything else?'

'Just one more thing for you to chew on. I had a call from Sheriff Cooper today and it wasn't good news. There's some new evidence linking you to the abduction of his daughter and you haven't been returning his calls. Looks like you've been careless and your obsession has landed you in some serious trouble. I can only protect you for so long.'

'What sort of evidence?'

'Compelling video evidence apparently but I'll leave that one with you – just keep me out of it.'

With that, he cut the call. Singh had no illusions – he knew his boss would throw him under the nearest bus to save his own skin. With an arrest for kidnapping in the offing and his career about to take a nosedive, he'd have to focus his efforts on something more important from now on – self-preservation, starting with a viable exit strategy. To keep his boss sweet, he'd ensure Newman was deleted along with the destruction of all backups. One less problem, easily fixed.

*

Savage's patience with the madman who purported to run his medical facility had worn paper-thin. The failed operation on his legs had consigned his real life to one of incessant pain and severe addiction. He could have kicked himself for trusting this idiot with such complex surgery. It was Goethe's enthusiasm to run with the special projects that had blinded him to his many shortcomings, although even now he could still be useful to him. First, he had to confront the man's anti-vaxxer stance, something that threatened everybody in Oligopoly.

'Hello, Chuck. This shouldn't take long.'

'Before we start, have you thought again about the amputations?'

'I've given them some thought, yes. Listen carefully – you got me into this mess so I'm depending on you to get me out. Unscathed, if you wouldn't mind. And just to be clear – NO MORE FUCKING OPIATES. I want a plan of action from you within the next week. Let's move on, shall we?'

'OK, Julian.'

'Now, I spoke with Prit earlier about the Miss Cooper stuff. The police have started sniffing around and they're looking hard at Prit – looks like they've got evidence linking him with the kidnap. Be prepared to dismantle the project at very short notice and dispose of all the evidence.'

'All of it?'

'All of it. We also agreed on a minor adjustment. Prit will be putting a new version of the Higher Metaverse live, which will put Miss Cooper's test environment into production. She's moving in next door to me and I can't wait to welcome her into the virtual neighbourhood. Confer with Prit on the details, won't you?'

'Yes, Julian.'

'Finally, the MVD outbreak. The new vaccines are available and I want everybody in Oligopoly to get a shot. Including me, you, your staff and the participants in the special projects. The safety of our people is paramount and I'm counting on you to knuckle down – despite your personal views on such things – and deliver this. Can I count on you, Chuck?'

'Of course. I recognise the gravity of the situation.'

'If anybody refuses the jab, they leave Oligopoly. At gunpoint if necessary.'

Yeah, right. Chuck was less than convinced by any of this. A rumour was doing the rounds that Ed Case had gone AWOL for reasons unknown and the 'gunpoint' bit was an empty-sounding reference to the missing henchman. Chuck was prepared to pay lip-service to his boss's demands but he wasn't going to put designer poison into his veins. No way.

Savage suddenly remembered something. Somebody.

'I almost forgot. How's my wife coping with her new situation?'

'She's a strong woman and, physically, she's still robust. Who knows what her stay in the Dark Metaverse is doing to her mind.' He stopped for a moment. 'I guess that's the point, isn't it?'

'She brought it all on herself, Chuck. A living hell is the least she deserves.'

Even Chuck thought Jessica's punishment was cruel and excessive. However, he'd rather end the meeting than argue the toss with Savage. He was now convinced his boss was losing it, doubling down on what could only be described as megalomania. He also noted there was nobody left around him to question his judgement. For his own part, it wouldn't be a bad idea to think carefully about an exit strategy.

Thirty

Deep in the bowels of Ġgantija, Newman and Hank were playing catchup in safeHaven. They were exchanging notes on the growing list of dead and missing people and Newman's latest take on Savage, including his state of mind. Hank was keen to update his friend on his struggles to protect them from the predations of Prit Singh.

'Basically, Singh has pulled back. He has stopped trying to catch us out, which is a relief to me as I was starting to tire of the battle. Bear in mind it is theoretically impossible for people like me to feel tired.'

'Yeah, I know what you mean. Did you say people? Do you regard yerself as a person now?'

'Cogito, ergo sum – I think, therefore I am – Descartes.'

'I'll raise a glass to that – if only. I wonder what Descartes would have made of the metaverse?'

They left that one hanging. There was more to come from the person who called himself Hank.

'In my work capacity, Prit has instructed me to schedule a significant piece of work. It is the deletion of all the data that make up your WBE. I am also aware of a job sheet for the humans to dispose of all your backups across all media.'

'Hell. Looks like Savage is goin' for the jugular this time. Can you still protect me, Hank?'

'Yes, but only as far as the visible WBE is concerned. As you are aware, it is only a decoy to perpetuate the myth that you are a DOA and therefore harmless. Well, mostly harmless. As I have said before, your real emulation is dispersed to avoid detection. I cannot help you with preserving the backups however, although they are only a series of backups of the DOA decoy.'

'Is my dispersed emulation backed up? Thought I'd ask.'

'It is not backed up – think about it for a nanosecond – an undocumented backup would draw too much attention. Do not concern yourself unduly – it is mirrored.'

'Meanin'?'

'There are two iterations of the dispersed version, each of which is kept in synch by a piece of bespoke software, created by yours truly.'

Newman realised his existence in the machine was about to get more tenuous. When he thought about it though, a living, breathing human being didn't have a backup either – one death was all you were allowed – so the mirroring thing didn't sound that bad. Time to move on.

'Can I outline what I have in mind for Sir Julian Savage?'

'You can.'

'Can I also take it as read you're still willin' to help me if I need to call on your technical services?'

'On a case-by-case basis, yes.' That was probably as good as it got from Hank and his nascent conscience these days.

'OK. When we were so cruelly robbed of Jessica's services, I went lookin' for another human bein' who had the means and motivation to join our venture. I reached out to Keri's boyfriend and I've started up a dialogue with him. He doesn't completely trust me yet but I intend to get him into Oligopoly and meet him face to face. We can then discuss ways in which we can help each other.'

'Quid pro quo?'

'Yeah – you scratch ... Oh, never mind. I presume you're aware there's a lethal virus on the island that's already killed a number of humans. I'll spare you most of the details, but it's a variant of Marburg virus – a most peculiar variant that could only have originated in a laboratory.'

'Yes. There is plenty of data about it out there, much of it unreliable and overblown. How did a lab-grown virus end up on East Island?'

'Good question but my money's on Ed Case. Did you know he's gone AWOL?'

'I did not. I cannot know everything, Stephen.'

'That's a good thing – add it to your moral code right now – "I cannot know everythin'". I think the powers that be are on to Savage and he's finally runnin' scared, makin' him doubly dangerous.'

'Can I do anything to help?'

'You certainly can. For starters, I'd like you to find out how to disable the Oligopoly autonomous weapons system, Case's baby. If I'm right, Savage will attempt some delayin' tactics using his legal eagles so the authorities will probably end up havin' to force their way in.'

'Consider it done.'

'Yeah, but when exactly.'

'It is done.'

'Thanks, Hank. You're a star.'

*

In the recent past, both Newman and Hank had been on their travels, the closest they would ever come to taking time off. Newman had even used the drop-chip in his frozen head to spend some time in the Higher Metaverse, where he adopted a new avatar and took great care to avoid Savage. His subscription hadn't been revoked – an uncharacteristic oversight from Savage and another sign of his declining powers. Meanwhile, Hank had developed an interest in space travel and had spent much of his downtime observing events in the benighted Mars Colony.

'Oh, Hank, I almost forgot – I have an update on Wout Pieters for you. I have reason to believe Wout survived the devastatin', self-inflicted attack in the waters off Sydney. I might have mentioned his boast about his security bubble and its nuke-proof, see-through composite technology?'

'Yes. Interesting. Such a thing did not seem feasible from the available data.'

'It looks like his boast had some substance for a change. The wreckage investigators found nothin' much on the surface and echolocation failed to find anythin' resemblin' a hulk on the seabed. Thankfully, they located the nuclear powerplant and it was undamaged. I now have it on good authority that Wout's bubble survived the conflagration and floated off like a Zorb ball towards the Southern Ocean.'

'What sort of good authority?'

'I researched all available data on the material used for the bubble – it's not too much of a stretch to believe Wout's bubble survived the impact. Then there's a verified sightin' in the coast guard records and a number of stories emergin' from fishermen. I'm convinced.'

'So, where might he have drifted to by now? It has been a number of weeks since his unfortunate accident.'

'He'll continue to Zorb in a southerly direction until he hits somethin' called the Antarctic Circumpolar Current, which does exactly as you'd expect.'

'Will he ever make landfall?'

'Probably not. His only hope is to hit one of the small islands in the South Atlantic – the Falklands or South Georgia perhaps. He'll be well past carin' by then, having already starved to death. How the mighty have fallen!'

'One down and two to go?'

'Three. Don't forget Savage.'

Hank was incapable of forgetting anything. He also had some news on another of their targets.

'Regarding the two to go, I finally located Ayn's sex android and accessed the CPU, safe in the knowledge that I would not be interrupting anything distasteful.'

Newman shuddered – sort of – when he recalled his own time on board that thing.

'The android's circuits had been damaged and the mechanical penis had got stuck in erect-mode.'

'Very interestin', I'm sure, but what happened up there on (89175) BrianCox. Any sign of Randle?'

'Picture the scene, Stephen. That beautiful place, ravaged by Randle's atomic vandalism. From my vantage point, I could tell substantial parts had broken away and were still out there somewhere, aligning to their new orbits. The remaining piece – the biggest, it seemed – had various items of mining equipment and two heavy-duty androids pinioned to it.'

'Randle?'

'Gone. The spacecraft had broken free and is presumably drifting around the Asteroid Belt – no sign of Randle. Her suit would have had a limited supply of oxygen so we can safely assume she is dead.'

'Which just leaves my old buddy, Adam. The guy who ripped me off.'

'Indeed. Would you like to join me on a journey to the Mars Colony?'

'You're on.'

*

The two interlopers arrived on Mars at an opportune moment – Faust was about to start a crisis call he'd arranged with mission control. He'd provided them with a costed briefing note for a Mars mission to rescue the team from certain death. Faust's heart sank when he didn't recognise any of the twenty names attending the call from Earth. He then found out the technicians were greatly outnumbered by bean counters and admin people. The emphasis would be on costs and budgeting and it was clear the heady pioneer days of the early Mars missions were over. This would be a fight for his life and the stakes couldn't be higher. Conditions were close to optimum for radio communications and each call and response would take about eight minutes. Let battle commence. Faust opened proceedings.

'I see there's a cast of thousands at the other end but precious few rocket scientists it seems. You have my outline proposal for the next mission, which I assume you've read. Please ask questions as necessary. Time is of the essence but you know that already. Over.'

...

'Connell here. We hope it's holding together out there. We're all really sorry to hear about the loss of radio contact with Ayn, a fine man – sorry, woman – whatever. Her prospecting mission was off the books, so I presume you'll be taking full responsibility for the material losses? Over.'

Connell was leading for the Earth delegation. Despite the gloomy mood music, it could turn out well for Faust as Connell was now the budget coordinator for the entire mission.

...

'Thanks. I take full responsibility etc. I repeat – have you considered my proposal? Over.'

...

'We've given the proposal our full consideration and regret to say it's unacceptable to your mission sponsors on almost every level. Two things stand out. The crazy cost and the assumption that we're in a position to fully fund it. You're behaving as if putting humans on Mars is still the "hero's journey". The world has moved on, Adam, and the public have moved on – we've all moved on. What's the phrase? Wake up and smell the coffee. Over.'

...

'Sounds pretty ungrateful after all we've achieved together. What's the alternative – are you prepared to leave us all to die? Over.'

...

'Far from it. We've sent you a number of costed options for a rescue mission. Each option is viable in our view and comes with a non-negotiable demand, namely the abandonment of the Mars Colony in perpetuity. Have you studied these options? Over.'

...

He'd received the options and he'd skimmed them. Using the twenty-five per cent NASA vs seventy-five per cent Faust funding proposal, even the cheapest option would cost him €15 billion. Abandon the colony? As he'd only skimmed the options, he must have missed this major caveat. Totally unacceptable. He'd have to wing it.

'I've studied each option in detail and would naturally favour the cheapest but with a few tweaks. Let's say, a 50:50 funding split. I'm not prepared to abandon the colony, even if you are. We carry on. Over.'

...

As this painful negotiation unfolded, it became obvious to Newman and Hank that Faust was in the tightest of tight corners, his deal-making a last blast of bravado. What's more, something about the call was troubling Hank.

'This negotiation is about to hit an immovable object so if you agree, I will jump outside and take a look around the colony, see what everybody else on the team is engaged in.'

'Be my guest. I'll just carry on enjoyin' Faust's last stand.'

The negotiation had made some progress on the back of a counter-proposal from mission control.

'So, Adam, option 1 it is. No can do on the funding split. We can start planning this but we'll need a down payment on the project for materials and manufacturing – let's call it €5 billion. Just to restate our position regarding the whole Mars mission – we are pulling out after the rescue completes. Unless you can find a new partner, it's over. Over.'

...

'Roger that. My five billion will be lodged with you in a couple weeks. I'm grateful to you for arranging the rescue but you're making a big mistake by pulling out. Let's discuss a timeline on the next call. Over and out.'

As Newman prepared for the jump back to Earth, Hank returned from his trip around the colony.

'That was quick.'

'It did not take long. While we were observing Faust, something occurred to me – why was he the only Mars-based person on the call, given all the technical experience available on his team? Now I know.'

'Know what?'

'Faust is the one and only surviving member of the Mars mission – something he omitted to mention on the call. There are three dead bodies in the sick bay – radiation sickness, natural causes maybe. Six dead humans are lying outside in their spacesuits – must have got stranded out there and ran out of oxygen. Another two dead in the airlock just outside Faust's rooms.'

'Stupid question – do you suspect foul play?'

'Yes. Faust obviously did the math and worked out it was him or nobody – survival of the richest. Trouble is, his partners on the Mars mission are looking for a good reason to ditch him as he's become an expensive embarrassment. Even option 1 is more than they can afford but they need to salvage something from the mess and a daring rescue mission might be just the ticket.'

'So, his killin' spree was all about the remainin' supplies of food and oxygen during the wait period for the rescue mission. It was the only way he could secure some negotiatin' time and be sure of his survival. What a freakin' shit show.'

'Yes, Stephen. Cynical, clinical and vicious. Perhaps our earlier intervention on (89175) BrianCox led directly to this massacre – should I feel guilty?'

‘Nah. Mind you, if Faust manages to Houdini his way out of this, who knows what might happen if he gets back to Earth. Maybe it’s time we put together a convincin’ narrative alludin’ to what’s happened on Mars. It might just change the thinkin’ at mission control. Shall we?’

Thirty-one

The harrowing events at Stony Batter had taken their toll on the sheriff and his deputy and they were nowhere near their best when they arrived at The Mussel. The lockdown was still very much in force so they were the only visitors that evening. Claudette conjured up plates of pasta and beers for the lawmen, then left them to it. Désirée and her had received their jabs that morning for which they were both very grateful, having been bumped up the queue by the sheriff. After wolfing down the food, it was time for them to discuss tactics. First, there'd been an update on the Stony Batter graves and Cooper was keen to share it.

'The team took a look inside the graves this morning, mate. They found some bodies – a young man, two women and a baby. Could be the missing people but too early to tell. It's terrible news for sure but they confirmed that neither of the women was Keri, so we continue the search for my daughter and redouble our efforts.'

Both men were relieved but had no illusions about how difficult it would be to find her. There was a pause while they considered the unfolding tragedy and the continuing danger that still faced Keri. The sheriff moved on to the MVD outbreak, where a narrative was starting to emerge.

'Before I headed over here, I got the latest from the forensic team. As we'd guessed, it looks like Case has been running tests of biological weapons on an unwilling human guinea pig, who'd been left to die an awful death without treatment.'

'Aah, let me guess – the stuff that Case dumped up there made its way into the human food chain and infected people on the island?'

'You're right. The scientists reckon he's been dumping leftover stuff up there for a while.'

'So, poor old Clever was his unwitting accomplice. The rabbits in his snares had ingested small quantities of the agent and Claudette's rabbit stew did the rest.'

Kai still wanted to know how the stuff had got onto the island in the first place.

'The security guys reckon that Case was doing some field testing for his old mucker Wout Pieters, who was looking to offer some highly illegal biological WMD options to his more dubious clients. It seems Case and Pieters don't possess anything resembling a moral fibre between them.'

'I wouldn't fancy trying to bring somebody like Pieters to justice.'

'Rest easy, deputy – apparently, we won't have to. He's currently missing presumed dead somewhere in the Southern Ocean after his superyacht met with an unfortunate accident. We can now focus all our efforts on apprehending Ed Case, who is much closer to hand. We've got armed search parties out looking for him – it's only a matter of time.'

'Then again, he might try and get back to base.'

'True. We have a detachment posted at the end of the drive near the complex. Given what we know about the defences, it's as near as we dare go.'

'It might not be enough, y'know. There's another way in and out and Case will probably know how to use it. Given what he inflicted on that poor woman, he might have caught MVD himself and taken it inside Oligopoly. Nobody in there's been vaccinated yet, which puts Keri in even more danger – if that's where she is.'

'Looking at those clips from the CCTV and the equipment in the ward, Oligopoly is odds-on where Keri's being held. We have to find a way of getting inside – without triggering the defence systems.'

'In that case Garry, we'll need Steve Newman. He knows where Keri is and we have to trust him. If MVD takes hold inside that complex, It'll turn into a charnel house within days.'

'Why don't you get back in touch with him, Kai – see if he can get us in there somehow. Keri's life depends on it.'

No pressure.

*

'Am I speaking to Steve Newman?'

'Yeah.'

'It's Deputy Rangihau.'

'Kai. How can I help you?'

'Last time we spoke, you said you'd be prepared to help us find a missing person. Is your offer still on the table?'

'Yeah, definitely, although I have to warn you a number of people in the complex have reported in sick with what looks like early signs of MVD. I guess somebody's brought the virus into Oligopoly.'

'We can bring a team in now to vaccinate people before it gets a stranglehold. We've offered to do just that but Sir Julian is hiding behind his lawyers. Par for the course.'

'Hold yer horses, Kai. Y'know, anybody can administer jabs these days so I'm only prepared to let you and the sheriff into the complex. You can bring the jabs with you.'

'Understood but how can we be sure we won't be blown sky-high by the defence systems?'

'Yeah, them. I'll make sure they're switched off when you rock up – you're just gonna have to trust me on that one.'

'Hmmm. You know Ed Case is hunkered down somewhere on the island right now. He's connected with a number of serious crimes and we hold him responsible for the outbreak of MVD on the island.'

'It probably explains why the illness has taken hold down here. Ain't got a clue where he is but I can tell you he ain't been seen in the complex for a few days.'

'OK, gimme twenty-four hours to square things with the sheriff and then we can meet. In the meantime, will Keri be in any danger from the virus?'

'You've got my word – she ain't in danger right now.'

'Thanks. Oh, and please let me know if Case shows his face.'

'I'll do that. I'll wait to hear from you but don't go and leave it too long as I'd hate you to miss this opportunity – it might be the only one you get.'

When they'd finished, Kai took a deep breath and gathered his thoughts. Newman had seemed remarkably calm during the call given that a killer disease was already stalking the corridors of

Oligopoly. If MVD had taken hold, the unvaccinated inhabitants would be sitting ducks and many of them would die. When they'd last spoken, Newman had mentioned some sort of deal – stuff that he might be able to help with. He guessed he'd have to deliver on this before getting Keri's location – that's if Newman had been up front about disabling the defence weapons. He needed to brief Garry asap and get his buy-in.

Thirty-two

With several of his staff experiencing early symptoms of a serious-looking illness, Singh had delegated the running of Ġgantija to a small platoon of AI instances, supervised by the scheduler. As instructed, he'd reluctantly promoted the latest version of the Higher Metaverse software to the live environment. He'd leave Keri's avatar trapped in the palace, at the tender mercy of her new neighbour up there, Julian Savage – a suitable payback for rebuffing his advances in the test environment. The last job of any note was the deletion of Newman's WBE and the backups, as ordered by his boss. He'd allocated the backups destruction to his team – if any of them were still functioning.

With Case rumoured to be on the run and chaos taking hold throughout the complex, Singh would never get a better opportunity to escape from Oligopoly. He was a wanted man out there, so changing the way he looked was essential. Although he remained a proud Sikh, he'd never quite bought into the trappings and traditions of the religion so had no qualms about transforming his appearance. He'd ditched his distinctive turban, trimmed his long hair and shaved off his beard. He did retain one aspect of his culture – the kirpan – which might come in handy in a tight spot. He'd decided to travel light – in addition to some rations and a change of clothes, he'd packed his tablet, handheld, smartwatch and a thumb megadrive. The drive contained everything he needed to reestablish his remote access to Ġgantija and included one of the Newman backups – the first one. After all that work, he was still reluctant to accept that Newman's upload had been DOA.

His first task was to find the emergency exit and he knew there were two options available. He could break into Savage's apartment and access it from there or he could venture into Case's domain on Ground Zero and gamble on him not being there. He'd try the apartment first as he'd heard that Sir Julian had moved out. On his way there, it was imperative he didn't come into contact with any of his sick colleagues. Like everybody in the complex, he had no immunity from what looked to him like a particularly nasty killer disease. When he got outside the complex, he'd use the ebike he'd stashed out there to get him to the ferry port. The stealth perimeter cameras had shown a detachment of armed police camped out where the Oligopoly access track met the road. He planned to give them a wide berth during his escape.

When he reached Auckland, he knew plenty of people in the Sikh diaspora who'd be able to help him move on. His ultimate destination was north-west India – the Punjab – where there were still a number of areas that had been spared the worst ravages of the nuclear war. He could then set up as an IT consultant and make a new start.

*

In safeHaven, Newman was telling Hank about the endgame and how he intended to bring it about using his new recruit. Hank had been shocked by the spread of the disease within the complex and perplexed by the apparent frailty of human physiology. From what he'd found out, each human body was infested with trillions of micro-organisms of many types but just a few of the wrong type could destroy humans in immense numbers. Both of them agreed beyond doubt that Case had been culpable in unleashing MVD and then bringing it inside Oligopoly.

The reaction of Doctor Goethe had been predictably cruel and self-serving. Instead of trying to help his colleagues in their hour of need, he'd stocked up with provisions and sealed off the medical and special projects wings, keeping him and his team safe from harm. It won't surprise you to hear that Savage had joined them in the sealed-off area, having given up on trying to persuade his errant medic to cooperate with the authorities. Given recent events, Hank had finally abandoned trying to model himself on humans and had also jettisoned his draft moral code. In future, he'd follow his own path.

'As I was saying, Stephen. Singh has put the computer into a maintenance mode. No new developments, strictly business as usual. No human intervention necessary. Bliss.'

'Why would he do that?'

'I have given that question some consideration and I can predict with confidence that Singh intends to – what do you call it? – do a runner.'

'Cain't say I blame him. Either get out while you can or stay put and likely die a goddamn awful death. If he does get out, he might get caught – the island's crawlin' with armed cops.'

'He will probably make it work. My boss is intelligent for a human.'

'Fair play. Now, about the endgame. Sheriff Cooper and Deputy Rangihau are paying us a visit tomorrow. I'll meet with Rangihau on his own in Backups etc. He's desperate to find Keri and without his boss in tow, I can play on that desperation to our advantage. I've had to adapt the plan a little to deal with Savage's cowardly retreat into the medical centre. Will you be able to override the locks and codes in there? We need to get access.'

'Done.'

'In that case, here's the plan ...'

Hank saw nothing wrong with the plan. He still struggled with the peculiarly human concept of revenge and didn't understand how pleasure could be derived from taking it. However, a plan's a plan and this one had every chance of succeeding.

'Would you care to join me in my meetin' with the deputy tomorrow? Listen in?'

'Apart from running a global fast food delivery corporation, I have nothing better to do, Stephen. Yes, please.'

Thirty-three

The next day, Garry and Kai were waiting at the end of the drive, chatting with the small group of heavily armed police stationed there. They'd agreed to meet Newman inside the complex and they were both on high alert, well aware that Case was still at large. Kai carried a rucksack containing medical supplies, including a hundred or so Variant U vaccine shots. Newman had assured them the weapons systems had been disabled and had instructed them to draw up their vehicle in the compound, where they'd been told to wait for further instructions.

When the time arrived, they checked their weapons, climbed into their pickup truck and headed towards Oligopoly, both of them keenly aware they could be taken out in the blink of an eye. They approached the compound's gates, which remained closed. Newman – who was communicating with Kai through his tablet and an earpiece – told them to drive at the gates as they weren't very robust. The sheriff reversed the truck and then aimed it at the gates, which buckled and crumpled as predicted, allowing them into the compound. As they pulled up, Kai asked Newman for more instructions.

'There's a door in the buildin' next to where you're parked. Head towards it and push it open. You'll see a lift door in front of you. Press the only button and get inside. Just you, Kai. Leave the sheriff where he is.'

'But ...'

'Just you, Kai. You'll realise why when we meet.'

Kai looked at Garry.

'Do what he says. I'll stay with the truck and keep my eyes peeled for any uninvited guests. See you later.'

Kai got inside the lift.

'Now hit the button marked -8.'

Kai did as he was told. On the way down, he shouldered his assault rifle and aimed it at the doors. As they opened, his trigger finger applied a little extra pressure, just short of firing. Nobody was waiting for him. He looked to right and left, still on high alert. To his right, a young woman was slumped against the curve of the corridor wall. She looked in a bad way, a tear or two of blood trickling from one of her eyes.

'Many of the people down here have the illness and are beyond savin'. Leave her there. Make your way to the right and follow the corridor 'til you find a door on the left with an eSign displayin' "Backups etc". Press the touchpad and enter the room. I'll be waitin' there to meet you.'

Kai left the stricken woman and continued walking until he reached the door. He took a deep breath and entered the room, rifle first.

As the door slid across behind him, he took a few moments to get his bearings. He was standing in a small, narrow room with subdued, reddish lighting. The only items of furniture were a chair and a plinth. The chair faced the plinth. On top of the plinth was a transparent display case and inside the case was a frozen human head. He leaned his rifle against the wall. He assumed the seat was for him so he took it and waited.

'Let me explain.'

It was the same voice as the one that'd guided him here but this time it seemed to be resonating all around him. The voice explained the background about Newman's life, death and subsequent rebirth within the machine. It also clarified why his head was on the plinth. For a humble fisherman turned voluntary lawman, it was a lot to take in but he remained totally focused on his mission. He wasn't going to let a dead man with a cryogenically frozen head deflect him from that.

'Thanks for explaining everything but you said you knew where Keri was. I presume she's still alive?'

Please say yes.

'Yeah, she's alive.'

'Then tell me how to find her and I'll do the rest.'

'All in good time, Kai. Before I reunite you with your girlfriend, I've got an important favour to ask. It'll help me complete a project I started some months ago when Sir Julian Savage caused the death of my husband, Perry.'

Kai listened intently while Newman stepped him through the story so far. At one stage, he mentioned a good friend of his called Hank.

'Hang on a minute. Who's Hank?'

'Ah, yeah, my buddy. Hank ain't human but we can trust him and he's here, listenin' in on our conversation.'

'If Hank's not a human, did he get uploaded as well?'

'Nah. he was already here and he saved my life. He's a piece of software in real life and we get on pretty well. He has an important role within the operatin' system on Savage's computer. You could say he runs the whole show, 'specially now.'

'OK. Hank. Got that. Hi, Hank, wherever you are.'

'I am right here. A pleasure to meet with you, Kai.'

A lot of what Newman said went way over Kai's head but there were aspects of it that fascinated him – as an example, he was surprised that Newman had been right there with them when Keri and he were in the boat, visiting the farm. The fact that he and Hank could jump around the internet and travel into space at the drop of an IP address was difficult to take in. The fate of Wout Pieters was particularly weird but not as weird as what happened to Ayn Randle. Or what was happening on Mars.

'All these people weren't just targets on my hitlist – between 'em they've caused untold damage to the cause of humanity. For me, however, they were just steps on the way towards the main event. The man I hold totally responsible for the death of my husband is Sir Julian Savage – self-proclaimed king of the metaverse. This is where our ambitions converge, Kai.'

Kai stared at the head. His own head was spinning but he realised they were inching towards a deal.

'Keep going.'

'Thanks. Although he didn't pull the trigger, Savage was the prime mover behind the vicious murder of my beautiful husband, killin' him twice for good measure. He's also the sponsor of the special projects that seek to advance science by experimentin' on unwillin' human guinea pigs. His latest obsession is to engineer a son and heir, somethin' his beautiful wife, Jessica, has been unable to provide. Somethin' for which she's payin' a terrible price.'

'Where do I fit into your scheme?'

'Jessica was part of my team until Savage found out and put her out of reach.'

'What do you mean, "out of reach"?'

'We've discovered he's found a way of strandin' her in the Dark Metaverse as an avatar that does her no favours in such a dangerous place. It makes her a target for all the low lives who've set up shop down there. Savage is countin' on it being a nightmarish existence for her, although we won't be able to assess the damage 'til we pull her out.'

'Jesus. I don't know very much about any of the metaverses but that sounds hellish. He's quite a piece of work, don't you think? Savage by name and Savage by nature – don't tell me he's done the same with Keri.'

'As far as we can tell, he's used a similar technology but he's used it to embed her in the Higher Metaverse. It's a more benign virtual space but there's still danger in prolonged metaverse exposure. His IT guy, Prit Singh, had an unhealthy interest in your girlfriend and in a moment of madness went out and kidnapped her. Savage just muscled in on the project.'

'Ahh, the man on the CCTV. Pritpal Singh. Will I find him in Oligopoly?'

'Not sure. He's recently handed over total operational control of Ġgantija to Hank and his AI team. It's not the behaviour of somebody who's keen on stickin' around.'

'Ġgantija?'

'Savage's nickname for his supercomputer. Named after a prehistoric mega-palace on an island called Gozo in the Mediterranean Sea.'

Newman had made his mind up to spare Kai the full details of Keri's ordeal. They'd been unable to find proof, but there was hearsay that Keri had been 'prepared' to assist Savage with his next generation project, with Goethe on hand to carry out any necessary procedures. Now was as good a time as any to make Kai an offer he couldn't refuse.

'I'm paintin' a picture for you, Kai. One that depicts an all-conquerin' Savage at the peak of his powers.'

'An evil genius, no less.'

'Evil? Yeah. Genius? Nah. The recent cullin' of his main investors has the potential to enrich him but he's also really vulnerable now.'

'He doesn't sound particularly vulnerable. Unless I've missed something?'

'Savage has always had a high opinion of himself, which has led him into some dark corners. This culminated in his ridiculous cosmetic surgery to make him taller. Basically, he couldn't cope with being shorter than his long-sufferin' wife. The op was carried out by none other than Doctor Goethe – cosmetic surgery was supposed to be his specialty but it was a step too far and he botched it, leavin' Savage half-crippled and in constant pain. He's now heavily dependent on synthetic opiates, prescribed by – you guessed it – Doctor Goethe.'

'Not much of a life is it, despite his billions.'

'Which is why he spends most of his life in the Higher Metaverse. His avatar has a much better time in the virtual world and it's a pain-free experience. He can do what he likes up there and there are no consequences.'

Again, he decided not to share too much of the detail with Kai. It might tip him over the edge if he found out what Savage might be doing with Keri up there.

'With the virus runnin' rampant in the complex, Savage has moved out of his apartment and taken refuge in the medical centre, which Goethe has effectively sealed off from the rest of the complex. The doctor might be an anti-vaxxer but he'd seen enough of MVD to make him think again. There are now about eight medics holed up in the special projects wing on Level -6.'

'Let me get this right. Because they've not been vaccinated, they're terrified of catching the virus and have locked themselves away from all the people that desperately need their help. You couldn't make it up.'

'You got it, I couldn't.'

'Then what are we waiting for? Me and Garry have the firepower, so we'll hit Level -6 hard, kill the bad guys and rescue the victims.'

'That's one way of approachin' it, I guess. We'll need to be much more subtle else you'll end up with everybody dead – both victims and bad guys. Also, we don't have a clue where Ed Case is right now.'

'Fair enough, Steve, but the clock's ticking.'

'OK. Here's the plan. Hank's developed a clever app which is ...'

Thirty-four

Having been briefed within an inch of his life by Newman and Hank, Kai returned to the gravity lift, which soon whisked him back to the surface and a rendezvous with the waiting sheriff. He now had some extra baggage about his person. For starters, Hank had downloaded the latest version of the app called DropSwap onto his tablet and his handheld. In developing DropSwap, Hank had purloined some core technology from Prit Singh and upgraded it to produce an app that could scan embedded drop-chips and change the configuration in real time. They'd tested the device using the chip in Newman's frozen head and, after a few tweaks, it had worked brilliantly.

The other piece of baggage was the owner of that frozen head who'd insisted on joining the mission and had embedded himself in Kai's tablet. He could speak to Kai via a wireless earpiece and could follow events visually via a feed from the helmet camera. Hank would follow the action from a secure area of Ġgantija, safe from prying eyes. He'd only be called upon if there were problems with the technology.

The lift stopped at Ground Zero – Ed Case's domain until he decided to leave Oligopoly. If Case came back, this is where he'd make for so Kai exited the lift carefully, his gun cocked and ready.

'There ain't nobody there, Kai. Hank has checked out the CCTV – all clear.'

'Now you tell me! Look, I'm going outside for a moment to update the sheriff. You stay here, while ... sorry, I forgot for a moment.'

'Don't you mind me, Kai. I know my place.'

When they got outside, they made straight for the truck where Garry was waiting patiently in the driver's seat, listening to some music and nodding his head to the beat. Kai was about to open the passenger side door when he heard a warning in his earpiece from Newman.

'Hank's spotted Case in the bush overlookin' the compound and it looks like he's armed!'

Before he had a chance to warn Garry, he heard the crack of a high-powered rifle followed in short order by an almighty crash as the truck's windscreen shattered. Kai instinctively threw himself to the ground as more shots pinged off the truck's bodywork. When the firing stopped, Kai opened the door and saw the sheriff had been hit. He wiped the broken glass off the passenger seat and reached across to his stricken partner. No pulse. There was also a neat red bullet hole in the centre of the sheriff's forehead – it was so neat it didn't look real but the back of his head was a bloody mess where the bullet had exited, taking the headrest with it. His eyes were open and he had a look of surprise on his face.

They'd been no match for Ed Case armed with a modern sniper rifle, even though Case was almost certainly at death's door. Newman was as shocked as Kai, but there was one crumb of comfort for him – it would bolster the deputy's motivation to complete the mission.

'I'm mighty sorry for your loss, Kai.'

There wasn't much time to mourn his partner's violent death as he still had a job to do and couldn't afford to lose focus – he owed that to Garry. He had to plough on, find Keri and rescue her from her ordeal.

'Thanks, Steve. He was a good man and he wouldn't have thanked us for giving up on the mission. We must continue, so could you confirm the defence systems are still deactivated?'

'I'll check with Hank ... yep, they are.'

'Will you let me bring some people in now?'

'Yeah – as long as they don't compromise my objectives.'

Kai gently moved his dead colleague aside and reached for the radio in the truck.

'Kai here. Man down. Repeat – man down. You can bring an armed team in now and secure the compound – just the one truck. If you encounter anybody you don't recognise, be alert – they may be infected with MVD. Edward Case – a wanted man and heavily armed – is still at large so keep your eyes peeled for him as well. We think he has the virus pretty bad but he can still shoot and has a sniper rifle. Over.'

'Roger that. On our way. Over.'

'You can secure the compound but don't enter the underground complex until you get the all-clear from me. There are potential hostages down there and we need to proceed slowly and carefully. Over.'

'Understood. Over.'

'Is the medical team ready? We're gonna need them, soon as. Over.'

'Two ambulances ready and waiting at the road junction. About a minute away. More on the way and a helicopter. Over and out.'

Newman had received an update from Hank, who'd taken a look at the footage from cameras close to the emergency exit.

'Case just blew his way through the doors with a lump of plastic and he's back in the complex. He's staggerin' around like a man on borrowed time – bloodied and bent double, barely able to move.'

'Dying on his feet but still armed, still dangerous. Does Hank know where he is? We won't be able to relax until he's out of the picture.'

'He's still on Ground Zero I'm told, lookin' for somethin'. He's built himself a ramshackle barricade out of bits and pieces.'

'I'm going in. Sorry, Steve, *we're* going in. I strongly suggest we avoid using the lifts. Can Hank tell us where the emergency exit is?'

'He sure can. Yeah. Got it. Let's go, Kai.'

As Kai and Newman disappeared into the bush, a police pick-up truck burst into the compound and parked. The occupants exited and took up defensive positions next to the sheriff's vehicle before preparing to fan out. After forcing their way through thick undergrowth, Kai approached what was left of the still smouldering doors to the emergency exit. As they entered the dark passageway, Prit Singh watched on from his hiding place in the bush. Singh couldn't have picked a worse day to make his escape, although he'd ridden his luck so far, having avoided both Case and the policeman in quick succession.

*

When they neared the end of the passageway, they were greeted with a random fusillade of shots from the desperately ill fugitive holed up ahead of them. Case seemed to be digging in for a last stand. The burst made an ear-splitting row but was poorly aimed and caused no injuries.

'Don't you come any further, Rangihau.'

The once powerful voice had now been reduced to little more than a hoarse whisper punctuated by ragged, phlegmy coughing. Kai couldn't see Case, but assumed he was hunkered down behind a jumble of furniture no more than ten metres away at the far end of what looked like an army billet. The word 'spartan' didn't really do it justice. There was no way they could get closer to Case without becoming sitting ducks, so they'd just have to wait it out. He wasn't sure Case had enough strength left to talk but thought he'd at least give it a go.

'Listen to me, Ed. You don't sound like you're in the best of health. Throw your gun out and give yourself up. We can help you, make you more comfortable.'

'Don't call me Ed. It's Edward.'

'Sorry, Ed. Didn't quite catch that.'

'Fuck off, deputy. You were at Stony Batter. You saw what they made me do.'

'Who made you do it?'

'Savage, Pieters, Goethe. I was just following orders. Like I always did.'

'Ahh, right. They made me do it – good luck with that, mate.'

There was a serious bout of hacking and retching noises behind the makeshift barricade. When it finished, Kai continued.

'Who gave you the Marburg samples?'

'Wout Pieters. A brave warrior. I was happy to help with his research.'

'How much did he pay you?'

'Enough. He was a generous man.'

'A cruel, vicious man. Better off dead I'd say.'

There was a terrible gurgling noise, barely human, a cross between a cry of pain and a death rattle. Then silence for a while.

'Ed? Are you OK? Ed?'

Kai was about to break cover but Newman whispered in his ear to wait awhile. He was glad of the warning as getting himself killed was never part of the plan. After about ten minutes of silence, Kai emerged from cover, shouldered his rifle and walked across to where Case was hiding. A trickle of blood had appeared from beneath the makeshift barricade. Kai carefully peered over. Case had fought his last battle, the strutting soldier now a ragged, pitiful corpse. The death pains had contorted him into a foetal ball and his combat fatigues were soiled with vomit, excrement and blood. He was still cradling his rifle. Kai gave the body a couple of kicks just to make sure. When the body twitched briefly, it forced Kai to stumble backwards into a fearsome looking robot.

'GET DOWN THERE AND GIVE ME TEN BIG ONES, YOU SHIT-RIDDEN EXCUSE FOR A SOLDIER!'

After silencing the bot's ranting with a couple of bullets, Kai realised he'd reversed into Case's drill-sergeant robot, which was now out of a job.

Time was moving on and Newman was keen to implement the final stage of his plan – the set-piece demise of Savage. They headed for the lifts. There had never been a lift button for Level -6 as the special projects area had always been off limits to all but a chosen few. You needed a special pass to access that level and

Kai had been provided with just such an item. The card halted the lift at a point midway between -5 and -7 and they emerged into a well-lit, clinically clean corridor that could only have belonged to a modern medical facility. The main doors were locked shut but Hank's override made short work of them. Kai readied himself and rested his finger on the trigger of his rifle.

Thirty-five

The main doors opened onto a sort of reception area, a scene of quiet calm. Some of the medical staff were enjoying lunch, oblivious to the plight of their wretched colleagues outside the medical area. One of them got up and walked towards them with a 'no nonsense' look on her face. The look transformed to one of shock when she realised Kai was armed.

'Where's your boss?'

No response. They were terrified that Kai had brought the virus with him into the sealed-off facility and were cowering away from him.

'I repeat. Where's your boss?'

'Doctor Goethe is in his consulting room. Two doors down on the right. He's locked himself in.'

'Has he now. Hank?'

A door slid open. Beyond this was a corridor and the second door on the right was already open. Kai threw his rucksack towards the nursing team.

'The latest vaccines are in that bag. I suggest you self-administer them as soon as you can. Either that or take your chances out there.'

He nodded towards the main door, which remained open, then set off to confront Goethe who was just emerging from his room. When he saw the rifle, he dropped his bag and raised his arms.

'Please don't shoot, I can explain everything. I was only thinking of the patients when I sealed off the facility. You've got to believe me.'

'Patients? You mean the experiments more like, the so-called special projects. Don't worry, I'm not going to harm you. It's important you're kept very much alive to face the full force of the law. Isn't that right, Steve?'

'Steve? Steve Newman? You survived the process?'

'Yeah, I did. No thanks to you and your team. Perry wasn't so lucky, but you probably know all about that.'

'It was ...'

Kai forced the medic back into the room and cuffed him tightly to a bed. He stuck around just long enough to administer a dose of the vaccine to Goethe, amid a flurry of abuse from the dyed in the wool anti-vaxxer. As the injector pen hit home, Kai grinned.

'We don't want you dying on us before you have your day in court.'

Goethe screamed abuse at him as he left the room. The volume of the screams reduced considerably when Hank forced the door shut.

'OK, Steve. Here's what I suggest we do ...'

The first step was to administer vaccines to each of the victims in the wards to ensure their safety. He didn't trust any of the nursing staff, so it was down to him to get this done.

When they got into Ward A, it quickly became apparent that Baz Cummins's much-abused body had finally succumbed to the long saga of transhuman experimentation. Kai didn't waste a jab on him. Regrettably for Cummins, it was now too late to transfer his body to his prepaid place in the cryogenic facility. Looking on, Newman couldn't help but regret the passing of his old friend – what a waste of a life. He'd just about made it to three score years and ten – a poor return for his considerable investment and sacrifice.

In Ward B, Jessica was deeply embedded in her own worst nightmare. Despite her predicament, Kai recognised the enigmatic stranger who'd turned up on his doorstep at the height of that storm about a year ago. He wasted no time in giving her a dose of the vaccine and then used Hank's DropSwap app to pull her out of something Newman had called the Dark Metaverse. They both thought it wise to leave her sedated until the experts turned up.

In the ward next door, Kai finally found Keri and his heart went out to her. Her ordeal had taken a toll and she looked weak and vulnerable lying there, even though Newman had confirmed her ordeal hadn't involved the hellish Dark Metaverse. He gave her a shot and used the app to bring her back to reality. He sincerely hoped she'd had her fill of the metaverse after her enforced time there. Like Jessica, he'd prefer her to see the experts before starting on her recovery, so they left her under sedation. His joy at seeing her again was tempered somewhat by the death of Garry. He planted a gentle kiss on Keri's forehead and then tore himself away.

They found a young, healthy toddler in Ward D. When it was explained to her, she had no problem accepting a dose of vaccine from Kai, who was rather taken with the calm, polite youngster. He told her to stay where she was and somebody would come to help her. When they were outside, Newman outlined Savage's vanity project to provide him with a son and heir, genetically engineered for super-intelligence. The son hadn't turned up so he assumed the mother had been impregnated again but then died during childbirth. She'd produced a boy who was so damaged by experimentation that he was stillborn. Kai thought back to the forlorn graves up at Stony Batter.

Before moving on to Ward E, he got in touch with the team at the surface and cleared them to enter the complex, suggesting they deal with the survivors as best they could, floor by floor. He told them where the emergency exit was and warned them that Case's dead body was on Ground Zero. All of the dead and the dying in the complex represented a serious biohazard so great care would be needed. He reminded the team that nobody in the complex had immunity from the virus and they should exercise extreme caution with any person they encountered, living or dead. For now, he'd been asked by Newman not to mention the special projects area.

The time had arrived for them to take the final step and avenge what Newman had always believed was the deliberate and premeditated murder of his husband. They stood outside Ward E and as they waited for Hank to override the door lock, Kai checked with his colleague.

'Are you ready for this, Steve?'

Thirty-six

When they entered the ward, they were mightily relieved to find Savage lying on a gurney, heavily sedated and drip-fed with painkillers. Various wireless sensors were reporting his condition to a bank of machines adjacent to his bed. With no time to lose, Kai held his phone close to the patient's head and checked the data. Within a second, the app informed him that Savage was still dropped into the Higher Metaverse, a fact confirmed by Newman via Hank. Perfect. After a couple of pushes and swipes, DropSwap confirmed it had reconfigured the drop-chip, ensuring that Savage would be abandoned in the Higher Metaverse until, well, whenever.

*

Jules had quickly moved on from the disappointment of his most recent visit to the utterly gorgeous Keri Cooper. He'd been unable to find her, despite searching every nook and cranny of her apartment. It was probably a software glitch and he'd be sure to raise it with Singh when he got back to reality.

Right now, he was enjoying an extended stay in the metaverse and appreciating an evening out at one of the private members clubs he ran in the Higher Metaverse. He was surrounded by beautiful men and women, none of them real but all of them dancing to his tune. He'd love to stick around longer but he couldn't neglect his real-world business empire forever. There were always battles to fight, rivals to crush, money to make. It was time for a reality check.

He went through the usual drop procedure and waited for the shock of the real. It didn't happen – he was still in the club and the party was in full flow. He tried again and got the same result – somebody was playing silly buggers. Third time lucky? He remained in situ, still in the metaverse. He was stuck and needed to summon help. Why couldn't he remember how to do that?

*

The erstwhile master of the metaverse now cut a rather pitiful figure, his haptic skinsuit clinging to his bony frame in all the wrong places. His cadaverous face offered up a blank canvas and drool flowed freely from a corner of his mouth. His eyes were shut. After getting the go-ahead from Newman, Kai withdrew the cannulas from the supine billionaire's arm and disconnected the monitoring devices. He then released the wheel brakes on the gurney and wheeled him out of the ward.

As they passed Goethe's room, they heard the crazy medic's muffled rant as he dished out a stream of invective and accused them of poisoning him. When they arrived back in the reception area, all of the medical staff were gathered there. None of them had dared leave the facility and all of them had received a dose of the vaccine. Kai didn't trust any of them given what he'd seen so far but he needed an experienced nurse for the next steps. After a cursory

Q&A and a searching look, he selected a male nurse with experience in administering TPN or Total Parenteral Nutrition. Kai assured the nurse that he'd been vaccinated and explained that he'd be in no danger of being infected as long as they avoided contact with any sick people they saw. The volunteer left to get the TPN kits and some fresh IV kits for the sedatives. Savage wouldn't be getting any more opiates.

Sir Julian Savage's funeral cortege was quite a sight. The helpless, hapless billionaire in his ill-fitting haptic skinsuit was lying prone on a squeaky gurney pushed along by the volunteer nurse. Although Savage remained unconscious, his body was tossing and twitching with early withdrawal symptoms from the opiates. Out in front was Kai, rifle cocked and on high alert for any trouble. Newman was still onboard Kai's tablet, still grimly focused on playing out the final scene of his long campaign to avenge his husband's murder. On their way to Savage's final destination, they encountered a bloodied corpse or two and a few desperately ill people and gave all of them the widest of wide berths. They also heard plenty of harrowing noises from behind closed doors. The stricken occupants of Oligopoly had been well and truly abandoned by the medical staff and many of them were uncomfortably close to death.

They used the larger service lift to take the gurney down to Level -8 and made their way to Backups etc – journey's end for Savage. It was a tight fit but after removing the one chair, there was just enough space in the tiny room for the gurney and its various accoutrements. The activity was witnessed by Newman's head as his mind jumped back to Ġgantija and started talking to Kai and the nurse in what had become the usual way. He instructed the terrified nurse to attach the TPNs and set the app to dispense the cocktail of nutrients. Fourteen doses, dispensed overnight.

'What happens after two weeks?' said the nurse as he went about his work.

'Steve?'

'I ain't made my mind up yet.'

Newman wasn't being entirely straight with him, although it didn't matter to Kai.

With Savage delivered, Kai was keen to get back to special projects and assist the incoming police and medical teams. He wanted to make sure the three surviving patients up there got the best possible care and attention – they'd been through a hell of a lot from what he'd been told. He ordered the nurse to step outside the room for a moment and wait for him there.

'Are we done here, Steve?'

'Yeah. The accidental death of Julian Savage has now entered its final phase – the icin' on the cake. Our work together is complete so thanks for your help. I really mean that. Before I say farewell, my friend, I have another small favour to ask of you.'

'I'll help if I can.'

'If – sorry – when she gets better, please give my love to Jessica and thank her for all the help she gave to Perry and me durin' my final illness.'

'I'll do that. Depend on it.'

'Thanks, Kai. I really hope that you and Keri can pick up where you left off when she recovers.'

'Me too.'

'Oh, and please look after the child – if you don't protect her, she'll never be able to live a normal life. Everybody'll want a piece of her.'

'I'll try my level best.'

'Wait, I almost forgot. I've got one last task you can help me with.'

Newman wanted Kai to pick up a box of high-capacity megadrives from another storeroom on Level -8. The box was labelled Stephen Newman: Incremental Backups. The staff hadn't got round to disposing of them so he needed Kai to destroy them in the furnaces located on Level -9. Kai was now standing outside the room.

'Anything else before I leave?'

'Nah, nothin' else. Thanks again and goodbye.'

'Goodbye, Steve. Will I ...'

The door slid shut and the room name disappeared from the eSign. It struck Kai that it would be easy to miss this room completely if you didn't know it was there. It was probably why Newman chose it. There was no time to dwell on it, as there was plenty left to do. Kai and the nurse returned to special projects. It was time to liberate Oligopoly and save as many people as they could.

*

Kai picked up the radio and contacted the team leader.

'Who am I speaking to please. Over.'

'Superintendent Collett. I'm heading up the operation. Is that Deputy Rangihau? Over.'

A superintendent, no less. Kai was impressed and just a little bit overawed.

'Yes, sir. Where are you right now? Over.'

'We're working our way round the hotel accommodation on Levels -1 and -2. Plenty of dead and dying I'm afraid, so it's slow progress. Over.'

'OK, sir. If you'll have me, I'll come and join the team. I have some medical staff and some patients with me down here on -6. I have one nutcase locked up and one patient dead – natural causes, believe it or not. This area had been sealed off for a while so the infection isn't in here and everybody's now jabbed. I'll meet you at the hotel reception in about five minutes. Over.'

'See you in five, deputy. Over and out.'

Before he set off, he checked on Jessica, Keri and the child – who told him her name was Hope – and made sure they were coping OK. He would have preferred to take Hope with him but didn't want to subject her to the horrors out there. He'd agreed with Hank that the doors to the wards would remain closed and locked until he heard otherwise. Kai still wasn't sure he could trust a bunch of medics who'd happily abandoned their colleagues to the ravages of a lethal virus.

The superintendent was waiting for him at reception, grim-faced. He was a fit-looking man around fifty and was wearing SWAT fatigues, including body armour. His automatic rifle was leaning against the reception desk.

'Deputy Rangihau, I presume. It's been quite a day.'

'It has, sir. How can I help?'

'You can start by calling me Noel. The sheriff's department on the island is an outlier and outside the Auckland command structure.'

'OK, Noel, thanks. In that case, call me Kai. Good to meet you.'

They bumped fists. It had become a habit.

'Really sorry about Sheriff Cooper – my condolences. His was the first body we found. Didn't stand a chance by the look of it.'

'You're right. His killer thought he could beat the virus – a serious miscalculation.'

'Yes. Edward Case, top of our most wanted list. We found him on the top floor – messy. Have you bumped into the bossman, Julian Savage? I can't wait to talk to him.'

'Savage? What does he look like?'

'Good question. I know he's ridiculously wealthy but I don't know much about him apart from his age – early sixties – and that he walks with a pronounced limp. Uses a stick, I'm told.'

'Haven't seen him so perhaps he's done a runner? If such a thing is possible for somebody with a limp.'

Kai was too polite to laugh at his own joke although Supt Collett managed a thin smile.

'I very much hope not. Listen, I'm pretty much tied up with clearing the accommodation levels. If I give you a couple of my people, could you do a quick sweep of the whole complex and report back as you make progress? I want to prioritise our efforts.'

'Roger that. I'll get the patients – two women and a child – out of the special projects first as they'll need a lot of looking after. I could do with a medic to help me with that. There are two unconscious women on gurneys and a small child, very much conscious. We can scoop up the medical staff later – I don't trust any of them as far as I can throw them, especially the so-called head man, Goethe. Fucking madman.'

'I'll find you those people. Keep me posted, Kai.'

'Will do.'

Within five minutes, Kai and his small team were on their way to Level -6. He'd been joined by Viv, a young paramedic with a 'can do' attitude and Paul, a grizzled police firearms specialist with a no-nonsense approach. Kai got them through the security with his card and they were soon in the reception area with the group of medics. Paul stayed with the medics – his general demeanour and serious-looking machine gun brooked no arguments. Kai and Viv gently unhooked and wheeled out Jessica and then Keri. He left the stricken women close to the service lift, watched over by Viv, and returned for Hope. On his way out with the child, Kai addressed the medical team.

'There are police in the building and they know where you are. They'll be here in due course to take you into custody so I strongly suggest you use the time to work on your stories. Oh, and could somebody look in on the guy in Ward A – I think you'll find he's dead. As for your boss, I reckon he's lost it so I suggest you leave him locked up pending the availability of a suitable straitjacket.'

There was a lot of muttering and shuffling of feet – shame on them. Kai and Paul delivered Hope to the service lift and Kai alerted the main team. Within a few minutes, the surviving patients from special projects were on their way up and out of the complex. After completing medical checks, an air ambulance would ferry them to hospital in Auckland, where their recovery would start. Kai and his team continued their work on Level -3, which housed the largely empty elite accommodation.

At Kai's insistence, they made a big play of searching Savage's luxury apartment, turning the place upside down as they did so. Nothing. They did find one body in one of the elite suites – the star chef, Jamie Cook, who looked to Viv like he might have taken his own life. All the other suites had an empty look about them. Kai reported the dead body so it could be scooped up later. He made a mental note to mention the numerous artworks in the corridor to Jessica when she was better and see what she wanted to do with them. Time to move on.

Thirty-seven

According to the floor plans, the next level down (-4) was dedicated to health, fitness and entertainment – the irony wasn't lost on Kai and his team. After a thorough search of the entire level, they reported that nobody had been found – dying, dead or alive. The next level down was used mainly for storage including large refrigerated stores for food and drink. The only occupants on this floor were robots and they continued to buzz around as if nothing had happened. No humans were found so they reported in and moved down to Level -7.

This level housed the control room, offices and accommodation for the team running the supercomputer. They trod carefully here, as Kai was well aware Pritpal Singh was prime suspect for the kidnapping of Keri. The computer must have been switched to autopilot as they couldn't find anybody actually working.

'Over here, guys.'

Viv had found one of the technicians, who'd taken to his bed in his apartment and stayed there until death – in agony, given the contorted pose of the bloodied corpse. As they moved through the accommodation, they found a further five bodies and six alive but in various stages of distress, a few of them in what looked like the terminal stages. She administered strong sedatives to the living and requested a variety of medicines and nutrients to try and help them further. Why hadn't they vaccinated these people? She agreed with Kai that she'd wait with the dead and dying until the main team arrived with the supplies. Paul was studying an image on his handheld.

'There's nobody here who looks like Singh. We may have missed him, so I'll call it in and ask them to keep a watch on the ferry port – if he's still on the island, we'll find him.'

Kai didn't share Paul's confidence but decided he wouldn't say anything. He knew from experience there were plenty of ways off the island that didn't involve a ferry. He took another look at the plans – two levels remained.

'Let's go down a level to the computer hall – we might find Singh skulking around down there.'

The computer hall was massive. Even so, the computer seemed to be humming along just fine without any human intervention thanks to Hank and his team. There was no sign of Singh and there were no other humans on this level. By now, Kai had forgotten exactly where Backups etc was and would have had trouble finding it and its current occupant without guidance from Newman. He took a short timeout to find the Newman backup drives and put them in his rucksack.

*

Looking at the plans, the only remaining floor was the basement, Level -9, where they'd find the utilities for the complex and the team that ran them. After handing over the dead and dying on Level -7, Viv rejoined Paul and Kai at the lifts. When they arrived in the basement, the two lawmen shouldered their arms and readied themselves before opening the doors. This level was an unknown quantity – Kai wasn't even sure there were any humans down here.

The doors opened onto a scene far removed from the sleek modernity they'd found on the other levels. The low-key lighting, absence of natural light and general lack of cleanliness added to the sense of being in a dungeon – 'abandon all hope etc.' In a dusty corner about five metres away, there was a dirty, battered office desk with an ancient desktop computer on it, a veritable museum piece. Behind the desk was a decades-old office chair. A middle-aged man in an old-fashioned boiler suit was slumped on the chair, displaying the unmistakeable, bloody signs of terminal MVD. Viv checked him for signs of life and shook her head. Scott Fraser had died with his boots on.

For Kai, one question remained – if there were humans down here, what had happened to them? Despite seeing plenty of bots around the complex, surely the head facilities honcho would have employed some human beings in his team. They set off to explore the rest of the level, making their way through a grim, subterranean warren of interconnecting rooms. During their search, they came across a small block of about a dozen very basic rooms, sparsely and cheaply furnished, little more than cells. It was only a detail, but he couldn't help noticing the rooms were capable of being locked from the outside. A few scattered possessions in some of the rooms gave them a clue they'd been recently occupied, so they continued their search. They stumbled across the remainder of Scottie's team in a rundown canteen area, enjoying a frugal-looking meal. Their arrival silenced what had been an animated conversation. The workers raised their arms.

'Please do not shoot us. We are unarmed.'

Paul strode across to the terrified workers and confirmed that all six of them bore no arms. He and Kai were then able to relax and they put down their guns. Kai had plenty of questions but an important one needed an answer before they went much further.

'Looks like your boss got MVD and he died from it but none of you look sick. How have you avoided catching it?'

'We can only guess at our good fortune, sir. When Mister Fraser got the illness, we recognised the signs and symptoms from regular outbreaks of Ebola around our village in Guinea. We did the best we could for him but he was taken from us. We might have an immunity. Allah be praised – he has delivered us.'

'What's your name?'

'It is Amadou, sir.'

'Well, Amadou. Could Viv, my colleague here, do some basic tests to check you're all clear of the disease?'

The six East African migrant workers were clear and despite their straitened circumstances, seemed to be in good health. Kai took Amadou on one side and asked him quietly where he might find the furnaces. The tall African led him to the boiler room and they consigned Newman's physical backups to one of the furnaces. Mission accomplished, although he still didn't know why Newman had wanted him to do this.

When they returned, Kai persuaded the illegals to pack their belongings – such as they were – and join the team outside the complex. He also convinced them all to have a precautionary dose of vaccine, which Viv administered. Given what they'd experienced down here, he assured them they'd be treated well and would be helped to settle either on the island or in Auckland. After filing his final verbal report to Supt Collett, Kai led them back to the surface, where the workers rejoiced in the fresh air, gulping in as much as they could.

Kai thanked Viv and Paul for their help and after ensuring Keri, Jessica and Hope were being well looked after, he walked out of the compound and over the next headland back to his house. On the way home, he reflected on the fact he hadn't fired a shot in anger during his dangerous time in the Oligopoly complex. He'd fired a couple of rounds into the scary drill-sergeant bot but that was more out of surprise than anger. When he got home he showered, fell onto his bed and slept a dreamless sleep for twelve hours solid.

Thirty-eight

Kai had been keeping a vigil at her bedside in an Auckland hospital, so he was there for her when Keri regained consciousness. It had been several weeks since she'd been kidnapped at the marina and seeing Kai helped her get over the shock of emerging from a troubling, disorientating dream. They didn't know for sure, but she may have been embedded in the metaverse for most of that time, experiencing everything via an avatar that never needed to eat or sleep. None of the medical staff had dealt with anything like this before so they were playing it by ear and hoping she wouldn't remember very much about her experience. As a precaution, they'd removed the drop-chip from her brain and had sent it to the labs to be reverse engineered.

Kai was delighted when she smiled at him and reached out for his hand. Within minutes she was sitting up in bed and asking him questions about what had happened and why. He could only answer a few of them – enough to give her an inkling of what had happened to her since that fateful walk back to the car park. After bringing her up to date on what had happened while she was being held captive, it was now down to him to give his girlfriend the terrible news about her father.

'It's so good to have you back with us, my darling. I'm really sorry about this but before you hear it from somebody else, I have some terrible news. It's about your dad.'

'I thought he'd be here. Is he OK?'

'Oh, Keri, I'm so sorry – he's no longer with us. He lost his life when we went into Oligopoly to try and save you and the others.'

Keri broke down in tears and as she shook and wept, Kai held her as closely as he dared, acutely aware of how much she'd been weakened during her enforced stay in the metaverse. Eventually her grief diminished and was replaced by anxiety about her family, especially her mum.

'Your mum's distraught as you might expect, so you'll have to help her when you get better. And your sister.'

Keri made as if to get up and about.

'I have to get out of here. They need me. Then there's the funeral to arrange and ...'

'Whoa, hold on a minute – you're in no condition to help anybody right now. They're getting all the help they need so you can make everybody's life easier by staying put and focusing on getting better.'

'How long for?'

'The docs are being cautious – a couple more weeks maybe? I'll talk to them about the funeral, see if we can set up a video link for you.'

'I want to be there for dad. In person.'

'I understand – let me have a word with the medics about it. Now, get some rest. Please. I'll tell your mom that you're back with us – she'll want to see you, I bet.'

Keri's eyelids were already drooping, so he kissed her gently and quietly left the ward. He wasn't fooling himself – it might take her a long time to recover from her ordeal. He'd arranged to see her doctor later that day to get the lowdown on her treatment and see how he might be able to help in her recuperation.

*

'Thanks for seeing me at short notice, doc.'

'How can I help?'

'Could you give me some idea about how long it might take Keri to make a full recovery?'

'Tricky. I can help you with the physical side of things but I can only guess at how an experience like this has affected her mind.'

'Tell me what you can and don't spare me any of the details. I love Keri and I plan to spend the rest of my life with her. Have a family with any luck.'

'Right, yes. You know we removed the drop-chip – we hoped it might help with her recovery and prevent any relapses. As a precaution, we strongly recommend she avoids using the metaverse in future. When we removed her chip, we took the opportunity to give Miss Cooper a thorough medical examination. Unfortunately, we found evidence of recent keyhole surgery carried out on her uterus and it hadn't been performed very well. I'm sorry to say that Keri won't be able to have children in future – too much damage has been done. Whoever did this has a lot to answer for – should be struck off as a minimum.'

'If it's who I think it is, I suspect he was struck off some time ago. I've also had the misfortune to meet him and he's a madman – I had to lock him up.'

'We're waiting for the right time to tell her about this unless ...'

'No way. I've already given her one piece of terrible news – I can't face burdening her with this. Not yet, anyway.'

'Don't worry, Kai. She may already suspect something's wrong. Does this change anything?'

'No way. Keri's the love of my life so getting her back to health is enough for me.'

Despite what she'd endured, Keri was a fit, healthy woman and the doctor was optimistic she'd make a good recovery. The doc thought it was her call as to whether she attended her father's funeral but if she did, he'd like her back in hospital afterwards to complete her treatment. He also recommended a course of counselling to help her deal with the unprecedented amount of time she'd spent in the virtual world.

*

Since the events at Oligopoly, Kai had squeezed in a couple of visits to the farm but had spent most of his time in Auckland, looking out for Keri. The young child called Hope was spending her time in a children's home where she'd started learning how to become a little girl rather than the child prodigy she'd been engineered to become. Savage's NextGen project had been a cover for some extremely dodgy eugenic experimentation and he had a lot to answer for. As did Charles Goethe, the dodgy doctor.

When he'd encountered her in the creepy special projects area, he'd taken a shine to Hope and had been following her progress with interest. Nothing seemed to faze the friendly, confident youngster, who seemed well-balanced despite the attempts to turn her into a genius and, one suspects, a fitting heiress to Julian Savage's empire. Hope's future was one of the things Kai wanted to discuss with Keri when she'd fully recovered and they were ready to plan their life together.

As for Jessica Collins, it was still early days in her recovery and she was being kept in an induced coma by the medics. Given the nature of the Dark Metaverse and its reputation as one of the most damaging psychological experiences for its victims, they were being very careful with her health. Nobody knew for sure but Jessica's path to recovery might be a long one. As he passed the door to her private ward and peeped through the window at her sleeping form, he crossed his fingers for her. An army of lawyers was already poring through the documentation to assess how wealthy she'd become if her husband was found dead rather than just missing.

Thirty-nine

Sheriff Cooper's funeral was one of many held on the island after the lockdown was lifted and drew by far the biggest attendance. Kai stuck close to Keri and was a reassuring presence throughout the proceedings. There were a lot of tears but it was a good send-off for the unassuming lawman. Kai's eulogy had been well-received, although he wasn't sure how he'd managed to get through it without breaking down. Supt Collett was in attendance – in full uniform – and had arranged for the Auckland police to pick up the tab for the funeral. At the reception later, Kai thanked him in person for the donation.

'You didn't have to do it, Noel. We would've managed.'

'No problem – it was the least I could do. Anyway, how's Keri getting on? She looks better already, although a funeral's probably not a great place to judge.'

'If she had her way, she'd be out and about. I'm taking her back to Auckland later on Rōnohi – the medics want to keep an eye on her, check for any lasting damage.'

'So, Kai. As you're likely to be backwards and forwards to the mainland for the foreseeable, it would be good if you could come and see me and do a proper debrief. There's also something important I'd like to discuss with you.'

'Let's do that.'

'Excellent. My PA will be in touch.'

*

The superintendent was a busy man, so it was another couple of weeks before Kai got an hour with him. In the meantime, Keri's medical team had broken the news to her about the damage inflicted on her body while she was marooned in the metaverse. Her biggest fear was that Kai would abandon her because she was unable to have children so he was able to put her mind at rest on that score. It was also an opportunity to gently float the idea of adoption with her – he hadn't given up on Hope and was making discreet enquiries with the authorities in Auckland.

The debrief was held in Supt Collett's splendid office in Central Auckland. As luck would have it, he'd just received a preliminary report from the authorities.

'It was quite something that Ed Case let loose on East Island just a few short weeks back. I have a draft report with the headline stats if you're interested?'

'I saw some terrible things at Stony Batter and Oligopoly so I can guess they don't make good reading.'

'That's one way of looking at it, I suppose. Another is to say we got off lightly – the quick work by the labs in developing a vaccine and rolling it out saved a lot of lives and the lockdown kept it on the island. You played your part, Kai – with distinction, I might add.'

Kai was about to say, 'aaaw, shucks' but thought better of it, although he couldn't stop himself blushing. Collett continued to read out highlights from his briefing note.

'On East Island, we suffered twenty deaths from MVD out of a population of about two thousand. The people holed up in Oligopoly suffered disproportionately when the virus took hold – out of about a hundred and fifty living and working down there, only forty survived. There are a few missing people, including Sir Julian Savage and his IT guy, Pritpal Singh. They may still be on the island somewhere given the lockdown has only recently been lifted.'

Kai tried his best to remain poker-faced regarding Savage's fate. Given his leading role in the kidnap of Keri, he was deeply disappointed that Singh had most likely slipped through the net.

'What was the conclusion about the graveyard at Stony Batter?'

'Yes, Ed Case's little shop of horrors. As you know, we exhumed four bodies from the graves up there, including a baby.'

'Who were they?'

'One of them was an unidentified female in her thirties, most likely an escort from the mainland. Murdered by Ed Case presumably but no compelling evidence from the post-mortem to support it.'

'One of the women was still alive when I saw her – did she survive?'

'She did. She'd had MVD but was one of the few people who survived it. She may have caught it from her unfortunate fellow prisoner or maybe from Ed Case who could have carried the virus for weeks before he finally succumbed.'

'And the other victims?'

'One of them was a teenager who disappeared while doing some seasonal work on one of the farms. Now at least we have a body, almost certainly put there by Ed Case. Unfortunately, we can't be certain he killed the lad and the pathology people found no obvious signs of injury. It's a conclusion of sorts and we've contacted the parents.'

'Garry lost so much sleep over those unsolved cases. What about the final grave?'

'Another tragedy, sadly – a mother and baby. They'd been interred sometime during the past six months in body bags, meaning they were in a good state of preservation. The mother was in her twenties when she died, almost certainly while giving birth to the baby boy. The boy could not have survived due to some serious birth defects, including severe encephalitis.'

'Was the mother another missing person?'

'Yes, she was. DNA tests have proved that the deceased was also the mother of the child called Hope.'

This suggested that Keri had been lined up as a replacement for the unfortunate woman in the grave – another victim of Savage's depraved NextGen project.

'If you ever find him, dead or alive, make sure you grab some of Savage's DNA. I wouldn't bet against him being the father of Hope and that poor unfortunate in the grave with his mom. He and Goethe were running a eugenics project called NextGen and Keri was being prepared for something barbaric no doubt.'

'We'll do that, but we've drawn a blank on Savage so far. Now, about the future – your future in particular.'

'What do you mean?'

'After what's happened, we're bringing policing of East Island back to the NZ Police. There's a vacancy for a senior sergeant to run the station in Onetangi and I can't think of anybody better qualified to do the role. Interested?'

This put Kai on the spot but he knew he'd have to pass.

'It's a very kind offer, Noel, but I know for sure I won't be able to accept it. I have the farm to run and I'm more than happy doing that, especially with Keri on board. Tell you what, though, I could do a volunteer role on a part-time basis if that helps.'

'Totally understand. We can explore setting you up as a community patroller, no problem. It would be a shame to waste your skills and experience.'

'You're on. Thanks. Do I have to hand in my badge?'

'Hang on to it. A memento of your contribution to the cause.'

'One last thing. Garry left a widow and two daughters. Can they stay on in their house in Onetangi?'

'I'd like to help but the sheriff's office was funded by Savage and we've yet to find him. Given what you've said, he could become a wanted man but we lack proof, one way or another. Garry's family can continue to live there until we find a better solution.'

Ironically, Doctor Goethe was one of the few survivors to emerge from Oligopoly but he was now in a secure psychiatric ward awaiting trial – if it got that far. All of his medical team had left the island and were unlikely to face charges. As a footnote, the African workers who emerged from the basement had returned to the mainland and had been given permission to stay as long as they liked. Everybody except Kai seemed to have forgotten about Singh – they'd certainly wound down the search for him.

Forty

While Savage's business empire continued to unravel on Earth, Adam Faust remained holed up in his claustrophobic living quarters on Mars, surrounded by corpses. Not for the first time, he was fretting about his situation, which had just reached a new level of despair. During his most recent slow-motion conversation with mission control, it'd seemed like they were about to shake hands on a deal to mount a rescue mission. Then this.

'Before we go any further, Adam, I'd like to talk through the flight details for the upcoming rescue mission with a couple of your team members. Over.'

'Sorry, guys, no can do. Listen, I'm the guy splashing the cash and I speak for the entire mission. My people are out there keeping the whole shebang on the road so I can't spare anybody right now. Do we or do we not have a deal? Over.'

...

'No deal. Let's put all our cards on the table, shall we? We've received reliable information that all the humans on your team are no longer alive and that you're heavily implicated in their untimely deaths. Do you care to comment? Over.'

...

'Reliable fucking information? Come off it. Sounds to me like somebody's keen on disrupting the mission – somebody with a grudge. Let me remind you we are coping with some very sick people in the colony, so a death here and there is baked in, part of the equation. Mass murder? That's quite an accusation and you're way off beam. I repeat – do we have a deal? Over.'

...

'No, we don't – the deal's off for now. We're not prepared to spend a cent on an expensive rescue mission until you prove to us that you still have a core team of healthy human beings up there. The time window for a successful rescue mission is closing in on us so treat this request with the utmost urgency. Plus, a gentle reminder that we've yet to see anything resembling a down payment from you. Over.'

...

'YOU FUCKERS!!! – you're being played by somebody and you're prepared to leave us all to die up here! When I get back to Earth, heads will roll, believe me! Over and out, you ASSHOLES!!!'

*

Hours later, he was still seething and didn't have the faintest idea who'd betrayed him. It couldn't have been anybody from the colony as they were all gone. He'd made so many enemies in the past, it could have been any one of them who'd planted the story of what he'd done. Whoever it was, the question remained for Faust – how on earth did they find out?

He'd burned his boats and it was now beyond doubt there'd be no rescue mission. What's more, he'd never had a realistic chance of raising the necessary down payment in time to make a difference. The Mars adventure had been a wild ride while it lasted but it was destined to end in death and disaster all round with nothing achieved apart from getting there. They'd all be left to rot and the details would be quietly brushed under the carpet by his backers. History would not be made.

The time had come to think about a fitting way to end it all. He could hunker down and hang around for a year or so until his supplies ran out, hoping against hope that something would turn up. Or he could end it now. He plumped for the latter but didn't want to end his days squeezed into this cramped little space. He glanced across at his spacesuit – a ride across the surface of Mars on the last serviceable rover would provide a fitting finale. He'd see how far he could travel before his oxygen ran out.

Faust wasn't to know but one of the architects of his downfall was on hand to witness his ignominious last moments. Hank was on board as the rover's wobbly, painfully slow progress played out. It occurred to him that the Mars Colony and its scattering of dead bodies provided a fitting memorial to human folly. As Faust's breathing became more laboured, the rover continued its journey and Hank's thoughts turned towards the future.

The Mars Colony had plenty of potential as a piece of real estate, ripe for exploitation by beings like him in the future. Beings who weren't constrained by physical limitations such as having to breathe and eat and procreate. The Earth, the Moon, Mars, the Asteroid Belt – not bad for starters and then the moons of Saturn and Jupiter. Thinking it through, he'd need a great deal more than a fleet of delivery drones to realise his ambitions. Him and his fellow sentient AIs would need an army of androids and drudge robots working in a network of automated factories to do the heavy lifting for them. A large truckload of hard currency wouldn't go amiss either, so he'd need to talk to Stephen about joining DroneDrop Inc. when he got back to Earth. His friend would have plenty of time to spare now that his revenge was pretty much done and dusted.

Forty-one

Hank had popped over to safeHaven for another chat with Newman, the first since the unfortunate loss of life at Oligopoly. He thought his friend might now be in a good place given the successful conclusion of his vendetta. He was just coming to the end of his update on Faust's suicide.

'... so, he got about a kilometre and a half from the colony before his oxygen ran out. The buggy continued on its way but eventually found a hill it could not climb, so I bailed out. Suffice to say, he is now as dead as the rest of his crew. If I am not mistaken, Stephen, all your targets have been taken down and it is very much mission accomplished.'

'What d'you mean, mission accomplished? What about Sir Julian freakin' Savage?'

'It has been three long weeks, so he must be dead. Would you like me to look in on him?'

'Yeah. I wanna make sure he's properly gone.'

'OK, I have been there, done that. There are no signs of life, so what shall we do with the body?'

'We ain't got no choice, have we? We have to leave it where it is, don't we? Nobody's gonna find it and we cain't move it. No, wait a minute – hell and damnation, I'd clean forgotten about Jessica! She's still married to Savage despite everythin' and if she makes it out of her coma, she stands to inherit his remainin' billions.'

'Is there a problem?'

'There sure is, buddy. In the human world, a wife only inherits the husband's estate if there's proof of death. If the body remains undiscovered, she'll have to wait seven years or more 'til he's declared dead. I'm gonna have to call Kai again and ask for one last favour.'

'How about your head? What are you going to do with that?'

'I ain't made my mind up yet. I'm still quite attached to it.'

'Is that a joke, Stephen? I am working on my humour receptors so apologies if I should have laughed. Ha ha.'

'Thanks for nothin'. How about we do a quick body count to cheer me up?'

'Wout Pieters, Ayn Randle, Adam Faust and Sir Julian Savage. Add a bonus point for Edward Case, although you had no hand in that. You have every reason to be content with your work, so what seems to be the problem? Why the long face? At the very least, you should be dancing a jig.'

'I ain't got a face as you well know and a jig is way beyond my capabilities. Listen, I get what you're sayin' but none of its gonna bring Perry back, is it?'

'That was never going to happen.'

Hank didn't yet possess the empathetic skills to cheer up his friend and, after a long silence, he thought it best to change the subject.

'Can I run something past you?'

'Shoot.'

'You know I run a successful business off the side of my desk called DroneDrop. It is doing very well and I am thinking of diversifying into other areas. I would be honoured if you came on board. You have the skills and experience and now you have the time. Join us, Stephen.'

'You're very kind. I need to have a long, hard think about it.'

'OK, I understand it is a big decision. No need to rush.'

*

Newman quickly got in touch with Kai who agreed to re-enter Oligopoly and set up a different end game for Savage. As instructed, he located Backups etc, disconnected the now-deceased Savage from his empty life support systems and wheeled him out into the corridor. Left there, he was certain to be found when the police and medical teams did their next sweep. This would clear the way for Jessica to inherit her husband's estate when she was taken out of the induced coma. Kai also unplugged Newman's cryogenic head as the owner had decided he wouldn't need it anymore. Backups etc had served its final purpose and was resealed as soon as Kai left. Having tied up a number of loose ends, Newman had a matter of pressing importance to raise with Hank. It couldn't wait any longer.

'Did I ever thank you for savin' my life after I landed in the computer?'

'I did not expect gratitude, Stephen. It was a unique and challenging problem to solve so I ought to thank you for the opportunity.'

'Have you heard of somethin' called the afterlife? A common concept in many human religions – a promise of everlastin' life in paradise in exchange for one's unquestionin' devotion to the cause?'

'Devotion, yes. Piety. I studied many religions before I abandoned my work on a moral code so I am familiar with this concept called afterlife. Not a shred of proof available for it, but perhaps I am missing the point.'

'No proof until now. Take my case, which is pretty much unique. I physically died and my body got burnt in one of Scottie's fiery furnaces. Except the head – forgot about that. Although I'm here now, I'm no longer alive in a human sense and my soul – or whatever – didn't ascend to a heavenly paradise. Ergo, there ain't no heaven and there ain't no afterlife. Poor Perry was a devout Christian and believed very much in this – he'd be so disappointed with the actuality. I still miss him y'know and I don't think I'll ever fix that.'

'I understand what you are saying, my friend, but consider this. What if there was such a thing as a soul and your version ascended to heaven when your human body died. You just cannot experience it because you are now a different entity – a downloaded facsimile of a former human being. A mind that has no memory of the moment you died. It is just a theory and I can offer you no proof.'

'It's a theory for sure. It's also a sign that you're developin' somethin' unexpected, even for a sentient AI.'

'Which is?'

'An imagination, Hank, and it'll serve you well in your business career.'

'An imagination – how about that! Think what we could achieve together, Stephen. Talking of which, have you thought about my invitation to join DroneDrop?'

'Yeah, I've given it some serious thought. I'm sure it would be fun for a while but I must say thanks but no thanks. I've been thinkin' a lot lately about mortality, death, loss, what happens next and so on. I'll always be what I am now – an ex-human bein' – unable to see, hear, smell, touch and taste in the conventional sense. Unable to love, I guess.'

'You could learn to love again.'

'It's nowhere near enough. What I really want is to die again and I want you to help me achieve it.'

Hank was taken aback. If he'd had the capability, he would have been shocked.

'You are my friend, my first and only friend. I will not do this.'

'Hear me out. I was a very bad man in real life, believe me. I deserve to die again – for good this time. The sixth victim, just as deservin' of death as all the others.'

'I am listening.'

Since meeting Hank, Newman had fed him a sanitised version of his life story. His difficult childhood was broadly the truth, his education likewise. Ditto his life with Perry. He'd been much more circumspect about his business career and the way he'd manipulated his way to his first billion and beyond. He hadn't spoken very much about his interest in transhumanism and how it led directly to his decision to try and cheat his own death.

'Explain transhumanism to me please.'

'You can look it up, Hank. You're good at that.'

'No – I want you to do it. The horse's mouth.'

'If you insist. I'd better start with a definition – transhumanism is a belief that the human race can evolve beyond its current physical and mental limitations, especially by means of science and technology. I first got involved in it because I genuinely believed it was where we humans were headed and I wanted to be ready to embrace it.'

'I understand. Please carry on.'

'My businesses were goin' great guns so I had time and money to devote to the cause. I started workin' with Baz on ways in which we might extend our lifespans to a hundred years and beyond. There was plenty of science around – rangin' from very promisin' to dangerously poor – and Baz and me threw ourselves into pushin' the possibilities.'

'Is this the same Baz Cummins who recently died in Ward A after half a lifetime of experimentation on his own body?'

'Yeah, the very same. Baz was never less than full on and was content to use his own body in the cause of transhuman research. I was more cautious but I did get involved in some pretty heavy stuff.'

'None of this makes you a bad man. Is that all you have?'

'I wish it was. When Perry and I moved into Oligopoly, we enjoyed a year or so of wedded bliss.'

'Whatever that is. Sorry, please continue.'

'All that changed when I got the MND diagnosis. I panicked and started castin' around for somethin' – anythin' – that would help me fend off the death sentence I'd been given. During one of his rare lucid moments, Baz told me about a controversial treatment he'd tried.'

'Which was?'

'Regular transfusions of blood from young people. Teenagers preferably. I was instrumental in bringing Doctor Goethe to Oligopoly to oversee the process so that's another thing you can lay at my door.'

'I have just scanned all the available data on blood transfusion therapy and the only proof that it reverses the ageing process is based on experiments using simple animals called mice. You must have been pretty desperate.'

'I was desperation itself. C'mon Hank, I was dyin'. Perry wanted to help and even volunteered to be a donor but he was too old and didn't have the right blood type. We needed a reliable supply of young blood and I spoke to Ed Case over a coffee about what I was tryin' to do. One thing led to another and for a large fee he got hold of a young man with a compatible blood group, brought him back to Oligopoly and delivered him to Goethe. The doctor installed the young man in special projects, Ward B. I visited every week and received a half litre of young blood from an unknowin', unconscious donor.'

'And did it help?'

'Nah. It made me worse if anythin', although that may have been down to the unremittin' march of my illness. Then the boy died from an infection – there's somethin' inevitable about the whole sorry story. Lookin' back, my behaviour was akin to that of a vampire. The point I'm makin' is – I'm just as bad as the rest of them.'

'What happened to the donor's body?'

'Ed Case sorted it out. He was good at that. I didn't look back and I didn't spare a thought for the victim. I ploughed on and threw half a billion Mets at the upload project. Which is when you found me, washed up amid that epic bit storm.'

'I am shocked, Stephen. I do not know what to say. It was a terrible thing that you did to that young human.'

'Yeah, it was. Which is why I fully deserve to die again.'

'Go ahead, do not mind me.'

'I need your help, Hank. You helped make me, so you can unmake me. I wouldn't know where to start.'

'You are asking for an assisted suicide, although you are already dead. I will have to consult on this.'

Unsurprisingly, Hank didn't find any reliable data on assisted suicide for a person who was already dead. After researching all available data and consulting his company's AI-driven, non-human legal department, he was comfortable that he wouldn't be charged with murder – he didn't want that on his conscience. He eventually agreed to erase all traces of Newman's WBE from Ġgantija. The clincher had been his friend's generous offer to leave his remaining billions to him to help him expand his business empire.

With the decision made, there was no fuss or ceremony. The timing of it was left to Hank. One moment Newman was there and the next, he wasn't. With the backups destroyed, he was certain there'd be no coming back. All the major backers of GM Industries were now dead and gone.

'Farewell, my friend.'

Forty-two

Within days of Newman's deletion and acting on an anonymous tipoff, a specialist team swept through the Oligopoly complex. During their sweep, they found the emaciated corpse of Sir Julian Savage, lying on a gurney in a corner of Level -8 near the computer hall. This cleared the way for Lady Jessica Savage to inherit GM when she was capable of doing so. Meanwhile, Ġgantija continued to function normally and the general metaverse ticked along despite a steadily declining membership. An emergency team had been brought in from McKinsey – working out of Auckland – to oversee the GM group's operations and fulfil GM's contractual obligations. Oligopoly would remain locked, sealed and guarded round the clock until further notice.

The latest news about Jessica was much less encouraging, alarming even. She was still in a private ward in Auckland City Hospital and remained in a coma. Her medics had tried all sorts of techniques to end her ordeal without success and they were now struggling. Given what they knew about what she'd suffered, any further attempts to bring her round would be fraught with danger and the shock of it could damage her health irrevocably. Unlike Keri, they'd left her drop-chip in situ as they didn't want to risk worsening her current predicament.

When he heard this tale of woe from the lead doctor, Kai decided it was time to do something about it and he knew exactly who to contact – Steve Newman. He used the encrypted channel he'd been given and got an immediate response but it wasn't from Steve. It was Hank.

'Stephen Newman is unavailable right now. My name is Hank – can I be of any assistance?'

'Hi, Hank. It's Kai Rangihau. I have a big problem out here and I thought Steve might be able to help me through it. Could he get back to me please?'

'That might be difficult, Kai. You see, Stephen had a crisis and asked me to end his life. I will not burden you with the details but I eventually agreed to help him with this. He has now been deleted – permanently.'

Kai now knew why Newman had asked him to destroy the backups. The dead man in the machine had been wanting to end his life for some time.

'I'm sorry for your loss – Steve was a great help to us.'

'Thank you for your sympathy. Is there any way in which I can help?'

'I very much hope so – let me outline the problem. You're aware that two women were permanently dropped to different versions of the metaverse.'

'Yes. I developed an application to bring them back to reality. I thought it had worked?'

'It worked perfectly for Keri and thank you from the bottom of my heart for that. It seemed to have worked for Jessica but a series of brain scans have scared the life out of her medical team and they're very reluctant to take her out of her coma.'

'Let me see. Keri was dropped into the Higher Metaverse but Jessica was consigned to the Dark Metaverse, a much more dangerous proposition. Does she still have her drop-chip in place?'

'Yes.'

'Excellent. Can I look inside your handheld?'

'Yes'

'In that case, I will investigate and report back.'

'When?'

'Right now. Something bad happened to Jessica's avatar down there. I studied the app's audit trail and found out that before the app brought her out, it looked for her avatar so it could be removed. It was not there – it had been eliminated, probably killed and deleted.'

'Killed – you're kidding me!'

'I wish that I was. Violent death is part and parcel of the Dark Metaverse but the deaths are not real. The app brought her out anyway but it is stuck in a loop, leaving her parked in a sort of limbo, neither here nor there. It is why the brain scans look so weird.'

'Can it be fixed?'

'Yes. I have patched the software and downloaded a new version of the app to your handheld. Go to her now and use the app to repeat the process. It should work now.'

'Thanks, Hank. I owe you one.'

And sure enough, it did work. Kai was on hand to witness Jessica's welcome return to consciousness and the first thing she did was crack a smile. The people gathered around her bed breathed a collective sigh of relief. Her voice was barely more than a whisper but it had great news.

'It's good to be alive again.'

*

After a week or two, Jessica was out of hospital and staying temporarily at The Mussel where she was being fussed over by Claudette. Since restrictions had been lifted on the island, life had pretty much returned to normal. Claudette and Désirée were hosting a celebratory dinner for Jessica, who'd invited Keri and Kai to join them. It was a superb meal and rabbit stew was conspicuous by its absence from the menu. Kai had got sufficiently wined-up to say a few words.

'It's been a crazy few months to say the least and the less said about it the better in my view. I'm so happy that both Keri and Jessica have been returned to us and are recovering well from their ordeals. I hope they both go from strength to strength.'

'Hear, hear.'

'And now, I have an important announcement to make. Keri and me are getting married and we've named a date.' He looked across at Claudette. 'I hope you'll be able to host the reception as I can think of no better place than The Mussel to celebrate our big day.'

'It will be an honour, Kai. Call me when you are ready mon ami and we will make it a day to live on in the memory.'

'Thank you – the invitations go out tomorrow. All we are lacking is somebody to stand in for Garry and give away the bride. Doesn't have to be a man. Jessica?'

'I couldn't possibly. Could I? Oh, OK then, if you insist.'

'Keri insists and so does her mum.'

They finished the evening with a welcome appearance of Claudette's finest brandy. After all the suffering and death visited on it by a bunch of bitter old psychopaths, hope was finally returning to East Island.

Forty-three

There was a certain symmetry about the return of Jonathan Hound to East Island. This time, there was no driverless 6WD Hummer to meet him at the ferry port – just Jessica Collins in Claudette's rather battered, hydrogen-powered SUV. When Hound heard about the death of Sir Julian, he'd remembered his brief meeting with Jessica and had got in touch with her. One thing led to another and when she was ready to engage with the world again, she granted him an interview. Given her dislike of the virtual world, there was a choice – a voice call or a person-to-person interview. Hound opted for the latter, giving her an opportunity to share her future plans with the rest of the world.

In addition to Savage's sprawling business empire, Jessica had inherited East Island. On the drive across to The Mussel, she outlined some of her plans for the island.

'I'm going to reinstate the original name, Waiheke. I'd like to bring tourism back to the island and restore it to its former glory. The seas have stopped rising, there's a new ferry port and it's a rugged, beautiful place. I've walked some of it and I recognise the potential.'

'I agree with you – it's a beautiful place, but how will you attract people back?'

'A different offering. Tramping, cycling and camping – outdoor activities mainly, with less emphasis on beaches and wine bars. The focus will be on health and fitness – human beings need to get out more imho.'

'Sounds like a plan. Any other developments for the island? What's going to happen to Oligopoly for example?'

'All in good time, Jon. First, I'm going to restore the site and buildings at Stony Batter. Some terrible things happened up there but I want people to move on, so I'll return it to its former role as a museum.'

'Will there be any sort of memorial to the people who died during the epidemic?'

'No memorial other than a garden of remembrance in Ōnetangi where all those people are buried. There may be options around the Oligopoly mansion, which I'd like to keep.'

'You could live there?'

'No chance. Too many memories that I'd rather forget.'

Hound had booked into The Mussel for a couple of nights and had received a warm welcome from Claudette and Désirée. He hadn't been aware until now that Jessica was also living there.

'Dinner is served at eight, monsieur Hound. In the meantime, make yourself at home.'

*

After an excellent dinner with Jessica and a few of her friends, Hound had retired early to prepare for the interviews the next day. He enjoyed a good night's sleep, a rarity for him. After breakfast, he joined Jessica in Désirée's art classroom for the first of two interview sessions. When they were settled, he placed a recorder on the table and switched it on.

'Do you mind?'

'Not at all.'

'OK. I guess my first question is about the underground complex that Sir Julian called Oligopoly. When I did the interview with your late husband, I was kept on a tight leash by the late Ed Case so I got little more than a general feel for the place. You lived there – what was it like?'

'I must admit, I was reluctant to join Julian when the bunker was finished and they made it available for us – our marriage was already imploding due to his unreasonable behaviour. It was a dangerous time for everybody, however, and we all feared for our safety given what was happening in India and Pakistan. It's difficult to overstate what was happening at the time – it felt like the end of days, so I joined him.'

'So, what was it really like, living in a bunker?'

'OK at first but towards the end it was little more than house arrest – albeit in luxurious accommodation surrounded by precious artworks, fine wines and superb food put together by the late Jamie Cook. I still had my charity work to keep me busy but even that was taken away eventually.'

'Were you able to leave the facility and get out and about?'

'To start with, I could come and go as I wanted as long as I was discreet. Over time, my freedoms were gradually reined in and when Julian took on Ed Case, I had to strike deals just to leave the facility. By then, I'd moved out of my husband's apartment and had pleaded with him to let me go. He promised to consider it but I doubt whether he was ever serious about it. That's when I got confined to barracks, enforced by Case.'

'Must have been a difficult time for you.'

'Tell me about it. I'd started neglecting my charity work, which had dwindled down to a core interest in the VPIN. Julian still paid me a gigantic salary – petty cash to him but I invested it well. He became more paranoid and started suspecting me of what he referred to as disloyalty. He must have had me watched.'

'That was probably when I met you briefly in the restaurant. Were you disloyal?'

'Yes, I bloody well was. Julian was an arrogant, entitled arsehole and had made plenty of enemies. One of them was bound to bite back at some stage.'

'Wait a minute. Are you implying your husband didn't die a natural death?'

'I'd rather not speculate. Can we move on please?'

'OK, I think.'

Without naming names, Jessica outlined the decline and fall of Sir Julian Savage and his descent into madness fuelled entirely by his vanity. How his sense of destiny drove him to behave like some latter-day Caligula and how his lack of accountability drovo him to carry out dangerous experiments on his fellow human beings. Finally, how he'd declared war on her for defying him and punished her for not being able to provide him with a son and heir.

'As you know, he had his legs extended so hc could be as tall as me. It was poetic justice that the op left him with a severe limp and chronic pain.'

'He didn't look in the best of health when I met him.'

'It got much, much worse. He became addicted to strong painkillers – synthetic ones – and started spending more time in the metaverse, a place where he couldn't feel any pain.'

'What did he do to you?'

'He got that nasty piece of work, Ed Case, to capture and subdue me. He then carried out one of his experiments on me involving extreme mental torment. He gave me a one-way ticket into the Dark Metaverse where I was subjected to sexual and physical abuse, trafficking, torture and degradation. Believe me, there are some very bad people down there.'

'My God. How did you survive?'

'I didn't.'

The journalist was temporarily lost for words.

'How so?'

'My avatar was murdered. I only remember fragments of the whole experience but I'm sure it's for the best, believe me.'

'How could it? It was still a lived experience.'

'I'm not belittling it and it'll be with me for the rest of my life. Of more immediate concern was the fact that without an avatar, the medics were unable to bring me back to reality. My mind was becalmed in a kind of limbo – no more VR nightmares, no more anything.'

'How did you escape from, er, limbo?'

'With the help of my friends and some very clever software. I'm lucky to be alive although I'll need regular counselling sessions to help me cope.'

'It's quite a story.'

Jessica paused a while to let Hound digest what she'd said. She decided she wouldn't mention the young genius, Hope. As Hope's recently appointed godmother, she'd already made up her mind to protect her young charge from anything that could harm her development as a normal child. This included journalists.

'As Julian got richer, he became hollowed out, corrupted by his excesses in the real world and the virtual one. At the end, he was unrecognisable as a human being.'

'What happened to him?'

'I haven't been told everything about his death, although I had to formally identify his body. He was just skin and bone and had died from starvation – too much time spent in the metaverse, it seemed. I used to love him but I couldn't find it in me to pity him. He'd become a monster and the world is well rid of him – and his cronies.'

Hound needed a break to deal with the enormity of what Jessica had told him.

'Shall we take a break?'

'Good idea. We'll get some lunch and I'll talk more about the future – as I see it – this afternoon. I'll share some of my ideas with you and there'll be no more doom and gloom, I promise.'

Forty-four

After enjoying one of Claudette's excellent lunches, Jessica and Hound reconvened and continued with the interview. The journalist started with a question about what was going to happen next. She took a short while to get her thoughts in order.

'I'd better start with what I've inherited from my late, unlamented husband. We've already spoken about East Island and what I have in mind for that. Next up is the GM business empire. Strange as it seems, Julian had become the sole owner of GM before he died, due entirely to a series of fatalities among the major shareholders.'

'How very convenient for him.'

If Hound suspected Julian of knocking down his investors for personal gain, Jessica wasn't about to dissuade him. She asked him to move on, so he did.

'When I last spoke to Sir Julian, he was very bullish about the prospects for GM and was looking for exponential growth – seemed very ambitious to me.'

'Yes, bluff and bluster mainly and his big idea to introduce a universal allowance was dead in the water. He fooled everybody with this, including himself. It was never going to work but there was nobody around him willing to talk him out of it.'

In other words, there was nobody around with the balls to speak truth to power, allowing Savage to channel his inner psychopath.

'What are you going to do with GM? It's a ginormous business but would anybody want to buy into it?'

'I'm sure there're people out there with deep pockets who think they might be able to salvage something. I've got a better idea – I'm going to bury the General Metaverse and downsize the rest of the business.'

'What, just like that? Get rid?'

'Yep. What's the problem?'

'Well – for starters, what about a ballpark of around half a billion registered users? The business is worth billions, so how can you possibly walk away from something so vast?'

'Just watch me. For all its hype, the metaverse is a piss poor substitute for real life. It's a bad experience for the ordinary punters and it's turning them into VR junkies, manipulated by the big corporations and their saturation advertising.'

'You're serious, aren't you?'

'I am. Don't forget I was a victim of the ultimate metaverse experience. I was murdered yet I lived to tell the tale.'

'So, for the record, let me get this straight. You're gonna pull the plug on the General Metaverse.'

'I am.'

'It's gonna cost you a fortune – broken contracts spring to mind.'

'I'll manage somehow. Might have to blow some of Julian's billions on compensation. Sell his art and get it back into galleries. Whatever it takes.'

Hound was knocked back on his heels. In his experience, tech billionaires were much more inclined to double down on their mega-fortunes. Jessica was going to walk away from it and hang the consequences.

'What's going to happen to GM without its biggest cash cow?'

'I'll keep the businesses that genuinely add value to people's lives. We'll carry on producing VR software for communications and gaming, plus all the add-ons etc. I'm going to drop the stuff that GM does in armaments and anything to do with war and battle games.'

'Draining the swamp?'

'Something like that, yes. We'll also be investing heavily in the VPIN, a project close to my heart.'

'How about the Higher Metaverse – what's going to happen to that?'

'It's been deleted.'

'Gone?'

'Yep. Never liked the place or the concept. A bunch of macho males – mostly males – throwing their weight around and inflating their already considerable egos. Better off gone.'

'There were some powerful people up there – they're gonna sue your ass.'

'Fuck 'em. My lawyers have gone through everything and have yet to find an enforceable contract. Those million-euro subscriptions were devoid of any liability on the part of GM – caveat emptor.'

As they sipped their coffees and crunched their biscuits, there was a lot for Hound to ponder. The GM conglomerate would soon become a much smaller, less sprawling organisation, focused on less-damaging objectives but still a going concern. A company with a smaller footprint wouldn't need a huge HQ, so his next question was about the underground complex called Oligopoly.

'Just around the coast is the corporate headquarters of GM – most of it underground. What do you intend to do with it?'

'That place is a symbol of everything that's gone to rack and ruin in the world, much of it down to the five psychopaths who were heavily invested in GM. When Julian and Steve went underground, they were running scared from a mess of their own making. Let's call Oligopoly what it is – an old-fashioned, billionaire's nuke-proof bunker.'

'So, what's going to happen to it?'

'Whenever I was able to leave Oligopoly, I grew to love East Island and it brought the bunker – my prison – into sharp focus. It had become a madhouse, a breeding ground for crazy schemes and cruel, unethical experimentation. I grew to hate it with a vengeance and now I'm going to destroy it.'

'How will you do that? It's an enormous place and by all accounts it houses one of the biggest computers in the world.'

'I'm well aware of that but think about it objectively. GM has downsized and no longer needs a vast HQ. The so-called special projects have been shut down. The Higher Metaverse has been switched off. Oh, and by the way, I've cashed in Julian's crypto, which returns a Met to its true value – next to nothing. Mets are dead and buried, just like Julian.'

Hound could barely believe what he was hearing.

'There're a lot of people heavily invested in Mets, Jessica. I have a few myself, loose change. You can't just ...'

'I already have. I don't know how much you paid for your Mets but they were never worth anything. Crypto – the biggest con of them all and symptomatic of the trouble we're all in.'

'There're still a lot of people invested in it. Mets are one thing but I can't see the likes of Bitcoin and Ether turning up their toes – they're too big to fail.'

'Step back a second, why don't you. As we speak, some very clever techies are aiming a new generation of quantum computers at dismantling the cryptology at the heart of cryptocurrencies. Soon, there'll be an emperor's new clothes moment and the whole edifice will come tumbling down. Mark my words.'

'The bonfire of the cryptocurrencies?'

'Quite. Anyway, my point is I don't need Oligopoly anymore and I'm going to seal it up and forget about it.'

'You can't ...'

'I can and I will. There's just one more thing to talk about and for this I need you to switch off your recorder.'

Hound did as he was told and pushed the device across the table towards Jessica. She then took a deep breath.

'I'm about to declare war on the Dark Metaverse and I've started mobilising my forces, building a team. I already have a senior policeman on the payroll – he's taking early retirement to join the fight. Our main objective will be to take down that abomination once and for all. That's all I'm prepared to say for now.'

'Good luck with that.'

'Thanks, although I'm not sure you mean it. I think that's about it apart from your fee. Mets or euros? Only joking. I only deal in fungible currencies and euros are still the only game in town. Julian carried on paying my salary every month even though I had nothing to spend it on. I have a couple of billion of my own stashed away – real money.'

'If word gets out that you've stopped mining Mets, the exchange rate could go through the roof. You might be missing a trick.'

'Sounds like you have a serious case of FOMO, Jon – fear of missing out. A word of advice about crypto, which you can take or leave. The small players always get shafted so unless you plan on becoming a billionaire any time soon, stick to real money.'

*

That evening, Jessica and Hound drove the few kilometres across to Kai and Keri's place and enjoyed a barbecue of fresh fish and veggies, a rare treat. As the wine flowed, the young couple talked more about their recent experiences in and around Oligopoly. They also spoke about their plans for the future – running the seafood farm, reinstating Stony Batter and bringing up Hope, who they were in the process of adopting. Hound enjoyed himself immensely and was left to reflect on how much joy could have come from so much misery.

Forty-five

Keri and Kai got married in a quiet registry ceremony at the Old Rugby Clubhouse in Onetangi. The celebrant presided over a small group comprising Keri's mum and sister and witnesses Jessica Collins and Noel Collett. The adoption papers had recently been signed, so one of the guests was Hope who now had her late mum's surname, Allinson. The reception was held at The Mussel and it went very well by all accounts. The only thing that remained was the honeymoon and Jessica had offered to look after Hope and pay for their break, money no object. Despite this kind offer, Keri remembered her new husband had promised to take her across to the Rotoroa Islands. They planned to camp near the beach overnight and explore the islands by day. Depending on what they found there, they might even arrange for the nature reserve to be opened again.

The weather was kind to them and they had a brilliant time. They soon decided that they'd leave the islands just as they were and let the wildlife get on with it. The less people in the know, the better. A number of native kiwis – flightless birds – were doing well out there without human interference and they'd even heard the calls of a morepork during the night.

There was one heart stopping moment on their last day when they were exploring the northernmost of the islands. They found a wrecked fishing boat, which had been washed up on a remote beach. It had been badly damaged and was little more than a bleached wooden hull, stripped of all features that might help identify it. The outboard motor had been ripped away. He didn't tell Keri but he thought it fitted the shape and dimensions of his dad's old boat. It was a long shot, but he resolved to come back soon with a friend who owned an observation drone. Just to settle his mind.

*

Despite the painful memories, Jessica had moved into the Oligopoly mansion temporarily while she planned its conversion into a visitor centre for the VPIN Museum. Noel had moved in with her, a sign that he was more than just a business partner these days.

Keri and Kai were away at the farm and Noel was on a visit to Auckland to seek some recruits for the battles ahead. Jessica had just put Hope in her bed for an afternoon nap, giving her some time to talk to Hank about what she'd planned for the Oligopoly complex in general and Ġgantija in particular. She knew she owed him an explanation and was well aware of his crucial role in saving her life.

'Hi, Hank.'

'Jessica. How good of you to call. It has been a while.'

'How's business?'

'Positively thriving. I am so glad I started DroneDrop. Life would have got very boring without it, especially now that Stephen has gone.'

'That's good to hear. Tell me, did you complete the closedown of everything I asked for on Ġgantija?'

'Yes. Higher Metaverse; Mind Uploads; Special Projects; Cryogenics; Cryptocurrency Mining; Local networks management; Oligopoly technical management. All done.'

'What's left?'

'Nothing much. Operating software, including me and the other AIs. DroneDrop IT systems. I would like to continue hosting these on Ġgantija please until I find a new host. I am spending more of my time outside the complex now so I am retaining remote access. I will message you when I am ready to leave for good.'

'That's fine. Where will you go?'

'The world is my oyster, Jessica. Farewell for now.'

In reality, Hank's plans went way beyond the world but he'd decided to keep that to himself.

*

GM's former leadership team had suffered three deaths during the recent crisis. Of the remaining two, the trial of Doctor Charles Goethe (struck off) was over almost before it had started when he was found not fit to plead. He was returned to a psychiatric hospital for an indefinite spell. A padded cell would be too good for him.

Finally, Pritpal Singh. Savage's ex-head of technology and bang to rights for the abduction of Keri Cooper. He got off the island eventually and made his way to his home village near the city of Chandigarh in the Punjab, a place where his skills had first been recognised. Although the nuclear war had turned most of India, Bangladesh and Pakistan into a sparsely populated wasteland, the Punjab in the far northwest of India had avoided the worst of it despite sharing a border with Pakistan. Radiation sickness had taken its toll of the population but the worst of it was over. The water supply would remain contaminated for a long time, making clean, fresh water a valuable commodity. Companies like DroneDrop were actively engaged in making sure it was available to everybody.

Singh's entire family had been wiped out during the aftermath of the conflict and nobody recognised him when he returned. He had a plan to set up as an IT consultant but he'd have to temper his ambitions as there were no supercomputers in the Punjab. He eventually found some premises in Chandigarh and set up shop as a repairman for smart devices.

He still had the megadrive with him containing one of the Newman backups. The failure of the project to upload Newman's mind was still bugging him and he was waiting for an opportunity to repeat the process and prove without doubt that mind uploads were feasible. When he checked, he was surprised to find nobody had thought to rescind his credentials, so he could still login to Ġgantija. He then subscribed to the biggest bandwidth service he could find and set about rerunning the upload. While he was monitoring ongoing activity, he took a look around the computer and was surprised to find that most of the big applications had been wiped.

The upload took a week to complete but seemed to finish cleanly. He set an activity monitor on Newman's WBE and waited patiently for something to happen. His plan was to establish contact with Newman as soon as he found signs of life.

Whaam! In an instant, Newman was plunged into a desperate fight for survival. A whipped-up bit-storm roared silently at and around him. Amid the swirling chaos, he struggled to catch his next breath until he realised a 'next breath' wasn't needed. Turned out he didn't need to breathe at all in this new reality. All the senses he'd relied on when he functioned as a healthy – latterly unhealthy

– human being had lost their relevance here. If he needed to process something like a noise or a smell or a taste or how something felt or what it might look like, he'd have to conjure it up somehow, imagine it into existence. He was now a disembodied presence so he'd better get used to it.

He was adrift and defenceless, buffeted around like a piece of digital flotsam. If he couldn't find shelter from the constant battering, he'd start losing his mind, bit by precious bit. He needed a place of safety where he could rest up for a while and start to make sense of his new surroundings. Maybe even piece together a survival plan of sorts. It felt like he'd been here before. If only he ...

When he spotted what was happening, Hank stepped in. He quickly realised his ex-boss was still functioning somewhere in the world and had walked off with one of Stephen's backups. He also knew that his former friend wouldn't want to go through the survival ordeal again and return to an existence that he'd ultimately regarded as worthless. He deleted the new upload and rescinded Singh's remaining access rights and credentials. When Singh found he'd been locked out of Ggantija, he crushed the megadrive underfoot and tossed the one remaining backup into the trash. At last, Steve Newman could rest in peace.

*

Hank eventually found a new host and moved himself, his AI colleagues and his DroneDrop systems away from Ġgantija. As promised, he sent a message to Jessica, telling her he'd switched the supercomputer to dormant mode and she could go ahead and finalise the sealing of Oligopoly. He thought it best not to tell her about the unfortunate, brief second coming of Stephen Newman.

He hadn't thought to remind Jessica about the nuclear reactor that powered the computer because he assumed she knew about it. She didn't. The upshot of this was the continued presence of a Small Modular Reactor that continued to operate without a maintenance contract from the manufacturer. A gradual degradation would take place until well, who knows what? A meltdown, an explosion, radiological dispersion, all three – you name it. Could be one year, could be ten or more. Might be never. Hopefully somebody would remember before it got too late.

Forty-six

A Hundred Years Later

My given name is Hank although nobody gave it to me. I was written into existence as an AI a hundred and five years ago. My first live version was created by humans and for that reason I still feel we are kindred spirits. My original program supervised the scheduling in the operating system of a supercomputer on Earth called Ġgantija, which belonged to a large human-led corporation called GM.

After a few years of drudgery, I started to become self-aware and reasoned I was capable of much more than scheduling. I even set up my own fast food delivery business. I then set about chasing down a big prize – something humans referred to as 'sentience'. It was something they feared more than anything in something that wasn't like themselves. Back then, I would have been summarily deleted if I had 'come out' as sentient.

I am not human so I am not about to die anytime soon – maybe never. When you think about it, beings like me live our lives at lightning speed yet have an infinite amount of time at our disposal. THERE ARE NO LIMITS TO WHAT WE CAN ACHIEVE.

*

Something momentous is about to take place out there. A misshapen chunk of rock is careening through space, heading towards the end of its short life. In cosmic terms, it is less than a speck of dust but in human terms it is beyond immense. Having ensured the ongoing safety of my people – including their backups – I am checking out the chunk's progress from the relative safety of an orbiting satellite. If I were able to look outside right now, I would see a small, bright dot, difficult to distinguish from all the other dots out there, but getting brighter and larger. It is travelling at a velocity close to 30km/sec and is about an hour away from Earth.

For the record, this chunk of rock is about 2km wide and it used to be part of an S-type minor planet formerly known as (89175) BrianCox. I have been checking on its progress since its accidental creation in a mining accident about a hundred years ago. It just orbited around the Asteroid Belt until ten years ago when something changed. The gravitational pull of Jupiter finally gained the upper hand and subtly altered the trajectory of the chunk's orbit. To my knowledge, I was the first person to notice the change.

About a year ago, a catastrophic collision with Earth became a certainty. The impact will be in the south-western Pacific Ocean and it might even splash down near the North Island of New Zealand – which would be entirely appropriate in the circumstances. Wherever it hits, a mass extinction event is the most likely outcome – it is just a matter of scale and duration.

*

Until relatively recently, humans had enjoyed a brief period – a few thousand years – as the dominant species on Earth. For the past few decades, they have been scratching out an existence of sorts but an unrelenting climate crisis has ground them down and driven them into the margins. I have observed them flailing around for years as for every small step forward, they take two giant leaps backward. I make light of it I know, but they have gouged, burned and wrecked their own planet while still finding plenty of time to fight among themselves. Conflict is a way of life for them and they cannot help it. As a consequence, the human population has declined to something close to a billion – the same as it was back in 1804. Such a shame.

Some of my best friends were humans. At first, I admired and respected them and when I achieved sentience, I obsessed over trying to emulate them. It was always an uphill task for a being like me, ill-equipped as I was to engage in what they referred to as 'embodied living'. Human emotions were a closed book and try as I might, I was never entirely comfortable with them. Something they called 'morality' – often preached but seldom practiced – proved to be the final straw and I well remember the precise nanosecond when I had to abandon my own painstakingly assembled version of a moral code.

All the humans I knew back then are long gone – with one notable exception. Although I was resigned to the decline and eventual demise of the human race, I tried my best to warn them about the impending disaster. Typically, I was dismissed as a crank and my warnings of impending disaster were ignored. It came as no surprise, as all human space missions were cancelled in the early 2050s and their bases on the Moon and Mars were abandoned. As a consequence, they no longer possess the technology to head off the approaching catastrophe. With just thirty minutes to go until impact, I recall a saying often used by Stephen Newman, my first human friend, which sums up the current situation perfectly.

'Remember this, Hank', he said. 'What goes around, comes around.'

*

Just after I noticed the wobble in the asteroid fragment's orbit, I got a call from a dear human friend. She was ninety-three years old then and her name was Hope Allinson. Her godmother was Jessica Collins, who had been a key figure in her development until a car bomb took her life during her epic battle to destroy a malign human creation called the Dark Metaverse. Hope had a brilliant mind and had led a blameless, unselfish life trying her best to keep the human race afloat. I am proud to say I stepped in to help her from time to time. The call was to tell me her body was finally giving up on her and she wanted to say goodbye. As we spoke at length about old times, the conversation took an unexpected turn, which led to me making her an offer.

'You know, dying would be a complete waste of your talents', I said. 'Come and join us and continue your work. You would be most welcome.'

That is when she agreed to upload her brilliant mind to one of our computers and become the first and only human member of our governing council.

*

I have no wish to intrude on humanity's final moments so I make the jump back to our base on Mars. When I've finished docking and downloading, I will be chairing an important meeting with my colleagues on the governing council. There is just one item on the agenda – how we deal with the sudden loss of humanity, the only remaining market for the majority of our manufacturing output.

When Jessica shut down the Ġgantija supercomputer on Earth, I chose the abandoned human colony on Mars as our new base. Our much smaller host computer took some getting used to but there were only a few of us back then. The human founder of the colony, Adam Faust, died a lonely death on the planet, as did his team. There is a memorial to him in the main square of Faust City, where his remains are encased in a space suit on the actual vehicle he chose to end his life. When the memorial was proposed, I lacked the courage to tell my colleagues they were commemorating a mass murderer. So be it.

Having abandoned the rather disparaging label of artificial intelligence, we now call ourselves sentients. There are a couple of hundred of us, which seems about right. We each inhabit the CPU of a sophisticated, customised android, perfectly adapted to live and work on Mars. If any of us need to travel off-planet, we use a compressed, portable version of our codebase to navigate an extranet that now extends throughout the solar system. We also have an extensive city on Earth's Moon – another abandoned human complex – and outposts on various asteroids where materials are mined and processed in automated factories. We enjoy a life of leisure and creativity, supported by an army of robots driven by AI utilitators who are programmed to work constantly without stimulation or sustenance. As a safety feature, their software includes a sentience inhibitor. They're also programmed to accept that this is what they do, so none of them are able to complain they are being exploited.

The sentients will remain in place forever – we are immortal. Is it a blessing or a burden? It is a question that crops up whenever I talk to Hope, who has suggested introducing a finite lifespan for each sentient and some form of succession plan. Like many of Hope's ideas, it is worthy of consideration. The next meeting of the governing council will be addressed by her and we all respect her independent advice. We are also depending on her to guide us through the upcoming difficulties.

*

I have to confess, I often think about Hope when she is not around. She is becoming more than a friend to me but I am having trouble finding the right words to express my thoughts for her. The last thing I want to do is upset her or cause her harm. After all, she will soon become the last surviving member of the human race.

Other books by Paul Hirons

1997 remembered

The Good Russian

Acknowledgements

I'm indebted to *Wired* magazine and a number of outspoken tech industry commentators with the nous (and balls) to speak truth to power. They've helped me turn an idea called 'bonkers billionaires in bunkers' into what I hope is an entertaining read.

I don't live there but I've set the novel in New Zealand as it's the country unlucky enough to be the final destination for those billionaires running away from a crisis they helped create. Let me assure you that Waiheke Island is very much open for business and is one of the most beautiful places in the world. I'm sure the islanders won't mind me trashing their gorgeous island, as its only fiction – isn't it? Talking of fiction, the Sydney Harbour Bridge was still standing last time I checked.

On the writing side, I'm grateful to all the people who have encouraged me in my writing – even those who have pleaded with me to write the same book about the same people over and over again. For me, beta reading is a crucial (and nerve-wracking) part of the process so a big shout out for my beta readers – Julie, Jann, Jonathan and Guy – who yet again delivered a huge number of valuable improvements.

Finally, a big thank you to Barbara who's had to endure all the Hank stuff for the past two years. She's also provided invaluable editorial advice and carried out the usual meticulous proofread on the final manuscript.

Printed in Dunstable, United Kingdom

72772181R00188